Also by the author

Fire on the Island
The Fourth Courier
A Vision of Angels
Cooper's Promise

Praise for ***Fire on the Island***

"Smith offers the perfect blend of intrigue, romance, and travelogue." – *Publishers Weekly*

"Timothy Jay Smith's *Fire on the Island: A Romantic Thriller* follows a gay Greek-American FBI agent Nick Damigos to a gorgeous town in the Greek islands to investigate a mysterious arsonist. More than the mystery of who's setting the fires and why, Smith creates a sensitive portrait of a small Greek community set against the refugee crisis and Greece's suffering economy. It's the town itself – a chorus of voices – that is the most compelling character and our reason for 'traveling' to Greece." – Lambda Literary Review

Gold Medal, 2017 Faulkner-Wisdom Competition for the Novel

Praise for ***The Fourth Courier***

"Sharply drawn characters, rich dialogue, and a clever conclusion bode well for any sequel." – *Publishers Weekly*

"Smith skillfully bridges police procedural and espionage fiction, crafting a show-stealing sense of place and realistically pairing the threats of underworld crime and destabilized regimes." – *Booklist*

Finalist, Best Gay Mystery, 2020 Lambda Literary Awards

Finalist, Faulker-Wisdom Competition for the Novel-in-Progress

Timothy Jay Smith

Leapfrog Press
New York and London

First published in paperback in the United States by Leapfrog Press, 2024
Leapfrog Press Inc.

www.leapfrogpress.com

Cover design: James Shannon
Cover image © Michael S. Honegger

Typesetting: Prepress Plus

ISBN: 978-1-948585996 (paperback)

987654321

Printed and bound in the United Kingdom

The Forest Stewardship Council® is an international
non-governmental organisation that promotes environmentally
appropriate, socially beneficial, and economically viable management of
the world's forests. To learn more visit www.fsc.org

**LEAPFROG
GLOBAL
FICTION
PRIZE**

Past Winners of the Leapfrog Global Fiction Prize

2023: *Istanbul Crossing* by Timothy Jay Smith
2023: *The Aves* by Ryane Nicole Granados*
2022: *Rage & Other Cages* by Aimee LaBrie
2022: *Jellyfish Dreaming* by D. K. McCutchen*
2021: *But First You Need a Plan* by K L Anderson
2021: *Lost River, 1918* by Faith Shearin*
⠀⠀⠀⠀⠀*My Sister Lives in the Sea* by Faith Shearin*
2020: *Wife With Knife* by Molly Giles
2019: *Amphibians* by Lara Tupper
2018: *Vanishing: Five Stories* by Cai Emmons
2018: *Why No Goodbye?* by Pamela L. Laskin*
2017: *Trip Wire: Stories* by Sandra Hunter
2016: *The Quality of Mercy* by Katayoun Medhat
2015: *Report from a Burning Place* by George Looney
2015: *The Solace of Monsters* by Laurie Blauner
2014: *The Lonesome Trials of Johnny Riles* by Gregory Hill
2013: *Going Anywhere* by David Armstrong
2012: *Being Dead in South Carolina* by Jacob White
2012: *Lone Wolves* by John Smelcer*
2011: *Dancing at the Gold Monkey* by Allen Learst
2010: *How to Stop Loving Someone* by Joan Connor
2010: *Riding on Duke's Train* by Mick Carlon*
2009: *Billie Girl* by Vickie Weaver

* Young Adult | Middle Grade Fiction

These titles can be bought at: https://bookshop.org/shop/leapfrog

DAY 1

Ahdaf dropped a coin in the tip bowl and left the hammam. The hectic street quickly robbed him of the languor he had enjoyed stretched out on a hot marble slab. He dodged pushcarts and deliverymen, some shirtless in the warming day, and jumped out of the way every time a boy, clinging to the back of a wagon piled high with boxes, hurtled down the hill with nothing more to brake him than his heels in thin sandals.

He could hear the customers at Leyla's Café before he turned the corner. A dozen or so men, seated at outdoor tables, flailed at the smoky air around them as they gestured telling stories or making a point. Everyone was loud. A few vaped, exhaling volcanic clouds with sickly sweet scents.

Inside the café, the air was fresher but the room no less animated. The customers – mostly dark men like himself with some amount of facial hair – competed to be heard. Ahdaf squeezed between tables and dodged outstretched legs to reach the "cowboy bar" – a short counter in a cubbyhole so nicknamed because, on the walls around it, Leyla had tacked pictures of Hollywood's most celebrated cowboys. On the inside of an overhead arch, she'd nailed a line of cowboy hats.

The bar's three stools were predictably empty. Beer was acceptable to be drunk at the tables, but for that conservative refugee neighborhood – unlike most of cosmopolitan Istanbul – sitting at a bar drinking anything was an affront verging on sinful. That didn't stop anyone, however, from recharging their phones with the power strips that Leyla snaked across it. Only one socket was available, and Ahdaf claimed it before someone else did. His charge was in the red zone, down to three percent – suicidal, given that his own life depended on his battery's.

Leyla stubbed out a cigarette and flipped her black hair off her shoulder. "Are you coming from the hammam?"

"How can you tell?"

"You smell like soap."

"Is that good?"

"It's better than you smelled yesterday."

"Was it bad?"

"You're not wearing your usual blue shirt, either."

"I washed it. This is my backup while it's drying."

A stranger, pushing up to the bar, said, "Sounds like you could use a third shirt." Out of the corner of his eye, Ahdaf saw that he was older but not by much, and he could've passed for Turkish, though his accent said he wasn't.

"I only have two hangers," Ahdaf replied, not looking at the man. He didn't care to engage with anyone who wasn't a potential client, and the man was too well dressed to be a refugee.

"Do you want a mint tea?" Leyla asked him.

"*Tea?*" She knew Ahdaf would want a beer. Then it dawned on him that maybe there was something amiss about the stranger, and that was her signal. "Yeah, and with an extra sugar," he said. "My body weight tells me I'm undernourished."

"That's an extra *lira*."

"Okay, no extra sugar. I don't want you getting rich off me."

Leyla laughed. "Get rich off you? I couldn't get rich off all you guys in here put together, no matter what I was selling!" She dropped a third sugar cube into his glass. "On the house."

He frowned as he stirred his tea. "We had jobs in Syria. I could've made you rich then."

The stranger offered his hand. "I'm Selim Wilson. Sam, if you prefer."

Ahdaf ignored his hand. "Why would I prefer 'Sam'?"

"It's what I was called growing up."

"You changed it to Selim?"

"My mother's Turkish. Selim is on my birth certificate."

"While you guys decide on his name, I've got other customers," Leyla said.

"Before you go, do you have cold beer?" Selim asked.

She looked at Ahdaf when she replied, "Only one is cold."

"I only want one."

"It's mine," Ahdaf spoke up.

"You're drinking tea."

He took a sip and pushed the cup aside. "I preordered the beer. Very cold."

"I tell you what, you guys share it." Leyla uncapped the bottle and planted it between them along with two glasses, before squeezing around the end of the stubby bar to serve tables.

"It's all yours if you want it," Selim said.

"We can share it," Ahdaf replied.

"Then I insist that it's my treat." Selim angled the glasses as he poured, to produce only thin heads of foam. He passed one to Ahdaf.

"Thanks," he said and took a sip. "Are you American?"

"Is my accent that obvious?"

"It's an accent. I like to know where people are from."

"It's American," Selim confirmed.

"If you're an American, you must know who some of these

3

guys are," Ahdaf remarked, referring to the cowboy pictures.

"I know a lot of them. Not personally, of course, but from the movies."

"Maybe you should take a selfie in a cowboy hat and stick it on the wall," Ahdaf suggested.

Selim snorted. "It takes more than being an American wearing a cowboy hat to meet Leyla's standards. I think you also need to be a movie star."

"I think she just likes cowboys," Ahdaf replied. Now that they were talking, he couldn't help but notice how handsome Selim was, his dark beard groomed and his eyes chestnut-brown. "I don't think all those came from movie stars," he added, pointing to the cowboy hats nailed overhead. "Have you been to Leyla's before?"

Selim nodded. "Yeah, occasionally."

"I've never seen you in here, and it's basically my office."

"Obviously we work different hours."

"I've also never seen another American in here."

"I'm Turkish-American. Maybe that explains it. Or maybe the fact that I wanted to meet you."

Ahdaf's danger alarm went off. He'd met lots of strangers at Leyla's. Refugees were his clients, and her café was where they knew to find smugglers to help them make the crossing to Greece. Selim, he sensed, wasn't looking for that kind of help. "Why did you want to meet me?" he asked.

"I've heard you get things done."

"What things?"

"Moving people."

"Who told you that?"

"A lot of people could have told me."

"But who did? I like to know how people find me."

"He. She. It. I don't remember."

"Why the secrecy?"

4

"I need a reliable route for people to escape."

"Escape what?"

"Turkey."

"So you're a smuggler, too?"

"Not like you, or why would I need you?"

"You don't need me. Lots of guys do what I do." Ahdaf checked his phone. "It's charged enough," he reported and dropped it into his daypack. "Are you CIA?"

"I can't say who I work for. Not until we have an agreement."

"Then I guess I'll never know. Thanks for the beer." He slipped off the barstool.

"Just remember, Ahdaf Jalil –"

"How do you know my name?" Ahdaf interrupted him.

"Just remember," Selim started again, "what you call 'moving people' is trafficking to the rest of the world. Turkey could deport you back to Syria. Back to Raqqa and ISIS. Back to a push off a high rooftop."

"Why have you come looking for me?"

"I told you, I want your help."

"I don't want to help you." Ahdaf stood to leave.

"Take this." Selim forced a business card on him.

"I don't want it."

"Sometime you might need help. Not everyone is a nice guy like you."

Ahdaf glanced at the card. No name. Only a telephone number with a local prefix. "Do I ask for 'Sam' or 'Selim'?"

"You don't ask for anyone. You leave your name and a message, and where to find you if you need help."

"I won't need help," Ahdaf said, but he stuck the card in his pocket anyway. "Thanks for the beer."

"Maybe next time I can treat you to a meal," Selim offered.

"I'm never that hungry."

Ahdaf made his way to the door of the lively café. He knew

5

some eyes trailed him. Nobody's business here was entirely private, as most of it was conducted on the street. Everybody kept an eye on each other, and not always to be helpful. Selim hadn't said he was CIA, but he was somebody like that, and somebody in the café probably knew exactly who he was.

The door hadn't closed behind him before his phone started ringing.

An hour later, Ahdaf was pacing the loading dock at the central bus station. The family was late. Nothing had been easy for Ahdaf to arrange for them because they insisted on traveling all together, not letting the father go first to establish a beachhead where the others could join him. For Ahdaf, that meant more seats on a bus, more lifejackets, more spaces on a raft – all of which were in heavy demand. It was mid-autumn, and already on some days the weather made it treacherous to cross. In another month, it would be an option only for the very desperate.

Ahdaf had bribed the bus driver to save seats for the family. He tried to promise the same service to all his customers, and he pretty much could. He'd learned which drivers he could trust to save the seats until the door hissed and closed.

He checked his watch.

Ten minutes.

Ahdaf looked around. The driver wouldn't wait for anybody. Certainly the seat-jumpers wouldn't. The instant the door hissed, preparing to close, the passengers standing in the aisle would wrangle for the three vacant seats, claiming maladies they didn't have to assert their priority.

The driver blew the horn. Five-minute warning.

Ahdaf caught his eye through the windshield and shrugged. He didn't know where the family was. Then there they were, scurrying along the platform looking for the bus to Assos, rushed and encumbered; an infant in her mother's arms, the father and teenage son hauling backpacks.

"Here!" Ahdaf waved to catch their attention. "HERE! HERE!"

They hurried up to him.

He chuckled when he saw Meryem's inflated belly. "You weren't so big yesterday," he said.

"You told us to make her look more pregnant," Yusuf, her husband, reminded him.

"And you did! I hope her lifejacket still fits!"

"My lifejacket won't fit?" Meryem asked, alarmed.

"I'm joking," I reassured her. "A lifejacket fits around the shoulders, and it's your belly that's bigger."

Yusuf grinned. "It's a life preserver for our new baby. Extra protection!"

"A life preserver?" Ahdaf asked, puzzled.

Yusuf poked his wife in the side, denting the inflated tube hiding under her rust-colored robe, at the same time revealing the outline of a life preserver.

"Yusuf, don't!" she said. "People might be looking."

Two short toots of the horn. The two-minute warning.

"Call the number I gave you as soon as you get off the bus. Your contact will be waiting for you."

"Who is it?" Yusuf asked.

"I never know. You have a backup number if there's a problem, and if there's still a problem, call me. Here, take these." Ahdaf handed out bright pink caps with sun visors. He even had one for the baby.

Issa, a lanky fourteen-year-old with a wispy moustache, looked dubious. "I'm supposed to wear a pink hat?"

"It's the only color they had. Besides, you won't care when you get to Lesvos and have to walk 70 kilometers in the hot sun."

Meryem paled. "We must walk 70 kilometers? I really am

pregnant."

"I'll carry you if I have to," Yusuf reassured her.

Issa put the cap on backwards, having to pull it hard over his mop of curly black hair. "It's too tight!"

"Tight's good. You won't lose it if there's wind."

"Wait," the teenager said, and turned the cap around to pull some hair through the band in the back. "Cool or uncool?" he asked Ahdaf.

"Very cool. It'll never fall off." Ahdaf caught the driver's eye again, who nodded. Time to board.

"Thank you again, Ahdaf," Meryem said, and did an unexpected thing for a Syrian woman: she kissed him on his cheek. "You are a kind man to help my family."

Yusuf grasped his hand with both of his. "You've helped save my family," he said.

"It's you who saved your family. You got them away from the war. I'm only helping a little."

They touched their hearts and Yusuf followed his wife onto the bus.

Issa, the last to board, pointed to his cap.

"Are you sure?"

"I'm sure."

"*Pink?*"

"You'll be glad to have it, pink or not. Besides, you might start a trend."

The boy grinned. "Cool. Thanks for helping my family."

They shook hands before Issa bounded up the steps to sit across the aisle from his parents in the front row. As they all waved goodbye, the driver stared at Meryem's pronounced belly. He glanced in the rearview mirror to ask the passengers, "Is there a midwife on the bus?"

Ahdaf heard a few nervous laughs as the door hissed and closed. The driver backed out of the bus bay and drove off. Ahdaf waved again, though he couldn't see the family through the glazed windows. He hoped they saw him, because he knew how every act of kindness, no matter how trivial – if only a friendly wave or the offer of a sesame bar – could nurture someone's hope that what lay ahead mightn't be so bad.

He left the bus terminal and ran to catch the tram when he saw it pulling up. It wasn't full and he sat by the window, watching shopkeepers in the last throes of the day: dragging merchandise inside, flicking off lights, and lowering squeaky metal grates. Only the cafés had customers. Ahdaf felt deflated – how else to describe it? – whenever he sent people he'd grown to like into unknown hands and an uncertain future. He had learned it was possible to bond with other refugees very quickly, because that's all the time they had. Yusuf's family, too, had felt the bittersweetness of the moment. Meryem's kiss on the cheek had been poignant proof of that. Ahdaf smiled to think she probably wished she had made herself appear a little less pregnant to have more room on the narrow bus seat, but the ploy might win her some sympathy if she needed protection or a helping hand. The family's journey had already been tough. Ahdaf had made the same one himself, coming from Syria mostly on foot and braving scoundrels, traffickers and kidnappers along the way. But unlike Yusuf's family, he had opted to stay in Istanbul. He felt safe enough there, and anonymous when he wanted to be.

Or was he? How did the CIA man – that's how he thought of Selim even if he hadn't admitted as much – know about him? He even knew his last name; but then, Ahdaf realized, half the people at Leyla's could've told him. It was odd, though, if he'd come around asking questions about Ahdaf and no one mentioned it. On suspicious things like that, someone always had your back because they expected the same friendly protection.

Like many of the young guys who hung out at the café, Ahdaf played a minor role in one of many smuggling networks. He moved people arriving in Istanbul to Assos, a sleepy village five hours away on the coast, from where they'd cross the narrow channel to Greece. He organized bus connections, space on rafts, lifejackets, and overnight stays if needed, and fulfilled special needs such as medications or replacements for lost crutches. He wasn't much more than an efficient gofer. All the young smugglers who hung out in Leyla's were gofers, not the bosses who paid the bribes and bought the rafts that he and their other minions filled with desperate passengers. Ahdaf had little idea who the bosses were. It wasn't like there was a corporate headquarters where he could meet the team. Smuggling was managed by cell phone, and only in-person when money needed to be exchanged or a gofer disciplined. That didn't mean that he didn't hear the abusive stories from up and down the line. The worst, in his mind, were the smugglers who took money from refugees for crossings that never happened. The victims were left stranded in Istanbul, their dreams and money stolen from them. Ahdaf knew which of the smugglers not to trust, but he was powerless to stop them. He survived in an edgy world, which, translated, meant dangerous-verging-on-lethal.

"Next station: Aksaray," a recorded voice announced over the tram's intercom. "Aksaray. Next station: Aksaray."

Many people got off, and Ahdaf followed them. Aksaray, a working-class neighborhood, was a magnet for refugees. Families sat in clumps on the sidewalks, some ever alert to begging opportunities, but the majority just huddled in what little space they could find. For most, living on the streets was a fraught adjustment after losing their claim to middle-class. Many of them could have been Ahdaf's mother or father, as they too had once been teachers and dentists, or simply housewives who'd enjoyed luxuries like dishwashers until their neighborhoods were bombed. They had fled – none under Ahdaf's special circumstances, but for reasons also threatening enough to force them to uproot themselves and embark on a dangerous journey. Not everyone survived. They knew the risks when they started out, but their odds were worse if they remained behind.

Ahdaf resented the whole vocabulary of human trafficking, and Selim had all but called him a trafficker. He didn't traffic people. He *smuggled* people, because they wanted to be smuggled. Down a long chain, he moved them one link. If they could have done it themselves, they would have, but they needed help; and he didn't exploit them. The guys running the rackets made the money, which he always collected, but he barely got by on his meager cut. It was only enough to keep him working for them as a foot soldier in an ever-growing army.

People who'd already made the trip successfully sometimes sent word back to other refugees to seek out Ahdaf. At least for one leg of their journey, they could be sure someone wasn't going to steal their money. They'd feel safe, because safety was what Ahdaf had sought for himself. He would never buy an oligarch's palace on the Bosporus, so why not be an honest man?

Out of habit, his feet brought him to Leyla's Café when he'd intended to go home. Once there, he thought he might as well go inside, but then he looked through the window at the men slouched in their chairs, hanging out because they had no other place to go. It depressed him because he was one of them, also with no place to go, certainly no place he wanted to call home, and he'd be going home to no one. He didn't want to be depressed after he'd been feeling good about helping Yusuf, Meryem, and Issa. He'd saved their lives, Yusuf said, though Ahdaf knew it was an exaggeration. He also knew that the road ahead of them was still treacherous. He smiled, remembering the fourteen-year-old boy's worry about looking uncool. Ahdaf, only ten years older, could remember being fourteen. Before the war. Before having another birthday became chancy. He might not have saved their lives, but he was glad he'd given the boy a better shot at reaching fifteen.

He saw Leyla watching him through the window. She looked

11

puzzled, and he realized he'd been standing there lost in thought for a couple of minutes. With a short wave, he walked off. Five minutes later he turned a corner and opened the front door of the building where he lived. He climbed one flight of steps. That was the only thing he liked about his room: it wasn't on the ground floor, which made him feel safer.

He flipped on the light and looked for fleeing cockroaches. It had been a week since Ahdaf had seen one. He appeared to be winning that war. He dropped his daypack on the floor and went into the bathroom. At least he had a proper toilet to piss into, and didn't have to use the same sink that he'd later use to brush his teeth or splash his face. Having his own apartment, if only one long room with a tiny bathroom, was a far cry from when he'd first arrived in Istanbul and shared a basement room with nine other guys, one of them always smoking or farting while pissing in the sink. Without a toilet, they'd had to shit somewhere else. Café. Mosque. Sometimes an alley. He'd never known ten confined men could be so rank. He'd wake up smelling like them. Sometimes it stayed on him all day. That's when he started splurging on a hammam whenever he had a few extra *liras* to spend.

He pulled a beer from the refrigerator, popped its top, and took a swallow. It was only as cold as tap water, but that would do. Beer was Ahdaf's new habit. In Raqqa, it had been hard to find, and he hadn't drunk it more than a few times clandestinely, usually when he and his cousin got tipsy enough to seduce each other – if their experimental touching could be called seduction. In Istanbul, it helped him to fall asleep before bad memories or anxieties about his tenuous existence flooded him. He swallowed more beer. Being approached by the secretive American had un-nerved him.

He stripped to his boxers and turned off the light before crawling gently into bed. He'd raised it off the floor using stacks of books: sixteen stacks around its perimeter and eight more to support its center, atop which overlapping pieces of plywood the-oretically distributed the soft mattress's weight. He'd made sure that the stacks were as close to the same height as possible, and with a large enough footprint to bear his weight as well as absorb his movements while asleep. He found most of his books on the trams, forgotten by passengers in a hurry to get off, and at spots where people knew to put things for anyone who wanted them.

The evening was warm for mid-autumn. He heard a couple of cars go by, some kid clatter past on a skateboard, the low mur-mur of televisions and conversations from nearby apartments. He threw off the sheet and lay back on the pillow, waiting for the beer to dissolve the day. It didn't. Instead, smelling the lingering soap on his body, he became aroused as he recalled that part of his day at the hammam. Timur, the attendant he'd learned to ask for, had scrubbed him down. As usual, his hands, hidden under a mound of soapsuds, slipped up Ahdaf's thighs, brushing his cock, which was already hard with anticipation. He gripped him, and with a couple of jerks made Ahdaf come, all while acting with complete indifference. Only when he doused Ahdaf with cold water did his sly smile acknowledge their complicity. What Ahdaf also saw, not visible to anyone else, was Timur's own cock wagging behind his thin towel. He wanted to touch it – they both longed for him to touch it – but they also knew the danger of exposure as a homosexual. Now in bed, with no one to de-nounce him for his unholy thoughts, Ahdaf pulled off his under-shorts, and with his eyes closed, imagined it was Timur's hand again that closed on his cock and made him come a second time that day.

He let his satisfaction subside before going into the bathroom to splash his belly clean.

DAY 2

Ahdaf found a spot on a bench to claim one of the spigots on the long ablutions wall. "*Selamün aleyküm*," he said to the men beside him and slipped off his sandals.

"*Aleyküm selam*," they replied.

Turning on the faucet, Ahdaf let the cool water run through his toes as the call to prayer droned through overhead loudspeakers. Like Ahdaf, most men along the bench kept their cleansing ritual confined to their feet and forearms, but some went through the full procedure of rinsing out their mouths, cleaning their ears, and snorting water out their noses.

He dried his feet with a handkerchief and crossed barefoot to the mosque's entrance, where he left his sandals on a shelf. Stepping behind a heavy velvet curtain, he entered the vast prayer hall, with its many tiers of stained-glass windows rising to the dome. Except for worshippers kneeling on the expansive red carpet, it was bare; there was no furniture, no architectural features to break the eye's sweeping gaze. The praying men appeared inconsequential in the presence of Allah, which Ahdaf supposed was the architect's intent.

Ahdaf wasn't a believer, though he liked the notion of religion. He liked the superstitions and rituals for luck, health, and good fortune. He believed very few of Islam's tenets, especially as they had been used to justify his cousin's execution, which made it ironic that Ahdaf now used religion as part of his survival strategy. The mosque was a source of rumors and news, and he relied on both to stay informed.

That morning, there was no *imam*. No sermon. The few dozen men who'd come to pray knelt in loose lines, bobbing out of sync to touch their foreheads to the ground while mumbling holy words. Ahdaf joined one of the lines, not exactly to pray but to plead with his parents to manage to survive the civil war and beg his cousin's forgiveness if he had somehow contributed to his death. Those were his only prayers most mornings, but that day, he also thought about the family he'd put on the bus to Assos the night before, and prayed for them to be safe, too. When he finished, he sat back on his haunches, eyes closed, enjoying a meditative minute before rousing himself to discover what the day was going to bring.

Outside, Ahdaf retrieved his sandals and dropped them on the ground. As he wiggled his feet into them, someone said his name. He turned to Malik, the headmaster of the mosque's religious school, a scrawny man with a pronounced limp, a prophet's beard, and a dark brown kaftan the same color as his dull eyes. *"Selamün aleyküm,"* they both said, and touched their hearts.

"It is good to see you so often at prayers," Malik remarked. "It's apparent that you are a man of faith."

"Sometimes a habit can be mistaken for faith," Ahdaf replied. "My father insisted that I go to prayers once a day."

"It is not only habit in your case."

"What makes you so sure?"

"You still come to prayers even though your father is not here to scold you."

15

"Yes, it's true, though I wish he were. At prayers, I see many men who remind me of my father. That's one reason I prefer to pray at the mosque, not in a shop or on the sidewalk. Also, my father always spoke of the mosque as a place of fellowship as well as faith, and I'm alone in Istanbul."

"Does the fellowship you seek include drinking *khamr*?"

"*Khamr*?" Ahdaf asked, repeating the Arabic word for intoxicating drinks.

"Beer."

In one word, Malik sent a seismic jolt through Ahdaf's world. Someone had seen him at Leyla's having a beer, and for some reason that was important enough to report to Malik. Why was it important – and why Malik? As the *medrese's* director, he was certain to be a fundamentalist, but did he go so far as to spy on people? "It's rare that I drink a beer," Ahdaf lied, feeling the need to defend himself.

"Even one beer is still *haram*," Malik said. *Forbidden.* "I'm surprised a man with your strong faith would succumb to the temptation."

"Allah is forgiving," Ahdaf reminded him.

"The Most Forgiving," Malik replied, quoting verse.

"*Alhamdulillah*," they both said and touched their hearts. *Praise be to God.*

Ahdaf, wanting to end the exchange, smiled and took a step away. When Malik said his name again, it felt like a summons, and he turned around. "Yes?"

"What did Selim Wilson want from you?"

Ahdaf gulped. "Selim Wilson?"

"He didn't tell you his name?"

"Yes, but how do you know it?"

"He is an American spy. What did he want?"

"He wants me to help smuggle people."

"Who?"

16

"He didn't say."

"We want you to help him."

Ahdaf was baffled. "Help him?"

"We want to know what he's planning and who he wants to smuggle. If he wants information, what's he looking for? Anything you can tell us."

"Who are you?"

"Brothers in faith."

Ahdaf summoned the courage to ask, "Are you part of ISIS?"

"We help everyone who fights for Allah. Will you help us?"

"I told the American that a lot of guys move people. He doesn't need me, and you don't either. Obviously, you already have spies."

"Apparently, Selim Wilson thinks he needs you. He picked you. He didn't buy anyone else a beer."

"I won't help him for the same reason I won't help you. I left Raqqa to escape a war. I don't want to be part of a new war here."

"You can't escape it. We're in a holy war, and your faith makes you part of it. The West's only faith is greed."

Ahdaf, feeling ambushed, shook his head when he said, "I'm just trying to survive."

"Can you contact Selim Wilson?" Malik asked.

He couldn't lie. Whoever had seen him sharing a beer with Selim would've seen the CIA man press his card on him. "Yes, I can contact him."

"Do it. We have an operation coming up. We need to know if he knows anything about it."

"I need to think about it."

Ahdaf, about to turn away, stopped when Malik added, "Don't take so long thinking about it that you accidentally fall off a building like your cousin."

Their eye contact held for an extra moment. Ahdaf willed his eyes to be expressionless. Malik's were confident.

Contempt was their common denominator.

Ahdaf's days were all different in the same ways. He was always on the lookout for new clients while helping the ones he had. Some came looking for him, some he found on the streets, and some came to Leyla's, which everyone knew was a hangout for smugglers. What Ahdaf did – find rooms for short stays, buy onward tickets, get space on a raft with a guaranteed lifejacket – wasn't exactly illegal; but the refugee situation had become so politicized, it required an extra dose of discretion, which did nothing to reduce the number of refugees while inflating bribes all along their route.

He'd been smuggling people almost since he arrived in Istanbul six months earlier. Ahdaf had fled Syria not because he wanted to go to Europe but for safety, and he figured Istanbul was safe enough. The war was far away, and his combination of languages – Arabic, Turkish, and English – made him valuable to the smugglers. He'd barely mentioned that he was looking for a job before he was approached by one of the rackets. In the intervening months, he'd fine-tuned his discrete part of the operation: getting refugees from Istanbul to the coast and onto rubber rafts to Greece. To the distraught and scared refugees, he had made the process seamless and personal, down to arranging pre-sized lifejackets; and he was especially trusted by Syrian refugees because he was one of them. That fact, of course, earned him the animosity and occasional belligerence of his Turkish peers competing for the same clients. In the pecking order of refugees, Syrians were at the top. No one could dispute their status as war refugees, and most had been middle class, which meant – more often than not – that they had enough money to buy their way to the front of the line.

No smuggler operated entirely independently in the refugee

business. The routes were too long, bribes too varied, and refugees too many for each step in their flight to be planned *ad hoc*. The business was multinational, which meant big, and lucrative for the rackets that controlled it. For his own protection, Ahdaf had aligned himself with one of them; but on a day-to-day basis, he operated independently. He found his own clients, decided how much handholding they needed while arrangements were being made, confirmed their onward contact, and made a backup plan for anything that might go wrong.

That day, after Malik's unveiled threat, Ahdaf could have used a backup plan for himself. His stomach was in knots. He couldn't think of anything else. *How had everyone learned so much about him?* he wondered as he entered Leyla's, which he now concluded must be a spies' nest. He wondered if someone might give himself away with an ardent stare or curious glance, but Ahdaf had forgotten that it was Comedy Night at Leyla's. The place was crowded, and the mood lighthearted. Comedy Nights were a balm for even the harshest lives.

Ahdaf dodged his way to the cowboy bar, skirting tables too small for the men crowded around them. He slipped onto a barstool. "It's a big crowd tonight," he said to Leyla as she emptied a miniature dishwasher, dried off glasses, and lined them up on a side counter.

"I have a beer in the freezer for you," she said.

Ahdaf briefly worried about being caught drinking a beer again, but said, "What the fuck, why not?"

Leyla frowned. "I don't like hearing you say that word. You're too nice a guy."

"It's not been a nice day."

She popped the beer bottle's top and set it in front of him. "Maybe this will get you to smile."

"Can I have a glass?"

"You always say it stays colder in the bottle."

"If I'm going to sin, I might as well do it with a proper glass!"

Leyla handed him one. "Since when is drinking beer a sin for you?"

"Since some guy at the mosque reminded me that it is."

He poured beer into the glass and toasted the room. *Let Malik's fink report me!* he thought, and took a swallow.

More women came to Leyla's on Comedy Night than other nights. The roving stand-up comedians – all Syrian refugees – had become trendy in the neighborhood. Sought after by the cafés because they had loyal followers, they plied on the dark humor of their refugee status and cross-cultural misunderstandings with real Istanbullus. When word got around about how funny they were, it was enough to lure those "real Istanbullus" to their shows. In the end, despite their differences, everybody in the audience laughed at the same jokes. Comedy gave them perspective and revived them on weary days. Its respite lingered well beyond the last joke.

"Omar's arrived," Leyla said, and muted the overhead television as a young man with an olive complexion and short beard entered the café. A spreading silence followed him to the bar as people recognized that evening's comedian. "Ice water," he said to Leyla, loud enough for everyone to hear. Turning to his audience, he added, "And make it a double!"

When the polite laughter subsided, he said, "My name is ..." He opened his arms, inviting the crowd to respond.

"Omar Vedit!" his fans cried.

"That's right, and if I don't make you laugh tonight, you can't ask for drinks on the house because you all just laughed!" He raised his ice water, toasting the crowd, then took a swallow and set the glass back on the bar. "So, I confess, I'm a guy who thinks a lot about girls, and when I walk down the street, I try to check them out. I'll make another confession: I like to see more than eyelashes on a woman. I don't mean that disrespectfully. I mean that in the way that you might like to hold your husband's hand in public. Haven't you all wanted to do it like you've seen on television? Fingers entwined, swinging your hands, maybe tickling each other. I see those smiles you're trying to hide. Go ahead, try it. Someone go first. Go ahead …"

A couple of women exchanged eye contact across a table; giving each other permission and giggling, they took their husbands' hands while the men feigned boredom. Then more women took the initiative and the men loosened up, too. One couple swung their arms; others found funny ways to tease each other, revealing a playfulness rarely exhibited in public. Ahdaf noticed a few disapproving scowls coming from tables of only men whose long beards signaled their conservative religiosity; but everybody else, if not playful themselves, enjoyed the merry moment.

"Wow, I wish my night last night had been as much fun! And since you didn't ask why it wasn't, I'll tell you. I met a beautiful woman, an American. I immediately thought: a perfect chance to practice my English. Right, guys? She seemed to like me, laughed at even my bad jokes, and I thought, maybe we could keep the language lesson going over dinner. It's true, no groans, I just wanted to conjugate a verb or two, eventually get past the conditional tense to superlatives with a few commas along the way. So, I asked a very simple question. 'Would you like to have dinner with me?' I can't think of a simpler question between a guy and a gal. Even if you only know the word *dinner*, you'd get the gist of it, right? And you know how she responded? 'It's complicated.' Okay, according to Facebook, relationships are 'complicated,' but an eight-word question about going out to dinner? 'How can that be complicated?' I asked, thinking it's impossible that she's poorer than me. 'I'll pay. My treat,' I offered. It turns out it wasn't the money, but her diet. Okay, so if she's on a diet, I suggested we eat light. 'We'll share a döner kebab,' I said, mispronouncing it and trying to make it sound funny, thinking if I talked funny, she'd think I *was* funny. She didn't. She was very earnest about her diet. 'I'm a vegan,' she declared, which, it turns out, is the atomic bomb of diets. Once veganated, everything is off the menu. Maybe salt's allowed. I was afraid to ask. When she finished listing what she couldn't eat, I told her it would surprise a lot of refugees to know they they're vegans. She didn't get that I was joking. Maybe because she knew it wasn't exactly a joke. Instead, she wanted to know if I was a Syrian refugee. To some people, there's a hierarchy with refugees, but to refugees, we've all fallen off whatever ladder we were climbing. I told her my whole family was Syrian except me. I was a Vegan refugee from Veganlandia. She processed that, and you know what she said? Nothing. Not even a smile. She looked at me, like –"

An image on the muted television caught Omar's eye, stopping him mid-sentence. Everyone looked up and fell silent, too, watching bodies being lifted off fishing boats onto a dock in a small harbor. Others who had survived an apparent capsizing stumbled about, distraught, desperate to find loved ones and friends. Leyla turned up the sound as the camera swung to a reporter. "All we know for certain is that a raft capsized with at least two dozen drowned and many missing," she said. A ticker at the bottom of the screen identified her as CNN SPECIAL CORRESPONDENT DERYA THOMAS. "Some of the survivors claim they were rammed. The mystery is, where *was* the Coast Guard, and where *is* the Coast Guard? All we know is that this is a terrible tragedy. I've seen bodies of several children."

"This is why they drowned!" a man shouted offscreen.

The cameraman found him on his knees next to a dead woman whose lifejacket he'd cut open. He reached into it and threw into the air soggy globs – of what, Ahdaf couldn't tell. "They're filled with shredded newspaper!" the man cried. He lurched to the side to cut into the lifejacket on another body and flung more of the muck into the air. "It's their lifejackets that killed them! The newspaper was heavy! They sank as soon as they hit the water!"

The cameraman swung to a woman seated on a wooden crate with a man's lifeless body draped across her knees. Ahdaf fixated on the pink cap still clinging to his head because of the knot of hair he'd pulled through its plastic band at the back. It was Meryem, cradling her drowned son, Issa. Fourteen. A sweet and funny kid.

The camera swung back to the man shouting, "Look! More newspaper!"

Omar reached over the bar for the remote control and turned off the broadcast. "I've run out of funny lines. I live on your tips, but tonight, give them to someone who really needs it when you're walking home. They're out there on the sidewalks. And please, someone help that woman."

Polite applause followed the comedian out the door. Many others left, too. Ahdaf, shaken, groaned and leaned on the bar.

"What is it?" Leyla asked.

"That's the family I helped last night. I put them on that raft." Ahdaf wept, thankful that his tears disappeared into his short beard; he didn't want others to see him cry. "I think only the mother survived."

"The woman they showed just now?"

"Meryem," he choked out. "Her husband said I'd saved their lives. But I didn't. I killed them!"

Leyla touched his arm. "It's not your fault."

"I put them on that raft. I bought their lifejackets."

"You didn't fill them with newspaper. You can't control what other people do."

"I can control what *I* do." He grabbed a couple of napkins and headed for the door.

"Ahdaf, wait," Leyla called after him, but he was gone.

Back on the street, he blew his nose, wiped his eyes, and wished he'd taken more napkins off the bar. He kept recalling how grateful Yusuf's family had been, how the whole family – the whole warm family – had trusted him, but in the end he'd led them to their slaughter. Sheep in pink caps. *Get on this bus ....* *Call this person when you arrive ....* Raft, lifejacket, and possibly a harrowing crossing, but at the end, a new life. A rebirth. But not for Yusuf's family. Ahdaf's family. The one he'd liked the most. He was blubbering by the time he reached his building and climbed the stairs to his room. He heard his French neighbor's dog sniffing at her door and hurried to unlock his own, not in the mood to talk to anyone. His door closed just as Madame Darton's opened.

Mechanically, as he got ready for bed, he picked up his cell phone to set his alarm an hour before his next appointment. Then he remembered: he didn't have a next one. Today he'd been too distracted by Malik's threat to trawl the streets for refugees in need of his kind of help. Instead, he'd kept up a running monologue in his head, denouncing Malik for destroying his fragile sense of security. He'd threatened Ahdaf with exactly what had made him flee home, making him a refugee, too. Ahdaf had never seen his own plight as being akin to the masses of people fleeing war. He hadn't fled because of the bombs. He'd fled because of ISIS's death warrants. That fear wouldn't stop until ISIS was defeated, and Ahdaf had no wish to live with that fear for the rest of his life.

Suddenly he knew what he had to do.

He debated whether to have a nightcap beer – his frequent sedative – and decided against it. His habitual anxiety had temporarily abated with the excitement of knowing he would finally fight back. Down to his underwear, he pulled the sheet over him, and just as quickly threw it off. Not sleepy, he lay flat on his back, recalling his horrible day, starting with Malik's curse and ending with drowned refugees. It didn't matter what little kindness he could offer refugees if what he did ultimately contributed

24

to their deaths. How many deaths caused by lifejackets heavy with sodden paper had gone unreported? Who knew their names, or cared? But he wouldn't forget Yusuf's family. Nor his cousin Sadiq. He'd loved him so much. Now maybe he could do something to avenge his death. No, it wasn't vengeance that Ahdaf sought. He wanted to stop such horrors from happening again, from his cousin thrown off a roof to Yusuf's family drowned by their lifejackets. He didn't know what he'd be asked to do, but he'd do anything to stop ISIS's cruelty.

For every Sadiq and every Issa.

He fell asleep with tears dripping off his ears.

DAY 3

Ahdaf was still asleep when they burst into his room. He glimpsed Malik before a pillowcase was pulled over his head. He kicked and swung blindly, but they overpowered him and tied his hands. They pulled him into the hall, but instead of dragging him down to the street like he expected, to be shot and left in the gutter, they yanked him up past eight landings and a final ninth flight of stairs to the rooftop. He could feel the fresher air on his face through the pillowcase. He relished it, and the sun, too. He knew they were his last sensual moments. It must have been midday. How had he slept so long?

They pushed him forward. Ahdaf didn't resist. What would be the point? A hand stopped him before he stepped into air, not to save him but to let him ponder that last step. His fear his sentence, and death his justice. From the street below, the repeated chant of a holy man reached his ears. The verse: when a man mounts a man as he would a woman, it is a sin so heinous that it shakes Allah's throne.

There it was, the palm on the middle on his back that, with a firm shove, sent him over the edge, falling headfirst, the wind whipping off the pillowcase from his face.

Just before he hit the ground, Ahdaf jerked awake.

Minutes later, coffee in hand, he pulled out Selim Wilson's card. No name, only a number. His call was answered by only a message tone, as Selim had told him it would be. When it ended, he said, "It's Ahdaf. I want to help you."

A minute later he had a message back.

One hour. Eminönü docks. Newsstand.

Already showered and dressed, he decided to have a second coffee near the docks. The tram was a quick ride. He crossed over its tracks, where he skirted the enormous Eminönü Square before ducking into a narrow passageway made barely passable by café tables lining both sides. He sat outside, where he could watch the news on a television inside. Two reporters, both women, appeared on split screens: one seated behind a high counter in CNN Türk's television studio, the other standing on the edge of a small harbor with colorful fishing boats behind her. A ticker identified her as Derya Thomas, the same reporter from the night before. Behind the studio reporter, a slideshow displayed images of the raft tragedy – not the capsizing itself, but fishing boats bringing the injured and dead into the small harbor; moments of anguish as people recognized loved ones who'd drowned; the widening line of bodies side-by-side on the dock, their faces covered by restaurant napkins. The slideshow stopped with another image of Meryem cradling her son's lifeless body. Had Yusuf survived, he would have been with her, so apparently he had not. Ahdaf hoped they wouldn't show the bodies on the ground; he didn't want to recognize him.

"Poor people," the waiter said when he brought his coffee. "Only trying to survive, and what happens? Dozens drowned. If they stayed home, they might be still alive."

Ahdaf snorted. "Or killed by one of Assad's chemical bombs. Or beheaded. Or thrown off a rooftop."

"You saw all that?"

"Not the beheading."

The waiter shrugged. "I don't know what is more risky for them, to stay home or to leave."

"They leave because it's safer," Ahdaf answered. "Staying isn't a choice for anyone who can manage to escape."

"You're the odd one, not crossing to Europe," the waiter remarked. "How long have you been here?"

"Almost seven months."

"Most of you don't want to stay seven days."

"I know, and I try to help them. For me, I'm safe enough in Istanbul."

"I hope it stays that way for all of us."

When the waiter returned inside, Ahdaf looked back at the television.

"We don't know exactly what happened," Derya Thomas was saying, "but the incident needs to be investigated, and not just because it was a tragedy."

"Are you suggesting it wasn't an accident?" the CNN reporter asked.

"Some of the survivors say that their raft was rammed."

"Rammed?" the reporter asked, surprised by the allegation.

"There were fishermen in the area, and maybe one of them accidentally hit the raft. Look at the facts: it was night, the sea was choppy, and most rafts carrying refugees don't have running lights for obvious reasons. But where was the Coast Guard? Who supplied lifejackets filled with shredded newspaper? Most refugees don't know how to swim. Their lifejackets drowned them. Was it all coordinated?"

The CNN reporter appeared to gasp. "Are you suggesting it was intentional?"

"I'm asking questions that need to be answered before we can know what happened."

"Indeed, they do need to be answered," the reporter agreed. "I also have a question for you."

Derya said, "I'll answer it if I can."

"You've covered so many incidents where people have drowned, sometimes whole families. On the screen behind me, our viewers can see the woman seated on a crate with, and I'm guessing, her drowned husband across her knees."

The camera zoomed in on Meryem. "It's her son, not her husband," Derya corrected the other reporter. "He was 14 years old. Her husband's body is in the line of bodies on the ground. She also lost an infant. She's also five months pregnant, but fortunately didn't miscarry."

The reporter, moved by Meryem's heartbreaking situation, clasped a hand to her chest. "I'm watching her on a screen and all I want to do is cry! So, my question is, you're there in person. How do you cope with all that sadness?"

"I cry at home," Derya replied. "Of course, some stories are harder to report than others, and hers is one of them. I know it's an odd comparison to make in a Muslim country, but she reminds me of Michelangelo's *Pietà*, the statue of Jesus's mother with his dead body draped across her knees. For me, Meryem – that's the woman's name – is the Syrian *Pietà*. From now on, at least for me, her image will always define this refugee crisis."

"As sad as that is, it's a beautiful thought," the CNN reporter replied. "You've given this tragedy a human face. An eternal face. Thank you, Derya Thomas, for taking the risks you do to remind us that this crisis is about people."

The camera lingered on Meryem before cutting to a commercial break.

Ahdaf took a last sip of coffee before walking back across the tram tracks to a newsstand, where he skimmed the headlines of newspapers clipped to wires hanging over stacks of them for sale. Only a couple of sensationalist tabloids, which always waited until the last minute to print, reported the breaking news that a raft of refugees had capsized off Assos with many drowned and missing. One had published the same portrait of Meryem that he'd seen on television with Issa limp across her knees. The Syrian *Pietà*. Of course, her photograph hadn't been given that moniker when it was published, but seeing the image again, Ahdaf realized how powerful it was. No doubt it would go viral.

The government-controlled newspapers made no mention of the raft incident; instead, they highlighted skirmishes in Turkish-occupied northern Syria, where ISIS fighters had attacked two police stations in a single day. Four policemen had been killed, and both stations' firearms stolen. The government tabloids downplayed these as minor incidents, nothing more than slingshot wounds on a mighty military, though they acknowledged that they represented a worrisome escalation in ISIS's war of attrition, which usually saw, at most, two attacks per week, not two in one day.

Ahdaf had never heard of a *pietà*. Guessing how to spell it, he googled it, and the first thing that appeared was a thumbnail of Michelangelo's *Pietà*. Instantly he saw the similarity of the two scenes, each woman grieving for a dead son stretched across her knees, but neither one wailing like the ululating grief he was used to witnessing. Instead, eyes downcast, they had nothing left but silence with which to mourn their slain men. Moved by the resemblance, he held his phone displaying Michelangelo's Mary alongside Meryem's picture in the newspaper.

"Excuse me," he heard as a hand reached around him to grab a paper off the stack. "Sorry, but I have a ferry to catch."

It was Selim, the CIA man. *Presumed* CIA man, Ahdaf reminded himself; Selim had never said. Ahdaf, less defensive than when Selim had first approached him in Leyla's Café, appraised him a second time, again thinking how handsome he was. Though stocky, he wasn't fat, and his quick movements suggested that he wasn't much older than Ahdaf. How could a CIA agent be so young?

"Let's meet on the ferry to Üsküdar," Selim said under his breath. "Less chance we'll be followed."

Selim paid for the newspaper and headed for the turnstiles. Ahdaf lagged behind as he followed him to the ferry, across a wobbly gangplank and up metal stairs to an open deck. Pretending to be strangers, they leaned against opposite rails.

As soon as the ferry was underway, the breeze gained strength. Selim turned his back to the sea, gripping the newspaper in both hands so it wouldn't fly apart. While pretending to read it, his eyes were scanning everyone on deck. He was practiced, and so discreet that when he made eye contact, Ahdaf almost doubted it had happened. When the wind became too gusty, Selim folded the newspaper and stuck it in his back pocket. He turned seaward and used his phone to take photos of the passing boats – or rather ships, as most were enormous freighters with only rare skiffs and yachts plying their wakes.

Ahdaf was unsure what he was supposed to do. Their brief eye contact – was it just a recognition that he knew he was there, or a signal to join him? He'd let Selim decide, and turned around to watch the view from his side of the ferry. Moments later, Selim joined him at the rail. Not looking at Ahdaf, he asked, "What changed your mind?"

"The story on the front page."

"The story about the raft?"

"The woman. I put her whole family on the raft. Only she survived."

Selim shook his head. "You're not responsible."

"In some way, I am."

"You'll eventually realize that you're not. Then you might regret changing your mind."

"No, I won't change my mind. I hate ISIS."

"ISIS hasn't claimed responsibility for the raft incident," Selim reminded him.

"It doesn't matter. Everybody was on that raft because of ISIS. I'm a refugee because of ISIS, and ISIS executed my cousin."

"Why did they execute him?"

"Someone denounced him."

"Denounced him?"

"They claimed he was a homosexual."

"Was he?"

"Does it matter? It shouldn't be a death sentence." Ahdaf paused, recalling Sadiq's fall from the rooftop. "We were like brothers. Only closer."

"Are you trying to say ... you were lovers?" Selim asked.

The unexpected question startled Ahdaf. He'd thought of Sadiq and himself as cousins with an affection unique to them. Even as their love deepened, they justified touching each other as satisfying male needs since girls were off-limits. The specter of shame perpetually haunted them, and inhibited how far they would go to express their love. They'd heard the vulgar terms for homosexuals, but those cruel words didn't apply to them because their affection for each other was perfect.

"We weren't lovers," Ahdaf finally answered.

"You hesitated," Selim replied.

"I was remembering my cousin. Why would you ask me that question?"

"I'm not sure what 'closer than brothers' means."

"It means we weren't born brothers, but loved each other as much. That's the only way I can describe it." Ahdaf reminded himself that Selim *was* a spy, and somehow might know a lot about him. "What do you think you know about me, anyway?"

"Not much, except I'm learning you're a sensitive guy. You're also street-smart enough to have a reliable network. And you're not jumping on a raft to Greece anytime soon."

"Why's that important?"

"You could be a long-term asset."

"Why would I want that?"

"I can help you."

"*Help* me?"

"Smuggling isn't a safe business. I can help you when you need it. You won't be safe forever."

Ahdaf snorted. "You don't look old enough to help yourself!"

"Yeah, I know, boyish good looks. Except for the fact that I'm four years older than you."

"How do you know my age?"

"It's my job to know things."

"Because you work for the C–?"

"Don't say it. It's the one word everyone hears."

"There's something else," Ahdaf said. "Someone approached me at the mosque. He wants me to help ISIS."

"Was it Malik Khair?" Selim asked.

"How did you know?"

"If there's an ISIS cell at a mosque, often the *medrese* is its cover. Or 'madrasa,' as you call them in Syria."

"A lot of mosques had one," Ahdaf replied.

"There aren't so many in Turkey. Not yet, but the number's growing. Atatürk made them illegal in 1924, wanting Turkey to be a secular country. President Erdogan made them legal again two years ago to attract religious voters. He declared he wanted to raise a 'pious generation' and he is. Certainly a more fundamentalist one and arguably more terrorist. While most fundamentalists aren't terrorists, most terrorists *are* fundamentalists, and the *medreses* make it possible for them to meet and plan their attacks with the excuse of gathering for religious studies."

"How did you know which is *my* mosque?" Ahdaf asked. As soon as he did, he realized, "You came to Leyla's Café because you wanted us to be seen together, didn't you? You fucking set me up."

"What does Malik want you to do?"

"Spy on you."

"Good. Do you want to do it?"

"Do what?"

"Be a double agent. Malik will think you're working for him when you're really working for us."

"What if I make it the other way around?"

"A triple agent?" Selim scoffed. "That's too complicated even for me to sort out."

Ahdaf hesitated. It felt like a commitment to ask, "What do I do?"

"You go to prayers every day, right?"

"How do you know that about me?"

Ignoring his question, Selim said, "Go to prayers today, because Malik will be looking for you. You've had a day to think about his proposal. Tell him we met again. Convince him I think you're working for me when you really want to work for him."

The ferry blew its horn as it approached the dock, interrupting their conversation.

"Everybody has to disembark," Selim said. "You can go back when you want. If we happen to be on the same ferry, we don't talk to each other."

"You're not going back?"

"I have some business over here." Selim offered him the newspaper. "Do you want this?"

"Sure." Ahdaf took it and stuck it in his daypack.

People started moving toward the exit on the lower deck. Ahdaf and Selim joined them, getting jostled on the narrow stairs. The gangplank scraped noisily on the dock. After they'd crossed it, Selim peeled off for a taxi without a goodbye. Ahdaf turned back around to reboard the ferry, and saw a man watching him.

He looked vaguely familiar, but that could be said about the millions of Turkish men sporting graying beards and beige kaftans. When he realized Ahdaf had noticed him, he looked quickly away.

Ahdaf, his mind reeling with what he'd just committed to, scarcely noticed the trip back across the narrow strait. Selim had joked that a "triple spy" was too complicated. A "double spy" sounded equally complicated and dangerous – but what choice did he have? Malik's threat was real.

Back in Eminönü, he shuffled his way along with the disembarking crowd onto the dock. A couple of times he glanced over his shoulder to see if he was being followed, but with so many people, he couldn't tell. When he thought about it, he realized it was more likely the man in the beige kaftan had been following Selim. He was the *real* spy.

Ahdaf pressed his way onto the tram at the busy Eminönü stop and managed to get a seat. Even better, it faced forward – he was less likely to forget to get off. With so much going on in his head, probably once a week he'd miss his stop and have to cross the tracks to go back.

He put in earbuds and streamed CNN Türk on his phone. By chance, Derya Thomas was again reporting from Assos. "The sea was choppy, putting every single raft at risk that night. It doesn't take much of a wave to swamp an overloaded raft, and they're *all* overloaded. So the question is, why was the Coast Guard not where the incident happened, which, after all, is where most rafts launch? Why had it been repositioned, and on whose order?"

"You make it sound like a conspiracy," a reporter in CNN's television studio commented.

Derya's response was blunt: "It had to be planned."

Someone touched Ahdaf's shoulder. He started, but relaxed when he saw Munir. "It's our stop, Ahdaf. Aren't you getting off?"

"Yeah, I am," he said, jumping up. "Thanks."

He followed Munir onto the platform. Munir was Syrian, and a smuggler like himself. At times, when they were overbooked, they'd refer refugees to each other. They were close enough friends for Ahdaf to expect an honest answer when he asked, "Are you managing okay?"

Munir shrugged. "As okay as possible."

"And the new baby?"

Munir frowned. "Do you know any tricks for a woman to make more milk?"

Ahdaf laughed at his question. "It's not my specialization, my friend."

"The new kid's always hungry, and she refuses to drink from a bottle. We need a wet nurse or she's going to die."

Ahdaf touched his friend's shoulder. "I'm sorry. I had no idea. Have you been to a clinic? Maybe they'd know what to do."

"We went and they told us to try formula, but we've already tried formula."

"And?"

"The baby won't drink it. We don't know if it's the formula or the bottle she doesn't like. Yasmin's online all the time, looking for tips for making more milk. She's starving, too, because she's giving her food to Samir, who's hungry all the time because he's three and growing. And I'm giving half my food to her, so I'm always hungry, too. At night, we listen to each other's stomachs growl." They'd been walking, but Munir stopped, staring at the ground as if he might find a solution for his troubled situation. "I might go ahead," he finally said.

Ahdaf knew that "go ahead" was refugee code for establishing a beachhead in northern Europe and, once employed, petitioning for families to be allowed to follow. Fathers separated from wives with young children had special priority. "I don't want to leave them, but I might," Munir said. "I know a lot could go wrong. What if they get sick? Or me?"

"Is it really so bad here?" Ahdaf asked. "At least you're safe."

"It's the cockroaches. We can't stop Samir from eating them."

Ahdaf shuddered at the thought. "You can't spray?"

"Then he'd be eating poison."

"Fuck."

"We can't afford a place that doesn't have them."

"I'll send more clients to you. Sometimes I have more than I can handle."

Munir grinned. "Are you listed on TripAdvisor?"

"Sometimes I wonder!"

"It must be nice. Sometimes I wonder if my ears scare people away!"

Ahdaf laughed. His friend did have big ears that stuck out, which he blamed on his father, who pulled them as punishment when Munir was growing up. "I doubt it's your ears!" he said. "Besides, I'm barely surviving myself, and I wouldn't be if I had four mouths to feed."

"Not to mention diapers to buy," Munir groaned. "If I did go ahead, do you think you could check on Yasmin a couple of times? Just at first to make sure she's managing. She has her own phone."

Ahdaf pulled up his contact list. "What's her number?" After he typed Yasmin's number into his phone, he asked: "Do you really think you'll leave?"

Munir sighed deeply. "It feels like the only solution."

"I'll miss you," Ahdaf said, and touched his friend's shoulder. "I don't have many friends as it is. Mostly accomplices! If you do go ahead, when you're ready for your family to join you, I can organize their trip to Greece."

"Thank you."

"I wish I could do more."

They touched their hearts and said goodbye with a sense of finality. They would miss each other when their real separation

came. They'd been safe companions in a rough trade, not only referring clients when personally overloaded but also sharing contacts, the lifeblood of a successful smuggler.

Munir walked off, stoop-shouldered, defeated by Istanbul,
forced into a decision he didn't want to make – yet part of Ahdaf
envied him. Europe had a pull on all the refugees. He always had
to remind himself that he was already *here*, across the Bosporus
on the European side of Istanbul, though the city's roots were
deepest in Asia. What he ate, the street life, the calls to prayer
were the same as at home … yet he never felt at home. How could
he, when all the welcome mats had been removed?

He wound his way through a crowded market, dodging people
and pushcarts. His hometown markets had been as lively, but
never as bountiful; certainly not in the year before he left, when
ISIS resurrected its insurgency and tightened the noose around
Raqqa, creating shortages until everyone was scrambling for almost nothing. How Ahdaf wished he could be leading his parents
through this market by their bony hands, throwing whatever they
wanted onto a vendor's scale. He was tempted by a beefsteak for
his dinner that night, but instead opted for a thick slice of *helva*,
a quarter the cost; moreover, its weight didn't include bones. His
mother, he mused, would consider it a lucky day in Raqqa if she
found some bones to boil for broth.

The call to prayer started. The *müezzin's* resonant voice,
broadcast from speakers atop the nearby mosque's minaret, drifted through the market. From every mosque in the city, the call to
prayer could be heard, mingling and covering Istanbul like a comforting blanket. Some vendors knelt in their stalls to make short
order of their dutiful prayers. Others joined customers kneeling
shoulder-to-shoulder in one of the market's wider aisles while
most shoppers wended their way past them. Only the men prayed
so openly; the women prayed at home or confined their public
display of faith to mosques. Before Ahdaf left the market, he

38

bought dates and olives to supplement the *helva*, then twisted his way along the crowded sidewalk until he reached the mosque's less chaotic courtyard.

He headed for the public toilets in a corner of the mosque's garden and waited in a short line for a free urinal. When finished, he dropped his kaftan, and, turning to leave, saw that the next guy in line was the man in the beige kaftan who'd been watching him on the ferry dock in Üsküdar. Had he really been watching him? Ahdaf had thought at the time that the man looked vaguely familiar. He realized they'd probably crossed paths at the mosque, and he likely looked familiar to the man, too. Maybe the man, staring at him, had just been puzzling over where he'd seen Ahdaf before. What had appeared menacing probably wasn't. Or was it?

Ahdaf found a spot on the crowded ablutions bench to wash his feet. Friday prayers, traditionally well attended, had become even more popular in the half year that he'd been in the city. They'd evolved into political referenda, the number of men praying inside the mosque a surrogate for opinion polls that were officially discouraged and rarely believed. Nothing had people especially riled up that day, so the crowd – mostly men, with women keeping to their allotted space – was simply evidence of religion's growing popularity, a trend the government encouraged for its own gain. It troubled Ahdaf to perceive how easily religion could be subverted by politics. For him, the mosque had always been a place where the rituals of religion – the common phrases and gestures – encouraged camaraderie. He found that to be less true in Istanbul, but never threatening until Malik had approached him, making him so paranoid that he'd even suspected a guy in line for the urinals of being a spy and trailing him.

Inside the small mosque, neat lines of kneeling worshippers snaked their way across the prayer mats. Ahdaf joined the end of one of them. Unusually, there was no *imam* for noon prayers, and the men bobbed randomly, touching their foreheads to the ground, murmuring prescribed scripture, then rolling back on their haunches before bending forward again. The noise was cacophonic, like an orchestra tuning up; the hum Ahdaf recalled from concerts he'd seen on television before debris from a bomb destroyed the satellite dish on the roof of his family's house.

Without an *imam*, there was no precise moment when prayers officially concluded. The men stood up, brushed their knees and left through the heavy drape that served as a door. Outside, Ahdaf took as long as he could putting on his sandals, hoping Malik might approach him – and he did.

"So again, you prove me correct," the *medrese's* director said.

"How is that?"

"You are faithful."

"Observant is not necessarily faithful."

"You needn't come for noon prayers."

"Habits are hard to break."

"Or perhaps you have changed your mind."

"Why do you think that?"

"There are other mosques where you could pray."

"But this is the most popular with refugees."

Malik smiled. "It's something I've encouraged. I'm from Raqqa too."

"But you can't be a refugee," Ahdaf protested. "Not a real refugee. You have a job!"

Malik chuckled. "Our Turkish brothers made an exception for me. When President Erdogan made madrasas legal again, there were no qualified headmasters in the country. I applied for a job and here I am. That's how I escaped our war. So why have you changed your mind?"

Ahdaf slid the daypack off his shoulder and pulled out the newspaper that Selim had given him. He unfolded it and showed Meryem's photo on the front page. "Hers was the last family I helped," he said. "That's her son across her knees. He drowned."

"And you want revenge?" Malik suggested.

"The Turkish government planned this," Ahdaf replied. "It's confirmed on the news."

"I still don't understand."

"ISIS is at war with Turkey."

"I never said –"

"You don't need to say it. Tell me what I can do to help fight Turkey."

Ahdaf left the mosque feeling fouled by his many deceptions, and fearful. He'd been tossed juggler's clubs, and any one he dropped could be fatal. Worse, if after all the lies and gambles, he ended up inadvertently aiding ISIS, he would never forgive himself. What had Selim dubbed him? A "double agent"? He was bad at lying once, let alone doubly.

Sweating in the unseasonably warm afternoon, Ahdaf entered Leyla's Café hoping she had at least one ice-cold beer. He planned to down it and go home for a nap. As he sat on a barstool, Leyla caught his eye and nodded in the direction of a disheveled young man watching him from a table. "He's been waiting for you."

The stranger noticed her signal as well, and stood to greet him. "Are you Ahdaf Jalil?" he asked.

"That's me."

"I'm Kalam."

They shook hands and touched their hearts. Ahdaf noticed that he had tried to pick his fingernails clean but not very successfully. He had streaks of mud on his neck and dirt in his ears; and his oily hair, the color of light caramel, was long enough to tuck behind his ears. Despite his grimy state, Ahdaf could see how handsome the lanky stranger was, with an open, pleasant face and forehead that furrowed when he smiled.

"Is something wrong?" Kalam asked.

"No. Why?"

"You're staring at me. Can I buy you a tea?"

Ahdaf would have preferred a beer, but he assumed he'd just met a new client and would spend the afternoon sorting him out. A beer and nap would have to wait. "Sure," he said. "Do you want to sit here, or at a table?"

"Why not here?"

"It's a bar. Some people don't like that."

"After walking for three months, I'll sit anywhere," Kalam replied, and sat on the stool next to him. "Two teas, Leyla," he ordered.

"How many sugars?" she asked as she poured steaming black tea into glasses.

"Be careful," Ahdaf warned Kalam. "She charges for sugar."

"The third one's free," Leyla clarified, and set the glasses in front of them.

"Only one for me," Ahdaf said unhappily.

"I'll take two and give my third one to him," Kalam said.

"You're a clever guy," Leyla remarked, and dropped two cubes into each glass. "My treat," she said, and squeezed around the end of the short bar to serve tables.

Stirring his tea, Ahdaf asked, "Are you from Raqqa?"

"How'd you guess?"

"Your accent – and I made the same three-month walk."

"I know. People talk about you."

Ahdaf grunted. "I bet they do."

"You have a good reputation for getting people to Europe."

"You mean crossing to Greece, right? Because I can't get you to Italy, for instance."

"Crossing to Greece," Kalam assured him.

"Why leave Raqqa now?" Ahdaf asked. "I know there's a war, but there's been a war for a long time."

When ISIS started kidnapping young men to fight for it, Kalam had fled. Like Ahdaf, he had traveled alone and walked most of the way. His sniffed at his shirt. "I know I smell bad. My last shower was over two weeks ago, and I'm desperate for one."

"You don't smell bad," Ahdaf lied. Yes, his clothes were crumpled, and his beard untrimmed and whiskery, but Ahdaf focused on his eyes — sparkling emeralds above his caramel beard.

"Did I say something wrong?" Kalam asked.

"No. Why?"

"You're staring at me again."

"Sorry. I'm thinking what to do first. Do you have a room?"

Kalam shook his head. "I only arrived today. Last night, I was outside of the city. I took buses to come here."

"And you want to continue to Europe?"

"*Inshallah.*"

"It takes time to organize."

"It's not possible tomorrow?"

"It usually two days minimum to organize everything, and now, before the weather turns too bad, it's not so fast finding a space on a raft."

"They can't find space for one more person?"

"That's the problem: they do. One more person, and one more, and one more, and soon the raft is overcrowded and sinks. You'll need a room for a couple of nights. Maybe three or four."

"How much does a room cost?"

"More than it should be, but you can't sleep on the street. The police will hassle you, or someone who hates refugees is likely to kick you in the side while you're asleep. Do you have Turkish *liras*?"

"Yes, and I want a shower. Definitely a shower."

Ahdaf shrugged. "It'll be what I can find. Why don't you take a piss while I find you a room?"

"I don't need to piss."

"I need 10 minutes to make some calls. In private."

"Oh, I get it."

"The toilet's in the back on the left."

"I know. I've been waiting for you." He checked his cell phone. "For three hours and 40 minutes to be exact."

"You know the exact time?" Ahdaf asked, suspicious why Kalam had noted the precise moment that they met. Had he needed to report it to someone?

"No one could say for sure if you were coming, and I kept checking how late it was getting," Kalam answered. "I was nervous, too, about what kind of person you'd be. Someone who'd help me, or cheat me, or cheat me and then kill me to cover up cheating me? You know the stories better than I do."

"And now that I've shown up?"

"I'm not nervous about you, only about what's next."

"What's next is finding you a room."

Kalam pushed back his chair. "A room with a shower, don't forget."

Ahdaf made a point of sniffing the air. "Me forget the shower?"

"I really stink, don't I?"

"It was a joke. But yes, you need a shower, though you're not the worst I've smelled."

"Who was the worst?"

"Other than me?" Ahdaf asked. "No one."

He watched Kalam walk off, surprising himself as he imagined the waltz of his bare buttocks. His mind peeled off his jeans as if he were used to seeing naked men, which he wasn't. Of course, he'd seen naked men in fleeting moments in hammams; and he'd seen his father, too, but even those glimpses over a whole childhood could be counted on one hand. Ahdaf had never been entirely naked with his cousin, despite their timid intimacy. He noticed men, but only in the blandest terms: *cute, handsome, short, tall*. Never consciously sexual. The only times he'd been aroused at the thought of a man had been in anticipation of a rendezvous with his cousin or the expectation of a handjob in a hammam. Had those simple encounters opened a Pandora's box of desire? More likely, he thought, it was Kalam's emerald eyes.

"You better get busy finding him a room," Leyla broke into his thoughts.

"You've been eavesdropping again."

"How else do I know what's happening?"

"Why should you know?"

"I worry about my boys. You're all innocent, young, and have bigger barks than you can deliver."

"Hav-hav!" Ahdaf grunted.

Leyla eyed him. "He needs a shower first."

"First before what?"

"Before anything else."

"He knows."

"So does anybody around him." She glanced toward the hallway to the WCs. "He's waiting for you to signal that it's all right for him to come back."

"It's not." Ahdaf held up his hand to stop Kalam and started making calls. After the third one, he shrugged his apologies at Kalam, and kept trying. Two calls later, he found a room with a shower and negotiated a good price. He gave Kalam a thumbs-up.

Kalam came back, grinning. "So, do I have a shower?"

"I forgot to ask."

"What?"

Ahdaf smiled. "Don't worry. It has a shower. It's what took me so long."

"How much?"

When Ahdaf told him, he shrugged, accepting the inevitable. But when he added that he owed Leyla five *liras*, Kalam complained, "For one tea?"

"Two teas," Leyla corrected him. "That includes Ahdaf's tea, since he's working for you."

Kalam shrugged and left the coins on the counter. "Can we go to the room now?"

All along the street, restaurant owners had pulled extra tables onto the sidewalk to take advantage of the sunny day. Waiters shouted orders at cooks inside while the smell of grilling meat permeated the air. At the corner, they waited for two motorcycles to roar past them before turning up the hill. In another couple of blocks, they turned onto a quieter street of mostly five- and six-story apartment buildings with laundry drying on most small balconies.

"What happens next?" Kalam asked.

"You wait for me to coordinate everything," Ahdaf told him." It's a lot of back-and-forth. I got you a room. Now I need to coordinate a bus, a raft, and a lifejacket."

"I don't need a lifejacket. I can swim."

"Not in the channel, if it's rough. Without a lifejacket, you'll drown."

"What's one cost?"

"When you need one and don't have one? Your life." Ahdaf stopped and rang a doorbell. "Here's where you're staying."

"The Tropicana?" Kalam asked, reading the sign over the door. "In Istanbul?"

"You'll see."

A buzzer unlatched the door and Kalam followed Ahdaf inside.

At the opposite end of a long hall sat a white-haired man behind a bamboo counter flanked by plastic palm trees. Under one stood two dusty pink flamingos. Under the other, a miniature beach umbrella. On the hall's long walls, men's swimming trunks hung on facing lines of hooks that ran all the way to the reception counter. Kalam laughed. "This is so weird! Do you think I can take a picture?"

"Hey, Fatih," Ahdaf called. "It's another one who wants a photo."

"New policy. Ten euros, unless you make me famous."

"He says it to everyone," Ahdaf whispered. "Just tell him you'll make him famous."

"I'll make you famous!" Kalam called back. "But I shoot video, not photos."

"I'll be a movie star! Or a *moving* one, and that alone should make me famous at my age! Come on and shoot your video."

Kalam pulled his phone, hanging on a cord around his neck, out from under his shirt, and started down the long hall. When he got close to the counter, Fatih made a funny face, and Kalam stopped recording. "Thanks. I want to make a movie of my journey."

"*Merhaba*, Fatih," Ahdaf said, joining his new client. " This is Kalam. Kalam, this is Fatih."

They shook hands.

"Why the décor?" asked Kalam. "Are you from a tropical island?"

The older man sighed. "Who wants to check into someplace that looks like a detention camp? The owner, he named the hotel 'The Tropicana,' probably thinking he could trick ignorant refugees into thinking they were in the tropics. I decided at least I could make them smile when they walk in." He held out his hand. "That's 15 euros, if you have euros. Twenty euros in *liras* if you only have *liras*."

"I have euros." Kalam pulled out a wad of new bills and paid him. "I got euros out of a bank machine! Can you imagine that in Raqqa?"

Ahdaf snorted. "There wasn't a working bank machine when I left. I'm not sure if there was still a functioning bank."

"Fortunately, I don't need a bank machine, but I do need a shower. There's one in my room, right?" Kalam asked the hotel-keeper.

"Yes, and you do need a shower."

"It's his first day in Istanbul," Ahdaf said, explaining Kalam's general unkemptness.

"I know what they smell like at the end of their journey. Human dirt." Fatih handed him a key. "Fifth floor on the left." He pointed. "The stairs are through that door."

"I'll show you the room," Ahdaf offered.

"Five flights up? You don't have to do that."

"He can probably find the light switch," Fatih said. "It's on the wall inside the door, and yes, it's a flush toilet. Please try to remember." Looking at Ahdaf, he asked, "Did I miss anything?"

Ignoring the hotelkeeper, Ahdaf told Kalam, "I'll still walk up with you. We need to go over some details."

The two young men, both fit, easily took the stairs.

"You've been here what, nine or 10 months?" Kalam asked Ahdaf's back.

"That's when I left Raqqa. Like you, it took me three months to walk here. So, seven months in Istanbul."

"You're not crossing?"

"I think about it. Maybe eventually. I'm surviving okay here."

"'Surviving okay' and 'living your dreams' are different things."

"It's your dream to live in Europe?"

"It's my big dream to make movies," Kalam replied. "I don't care where. Maybe Hollywood! Or France, Germany, Sweden, England. They all make good movies."

"That's a big dream, all right."

"Bigger than repairing car engines in Raqqa, which is what I was doing."

"You're right about that. Fifth floor."

He opened the stairwell door to a rectangular concrete slab

48

with flimsy doors to the left and right. "You've got the key."

Kalam opened the door. "Come in for a minute. I haven't talked to anyone I trust in weeks."

Ahdaf shrugged. "Sure."

"Great."

They went inside. The instant Kalam switched on the light, dozens of cockroaches scurried for the shadows. "All the hotels have them," Ahdaf said. "I can't do anything about it."

"I've slept in worse situations. Besides, I can eat them if I get hungry enough. They're mostly protein, did you know that?"

Ahdaf felt slightly nauseated at the thought, reminded that his friend's son ate them for exactly that reason.

"So far, it's only been a philosophical question," Kalam added. "I confess, I was hungry enough at times that I was tempted. Some days I ate grass. I know it's not nutritious for humans, but it's not a poison, and filled me up."

Ahdaf already knew the room. He'd been in dozens like it. None of the other fleabags had pink flamingos at the front desk, but they all had mattresses on the floor and sometimes a chair. Kalam's room had one, and he dropped his pack on it. "I want to check the shower." He stepped into the bathroom, and a moment later whooped, "There is one! And there's water! *Oh fuck!*"

"What happened?" Ahdaf peered around the door and saw dozens of cockroaches fleeing an open drain on the side of the tub.

Kalam pulled off his shirt. "I don't care. I gotta take a shower." He leaned against the wall to take off his shoes and socks. His eyes smiled when he asked, "You want to join me? I wash your back and you wash mine? I know mine needs scrubbing."

Ahdaf felt conflicted by Kalam's question. Of course he wanted to shower with the handsome stranger. He'd see those waltzing buttocks naked and maybe even touch them. But as soon as his fantasies verged on sexual, the paranoia that dogged him

49

returned. Other than a somewhat flirtatious suggestion that they wash each other's backs, it could also be true that that's all Kalam really wanted, and wouldn't welcome a hand on his backside or anywhere else.

All those thoughts were swirling in his head as Kalam stripped, stepped into the bathtub and turned on the shower. He gasped when the cold water first hit him, but soon became used to it, flapped his arms and laughed abundantly. With no shower curtain, he managed to splash Ahdaf at the same time. "This feels so good! It's cold, but it's also wonderful! Join me!"

"I'm good," Ahdaf replied. "I went to the hammam yesterday."

Kalam started soaping up. "You need to be careful at hammams. That's where Sadiq was caught."

Startled by the revelation, Ahdaf asked, "You knew my cousin?"

"We were friends."

"He never mentioned you."

"He often mentioned *you*," Kalam told him. "Sadiq loved you."

"He'd have said something about your green eyes," Ahdaf muttered, trying to make sense of what he'd just learned.

Kalam laughed. "He had a thing about eyes, didn't he?"

"His were beautiful," Ahdaf replied.

"Hazel, like yours," Kalam said. "Maybe he didn't say anything about me because he didn't want you to be jealous."

"Jealous?"

"We were secret friends, too."

"He called us that," Ahdaf replied. "How did you meet him?"

"Along the river."

"Along the *river*?"

"He never told you about that, did he? I told him he should, but he didn't want you going there."

"Tell me about what?"

"There's a place along the river where men like us go to

meet. Not to have sex – that's too dangerous – just to meet and make plans." Kalam reached for his briefs on the floor and dropped them in the tub. "I might as well wash these at the same time," he said, and started treading them with his feet as soapy water ran down his legs. "He never told you about that place, did he?"

"No."

"I told him he should, but he thought it would be too dangerous. He said you were too innocent."

"Innocent?"

"You might be led into a trap without knowing it. After your cousin and I met, we stuck to each other, and you had him, too. Until someone denounced him, we were all safe."

"Who denounced him?"

"I don't know."

"You said at the hammam," Ahdaf reminded him.

"It's only a guess, but I think that's the most likely for Sadiq. I don't think he had more than three secret lives."

"Three secret lives?"

"Him and me. You and him. And the hammam." Kalam turned his face to let the water run over it. *Ohhh …*" he moaned. "You don't know how good this feels. But of course you do."

Ahdaf smiled. "I remember my first shower after my long journey. It felt exactly like you're sounding."

"You sure you don't want your back washed?"

"I'm sure."

"There's still a piece of soap."

"I said I don't want my back washed." It came out terser than Ahdaf intended, but he let it stand. What he longed to do was to embrace Kalam, pressing their chests together, skin on skin. His cousin had never even taken off his shirt completely; he'd only unbuttoned it. Ahdaf came close to acting on his desire, but his natural paranoia stopped him. Thinking about it, how would

Kalam know where Sadiq had been caught when Ahdaf himself didn't know? Had Kalam denounced him? Ahdaf suddenly felt nauseated again. Maybe Kalam tracking down Ahdaf wasn't innocent, but a plan to entrap him, too? Who'd be the villain behind such a plan? Malik from the mosque?

Ahdaf, reeling from Kalam's revelations and his own suspicions, turned to leave without even a goodbye.

"Hey! Where are you going?" Kalam asked.

Ahdaf turned back to face him. Kalam made no effort to cover himself as the water ran down his bronze body. In five steps he could've cupped his cock in his hand. Had he seduced Sadiq in the same way? It was that suspicion that immobilized Ahdaf. "I've a lot to think about," he replied, "including getting you on a raft."

"I hope what I told you about me and Sadiq didn't hurt your feelings."

"I don't know what I'm feeling. Let's meet at Leyla's Café later. I might have more information for you."

"When, later?"

"When you smell better." Ahdaf grinned when he said it. He didn't want to leave on a sour note.

He took the stairs two at a time. He wasn't sure why he was running, except for a vague sense of betrayal by his cousin, but with every step he wondered: was any accusation warranted? There were so many ways to dissect the shame of homosexuality. It was a word burdened by injustice, not fidelity. Ahdaf, a novice in the gay world, had just learned that.

He slowed down as he approached the small hotel's front desk. The hotelkeeper, having heard his heavy steps, raised a worried head. "Is everything okay?"

"Yeah, I'm just late for another meeting. My friend might need directions to go back to Leyla's."

"You could drop breadcrumbs."

"Birds might eat them."

Fatih snorted. "More likely the refugees."

"In either case, directions are more reliable," Ahdaf replied.

He walked down the hall between the facing lines of men's swimming trunks on hooks and stepped into the balmy night. He paused on the sidewalk. His plans hadn't extended beyond checking Kalam into his room. Certainly he hadn't counted on watching Kalam strip naked, or facing him in conversation once he was, suggesting pleasures Ahdaf could now visualize. Dragging his tongue down Kalam's neck. Kissing a nipple. Nuzzling the patch of wiry hair below his belly. He longed to go back and join Kalam in the shower, but wouldn't Fatih be suspicious? Whom might he be reporting to, in Istanbul's pervasive spy web?

In the months since arriving in the city, Ahdaf had managed to construct a world where he felt safe, given his circumstances; he was coping, and not hungry—what more could he ask for? Yet, in a single day, his sense of security had collapsed, undermined by both ISIS and the CIA and finally toppled by Kalam, who showed up knowing so much about his relationship with Sadiq that it fed his paranoia. He wanted to shout at the injustice of the world and weep for his lost chance with the fair-haired youth.

Instead, he shuffled along on his feet, intending to head for Leyla's to arrange the details of Kalam's onward trip. His feet thought otherwise, however, and before Ahdaf realized, he was following another familiar route: the one that led to the hammam, which he supposed was his subconscious telling him he needed to relieve his anxiety. He was feeling it on two fronts: his fear that Kalam was there to somehow expose him, and his desire for him. At the hammam, he could count on Timur, his preferred attendant, to relieve his physical longing under a mound of suds with glancing touches and a final couple of jerks with his fist clenched around Ahdaf's cock. Timur, too, would grow aroused

53

and let Ahdaf subtly touch him, but that was the most he ever allowed, leaving Ahdaf unsatisfied in another way. He could always relieve himself but he craved affection.

He suspected that he wasn't Timur's only client enjoying his deft hands. His technique was too practiced, which raised the question: how was it possible that no one admitted knowing a homosexual? No one, in fact, acknowledged that homosexuality existed in their holy world. Faith had demoted it to a Western depravity. Until ISIS exposed it. By executing gay men, it let the public know they were still amongst them. The blinders people chose to wear could no longer excuse their ignorance as they watched their young men tossed from rooftops.

Ahdaf arrived at the wide marble steps leading down to the hammam's entrance. He took the first couple and stopped, recalling Kalam's warning to be careful in hammams. It's where Sadiq had been caught, he'd said, without elaborating on what he meant by "caught." But it fed Ahdaf's own question that he'd pondered so many times: had his cousin been indiscreet, or was he betrayed? Sadiq never mentioned his relationship with Kalam. Nor had he told Ahdaf about the place by the river where men met to set up encounters for sex. Who else had Sadiq not mentioned who might've betrayed him?

Ahdaf took another couple of steps and stopped again. Should he worry about Timur denouncing him to ISIS? He decided probably not. For months, Timur had an almost weekly excuse to denounce him, so why wouldn't he have done it already if he were going to? Unless, of course, something had changed, forcing Timur to denounce the men who especially liked his deft hands.

Ahdaf shook off that thought and went down the rest of the steps. He paused at the door. Whether Timur was risky or not, Kalam had made him desire more than a furtive hand job under a mound of suds. He wanted one long, unhurried caress. No

54

one before Kalam, in his uninhibited nakedness, had even inferred that gay sex might be more than something secretive and shameful. It could, in fact, *be* unhurried. It could be lovemaking. Though he hadn't experienced that yet, he knew that's what he wanted.

He turned around and climbed back up to the sidewalk.

Inside Leyla's Café, the tables were filled with the usual noisy men and a handful of women. Leyla passed between the tables delivering short glasses of tea and a few tall beers. Ahdaf aimed for the cowboy bar. Like the hotelkeeper's tropical touches, it reminded him that he'd escaped Raqqa, where nothing like a bar existed any longer, and certainly no place served beer.

He plopped onto a barstool. As usual, the counter was cluttered with cell phones plugged into power strips, seemingly abandoned – while in reality, they were always under the watchful eyes of their owners from wherever they sat. Ahdaf wondered who might be watching *him* instead of a phone. Who was Malik's spy? Who was Selim's? He scanned the room, looking for someone who might suddenly glance aside, giving himself away, but no one did.

He pulled his cell phone out from his jeans pocket and made a call. Mustafa answered on the first ring. "Hello, Ahdaf. *Selamün aleyküm.*"

"*Wa aleyküm selam,*" Ahdaf replied perfunctorily before he asked, "What the fuck happened last night? I put a family on that raft. *You* put a family on that raft. The woman they keep showing on TV is the only one of them who survived, and *you* supplied their lifejackets! They were fucking death jackets!"

"I don't make them, I buy them."

"They were filled with shredded paper!"

"Why shouldn't I think they're okay?"

"They didn't feel different?"

"Look, I pay for them; I don't hand them out. I'm nowhere near the rafts when they launch."

"Maybe you should be, for quality control."

"It gets chaotic," Mustafa reminded him, implying "dangerous" – as Ahdaf knew. "You want to try it?"

Ahdaf ignored his question. Instead he said, "I need space for one person as soon as possible."

"You?"

"Not yet."

"It's crowded now. Demand is up."

"Let me guess. It costs more."

Ahdaf could almost hear Mustafa shrug. "It's the law of supplies and demands. I didn't invent it."

"And I didn't invent or buy death jackets," Ahdaf said. "I want this guy to make it. I don't want to see him on tomorrow night's news."

"It won't be tomorrow night. Trust me. All the rafts are booked tomorrow."

"Then when?"

"A couple of days if the weather holds."

"Whenever it is, promise me a real lifejacket for him."

"I'll check it personally." Mustafa hung up.

Ahdaf put his phone in his pocket. His mind was racing, every thought making him more apprehensive. Rafts. Lifejackets. Juggling both ISIS and the CIA. A thought came that he should become a double spy for both. What would he be called then? A quadruple spy? He was too anxious to think his own play on words was funny.

Leyla returned, squeezing around the end of the bar with a tray of empty glasses.

"That's a serious face," she said to Ahdaf as she loaded her small dishwasher.

56

"I'm just thinking."

"You do a lot of that."

"Do I?'

"If that's your thinking face, you do."

Ahdaf looked cross-eyed at her. "Me? The serious guy?" he kidded, aware, however, that it was true. He'd been told before that his default expression was so somber that people often worried something bad had happened.

"You're a funny guy," Leyla grunted.

"I won't be funny if you haven't saved a cold beer for me."

"You're not the only person who wants cold beer."

"You gave mine away again?"

"And risk losing your big tip? No, I kept one back. In fact, I kept two back for you, so it better be a very big tip."

"I never drink more than one."

"What about your handsome new client?"

Ahdaf grinned. "You noticed?"

"I'm not blind." Leyla pointed her chin at the door. "Plus, he's here, and looking for you."

Kalam saw Ahdaf wave from the bar and wound his way through the tables to join him. As he did, Ahdaf noticed the glances he attracted – and no wonder. His height, good looks, and freshly washed golden locks would turn heads anywhere. "Do you always sit here at the bar?" he asked, taking a seat.

"I prefer it. Why?"

"You don't feel conspicuous? I can't imagine such a place in Raqqa. People drinking beer. Women not escorted by a man in a room full of men? The first time I ever sat at a bar was right here a couple of hours ago!"

"There used to be bars in Raqqa before ISIS took control," Ahdaf reminded him.

"I was only 16, and that was six years ago," Kalam told him, "so I remember them but not really. My father went and my mother disapproved, I do remember that."

"There wasn't much to disapprove of. They were mostly like here, like Leyla's. They weren't flashy bars like you can find in Istanbul. My parents allowed me to go but for tea only. My father's religious and told me I couldn't drink alcohol until I was old enough to decide for myself."

"How old was that?" Kalam wanted to know.

"Eighteen, and I had turned that just after ISIS closed all the bars."

"What about the bars here in Istanbul? Do you go to them?"

"I've never gone inside because I'm sure they're expensive, and there aren't any here in Aksaray," Ahdaf replied. "I pass them in other neighborhoods when I'm going to meet a client."

"I'd go inside at least once," Kalam said. "I want to make movies so I want to see everything."

"Movies about what?"

"I won't know until I see something to make a movie about!"

"There's a lot to see in Istanbul. Do you like beer?"

"I tried it with Sadiq, but didn't like it very much. Maybe I'll enjoy it better this time."

Ahdaf felt annoyed at the mention of his cousin. Jealous, in fact – and it surprised him. He'd never considered the possibility that Sadiq had more than one secret friend. Ahdaf had thought their affection unique to them. Also piquing his jealousy was the sense that his cousin had been more experimental with Kalam, but he didn't want to ask. Had they ever been naked together? He blocked the thought from his mind, not wanting his speculation confirmed.

"I think that's two beers," Ahdaf said to Leyla, and to Kalam: "Right?"

"Why not?" Kalam's smile revealed his big even white teeth. "Like you said, Istanbul is different!"

"How about you two share one? The second will stay colder

in the refrigerator." Leyla glared at Ahdaf, adding: "Some people complain when their beer isn't cold enough."

"Who?" he asked.

She filled their glasses. "You two talk your business while I go have a smoke."

They watched her go outside and light a cigarette while chatting it up with some customers. "I've never met a woman quite like her before," Kalam said, breaking into his thoughts. "She has a strong presence. I can sense it."

"She's different," Ahdaf agreed.

"Everything in Istanbul is different!"

"It's changing, too."

"What do you mean?"

"It's becoming more conservative because of the fundamentalists."

"Come on, look around. You call this fundamentalist? I want to take a video. Is that okay?"

Not waiting for a response, Kalam pulled his phone from his daypack and panned the room. "This is my first day in Istanbul in my first café after my first shower in three weeks," he said as a voiceover, "and while this part of the room looks like cafés everywhere in Turkey, this part" – he zoomed in on the cowboy hats – "looks like America! And there's beer, and already I have a new friend –"

Ahdaf blocked Kalam's lens. "No pictures of me."

"Sorry. I'm just excited." He turned off his phone.

Ahdaf stopped him before he could put it away. "I've never seen a phone case like that before," he said.

"It's waterproof."

"Waterproof? Why?"

"All my videos are on my phone. If I fall out of a raft, they'll be protected. They're my future."

"Your future?"

"I told you, I want to make movies. They're the proof that I can. So, what happens now?"

"I've already contacted someone to get you on a raft. Demand's high because people want to beat winter setting in. For the last two or three years, I'm told there have been fewer overall, but there's always a big wave of them about now wanting to cross before the weather becomes too bad. People cross even then, but it's dangerous. When I know you have a raft, I'll get your bus ticket."

"My bus ticket to where?"

"Assos."

"That's where the rafts are?"

"It's either Assos or Ayvalık, but I don't deal with Ayvalık. It's complicated enough to have one network. Besides, I have enough."

"Enough what?"

"Enough clients. Enough hassles. Something always changes at the last minute."

"How long do I have to wait for a raft?"

"Minimum two days, but it could be more."

"Good."

"Good? I thought you were in a hurry."

Kalam smiled. "I'm enjoying the company in Istanbul."

"Me too."

They sipped their beers while exchanging a meaningful look. Ahdaf glimpsed Leyla watching them from across the room, now standing next to a table of men, talking to them but with her eyes on him.

"When you arrive in Assos," Ahdaf said, shifting into work mode, "you'll have the name of the person who will meet you, his cell number, and a local backup contact. If something goes wrong, you call me."

"How often does that happen?"

"Almost never, but it still happens."

"Somebody takes me to a raft. Then what?"

"You'll be told who to contact when you land in Greece. Make sure your phone is charged, and make contact as soon as you're off the raft. They're usually waiting nearby."

"Usually?"

"Things can change, but you'll always have a backup contact."

"And if the backup changes too?"

"Call me. I'll find a way to help."

"That's not especially reassuring."

"I'm only one link in a chain."

"I've made it this far. I guess I can make it farther." Kalam shrugged and took a look around. "Is this where you hang out?"

"Yeah. It's like my office."

"And everybody knows that?"

"There are two cafés on this street where people know they can find guides."

"Guides?"

"That's what they call smugglers like me. It's not a big secret, and if the police get a cut, that suddenly makes it legal."

Leyla returned behind the bar. "Don't believe Ahdaf if he says the crossing is safe," she said. "It's his business to say that."

"He told me it wasn't safe."

"Then he must like you."

The café suddenly fell silent. The television, a moment earlier only a scratch in the background, became what everyone strained to hear. "Turn it up!" someone shouted. Leyla, punching a button on the remote control, raised the volume on a streaming live video of a panicked crowd fleeing a burning building. Behind them, people jump from the upper two floors. "This is coming from our affiliate station in Greece," a reporter said offscreen. "A regular contributor in Athens happened to be in the vicinity of the Spartacus Bar when the explosion ripped through it." At that moment, there was another explosion, followed by a collective gasp from Leyla's customers as the building started to collapse. Then the video went blank.

An instant later, a reporter in CNN Türk's newsroom appeared on television, listening intently to someone on a headset. He looked directly into the camera and said, "What you've been watching appears to be an ongoing terrorist attack in Athens at the Spartacus Bar, a popular nightclub for gays –"

"For fucking queers!" a customer shouted.

On the screen, the newsman cupped his hand over his earphone, straining to hear anything. "It appears we've lost contact with Dimitris Stefanapoulos. Dimitris, if you can hear me –"

"He's a fucking faggot too!" the hostile man cried and threw a beer bottle that shattered on the side of the television.

"That's enough, Burak!" Leyla snapped. "You leave now, or I'm closing the café for everyone."

When no one came to Burak's defense, he mumbled, "Fucking bitch," and headed for the door.

He was almost there when Leyla called out, "You forgot to leave a tip."

The hush in the room deepened. All eyes watched the hot-headed Burak. What would he do? But before he had a chance to do anything, another man spoke up. "Hear that, guys? Now Leyla expects us to tip her!" That elicited a few chuckles because, as everybody knew, nobody ever tipped more than nothing. The banter diffused the tension enough that Burak pushed his way out the door without feeling the need to exit with a final crude remark. Conversations started again, though muted, as they watched the emergency vehicles arriving and ambulance teams racing with stretchers while reporters tried to provide more details without having any.

"You boys ready for another beer?" Leyla asked.

Ahdaf glanced at Kalam to see what he wanted. Watching the news intently, his face was drained of color. "I think we've changed our minds," Ahdaf replied, and left money on the bar.

"Let's go."

They got off their barstools and started for the door.

"You forgot a tip," Leyla called after them. Ahdaf dug into his pocket, feeling for a coin. "Get out of here," she said.

Ahdaf followed Kalam outside, and they retraced their steps up the easy hill. After a couple of blocks, he said, "This is where you turn for your hotel. It's on the fourth corner."

Kalam stopped. "Do you want to come back to my room?"

"You know I do. But I can't."

"I can't persuade you?"

"I don't want the man at the hotel to know I'm in your room. He'll guess what's happening, and I don't know what he might do."

"What about going to your place?"

"I'm too nervous tonight. Ever since what happened to Sadiq, I've been scared, and what's happening right now in Athens only makes me more scared."

Kalam touched Ahdaf's shoulder. "I understand."

"I hope so."

"I do; but before we say good night, I have something to give you, and something to tell you." Kalam reached into his daypack and handed him an envelope with his name written on it.

Ahdaf recognized the handwriting. "It's from my mother?"

"Yes."

"You saw her?"

"Sadiq had mentioned the mosque where you and your father prayed. I went there to tell him that I was leaving for Istanbul the next day, and asked how I could find you. He said to pass your house in the morning and he'd have it written down for me. The next morning both your parents were waiting for me. Your father gave me your information, and your mother handed me the letter."

Ahdaf stared at the envelope. He'd had no direct communication with his parents since he'd fled Raqqa 10 months earlier. The town's telephone and postal services had been bombarded into oblivion. He'd given a letter for his parents to someone going to Raqqa, in which he let them know that he'd survived his journey and where others could find him: Leyla's Café. Occasionally, refugees from Raqqa had been able to report that his parents were alive, seemingly coping as well as anyone, and missing him. The news from Raqqa was never hopeful. Only the envelope in his hand proved they were still alive when Kalam started his journey some three months earlier. "You also said you had something to tell me," he reminded Kalam.

"After they executed Sadiq, ISIS fighters came to your home looking for you. If you go back, they'll come for you again."

"What did they say to my parents?"

"I don't know exactly what they said."

"But you know what they said."

"Does it matter now?" Kalam asked.

Ahdaf, distraught, said, "My parents must be so ashamed of me."

"They're not. They told me to tell you that they loved you, and nothing can change that. They both said it. Your father emphasized *nothing* a second time."

Ahdaf couldn't hold back his tears. They dripped onto the envelope, blurring his mother's ink. He rolled off his daypack and stuck her letter into it.

Kalam said, "Your mother explained that they wrote that letter but never mailed it because it was too important to get lost."

"So I owe you a special thank-you. I'll call when I have news about a raft."

"Call me anyway," Kalam said. "I like you. I'd really like to kiss you."

Ahdaf grinned. "You're the first client to say that to me."

"Who was the first guy you kissed?"

"Sadiq."

It was Kalam's turn to grin. "We're both lucky that way."

They touched their hearts, and Kalam walked off. Ahdaf turned in the opposite direction to go the short two blocks to his room. Outside the front door of his building, he braced himself for the stale air that hit him face-on as soon as he opened the door. The entry had no window to dissipate the cloying smells of fried fish or boiled cabbage or smelly toilets that gravity had sucked from the whole building to the ground floor.

On lucky days, the smell of his French neighbor's cooking – her tangy sauces and baked goods – masked the more offensive odors, but not that day as he climbed the rank stairs to his first-floor room. It was an apartment, technically, in that it had a separate bathroom and a kitchen – if a hotplate, midget refrigerator and sink constituted one. He propped his daypack on a cheap plastic table, pulled out his mother's letter, and set it aside. He was tempted to tear it open and read it immediately, but despite what Kalam had said, how could their love for him not be tainted by knowing his shame? He dreaded their probable words of disapproval and disappointment.

He realized he was hungry, and took the *helva*, olives, and dates from his daypack. He'd forgotten the newspaper Selim had given him. Impossible, that it had only been that morning! He pulled it out and flattened it. There she was, Meryem – the Syrian *Pietà* – perched on an upturned crate, her dead son heavy on her knees, her husband on the ground meters away.

He ate a chunk of *helva* and some olives, all the while wondering what to do with her photo. It haunted him. He felt the woman needed to be honored, especially by he who'd contributed to her tragedy. He had no scissors, but used a knife instead to score the photo's edges, making it easier to tear it out of the newspaper. From a drawer he retrieved a couple of pushpins he'd collected from flyers posted in the neighborhood, and tacked the photo to the wall. Then, as he bowed his head to Meryem, a prayer for forgiveness escaped his lips.

He went through the steps of getting ready for bed: brushing his teeth, using the toilet, pulling off his jeans and shirt. The whole time, he could see the white rectangle of his mother's envelope out of the corner of his eye, or reflected in the bathroom mirror. He worried it was an indictment. What did ISIS's fighters say to them? How had they described his relationship with Sadiq?

He took the letter to bed with him. After pulling back the sheet to check for the dreaded insects, he settled himself on the mattress, gently and steadily to avoid toppling it off its many bookstacks. When he was ready, he opened the envelope, took out the letter, and unfolded it.

To our beloved son,

Your father and I are writing this together. A child has no secrets from his parents, though we sometimes prefer to ignore the truth when it is difficult or inconvenient. Your father and I both knew your secret, but we never spoke about it to each other. The most important conversation we should have had, we never did until you were gone. We are ashamed of ourselves because we were ashamed of you. We no longer feel that shame. We long to embrace you as you are, our son whom we have always loved and always will.

Your loving parents

Ahdaf read their letter a second time before falling back on his pillow, pressing it to his heart. No shame. No recrimination. An admission that they had always suspected – no, known – his sexual orientation.

He put the letter on the floor next to him. He reached under his pillow for the bandana he kept there and, twisting it into a narrow band of cloth, tied it to cover his eyes so he could leave the light on, which helped keep the roaches away. He patted the floor to find the letter and raised his bandana to read it again. Another surge of tears wet his pillow before he fell asleep.

DAY 4

His telephone pinged and woke him up. That happened most mornings. What was unusual was that, when he pulled off his bandana, it was already bright outside. Ahdaf rarely slept that late, or, rather, was rarely allowed to sleep that late. His refugee clients had his telephone number, and, to a person, they were understandably anxious. *Had he found space on a raft? Could they go that day?* He tried to remember what he had to do that day and instead could only remember what had happened the day before. The bombing of the bar in Athens. His parents' letter. His phone pinged again, reminding him he had a message. He read it.

One hour.

Of course it was Selim. Of course he meant the Eminönü docks. Ahdaf had a choice: take a shower, then a tram – or not shower, and walk. He sniffed his pits and decided he didn't need a shower; but he wanted one anyway. He made it quick, dried off, and brushed his teeth. A hand through his black curls was the only comb he ever used. A cinched belt, tied shoes, and he was out the door.

In the dead air of the hallway, that morning's characteristic stratification of odors was permeated by something appetizingly fried, causing Ahdaf's empty stomach to growl all the way to the next corner. He bought a *simit* – a large thin bagel covered with sesame seeds – and ate it on his way to the tram stop.

The stop was mobbed. Like everyone, he used his shoulders to wedge his way closer to the turnstiles, where people backed up because half the time their tickets didn't work on the first swipe. Passengers pressed against him on all sides. Remembering to be wary of pickpockets, he slapped his hand against his back pocket and felt someone's hand quickly jerk away. He whipped around. Who'd it been? No one looked guilty. Then he saw the girl leaning against her mother's knees, maybe five years old and staring at him.

"I'm sorry," her mother said. "She lost her balance."

He transferred his wallet to a front pocket and kept his hand on it.

The platform was so crowded that people had to stand in the demarcated danger zone at the edge of the platform. It made Ahdaf nervous, the possibility that someone might bump him onto the tracks, and he let the crowd push forward around him as a tram approached. When its doors opened, a brief melee ensued as passengers pushed their way off while others pushed their way on. He was the last on before the doors closed, grazing his shoulders.

Getting off at the docks, he headed for the newsstand, assuming Selim would look for him there. The dozen or so newspapers clipped to wires all headlined the bombing of the nightclub in Athens. From what Ahdaf could read above the fold, most described the nightclub as trendy and popular with gays, but the right-wing press applauded the attack on queers and their perverted lifestyle.

"Excuse me," he heard.

Selim reached around him for the top newspaper in one of the stacks. "My boat leaves in five minutes. Maybe I'll see you on board." He paid the vendor and headed for the ferry.

Ahdaf held back to avoid appearing to be with him. He gave a quick glance around; no one seemed especially interested in him. When he pushed through a turnstile to board the ferry, however, the man in the beige kaftan – the man from his mosque – pushed through the turnstile next to him. Intentionally catching Ahdaf's eye, he said, "*Selamün aleyküm.*"

"*Wa aleyküm selam,*" Ahdaf replied nonchalantly, though he felt the opposite of calm as he boarded the boat.

No sooner had he got aboard than a bell rang, and two crewmen pulled up the gangplank. Ahdaf passed through the open doors into the main cabin and climbed the steep stairs to the upper deck. Always popular in good weather, it was crowded; nevertheless, Selim had secured a spot along the rail, keeping his space as wide as possible by opening his newspaper. Ahdaf pretended to look for somewhere to land, eventually squeezing his way to the rail beside Selim. "Excuse me," he said.

Selim feigned annoyance that he had to give up any of his space. When the ferry pulled away from the dock, rolling in the wake of other boats, Ahdaf looked out over the Bosporus while the CIA man kept his back to it. They stood that way for a couple of minutes until Selim loosely folded his newspaper and turned around. "You're being followed," Selim told him. "He's just come up the stairs."

"I know," Ahdaf muttered. "A man in a beige kaftan."

"That could describe a dozen men on this boat."

"He's from my mosque."

"Then he's Malik's man. Do you know him?"

"I don't know him, but he greeted me as we boarded just now. I saw him watching us yesterday, and he was at the mosque later."

"I saw him yesterday too, and this morning he was watching you at the newsstand when I showed up."

"Maybe we shouldn't be seen together," Ahdaf suggested.

The CIA man shook his head. "All he can report is that he saw us together. Malik thinks you're spying on me for him. How else would you get information? Besides, we'll lose your tail after we dock."

"Talk about what? You haven't explained why we're meeting."

Selim smiled. "Don't be impatient."

The ferry blasted its horn, signaling its approach to the Üsküdar landing, and turned a half-circle to approach the dock with its stern. Passengers started moving down the stairs and were soon backed up at the top. "There's no rush," Selim said, "and don't let your tail know that you're onto him. Never look at him."

"There he goes now," Ahdaf remarked.

"There's only one way off the boat. He'll be watching us."

They shuffled down the stairs and across the gangplank onto the wharf. Üsküdar's docks lacked everything the Eminönü docks had: the bustle of people, shoulder-to-shoulder fishermen on a bridge, shoeshine men, hucksters, and vendors galore. Üsküdar was only a place to arrive at and depart from, not linger.

Ahdaf glanced around. "Now what?"

"Now we go somewhere to talk. I know a good spot." Selim hailed a taxi and they got in the back.

The driver glanced at them in his mirror. "Where to?"

"Çinili Mosque. "Have you been there?" he asked Ahdaf.

"No."

"It has a pleasant garden in front, where we can talk."

The road wound up the hill, passing a mixture of three- and four-story apartment buildings and artisan shops – tailors, pot repairers, leathermakers. Ahdaf had been to Üsküdar a few times, always for something to do with clients; and he always felt it was more of a sprawling village than a neighborhood in self-consciously modern Istanbul. The call to prayer started as they made a last couple of turns and pulled up in front of the mosque. Worshippers had started arriving, mostly older men with mustaches stained yellow from a lifetime of smoking.

Selim looked annoyed. "I hadn't considered the crowd for noon prayers."

Ahdaf shrugged. "Everyone will be inside in a few minutes." They got out of the taxi. "It's small, isn't it?" Ahdaf remarked. Looking up, he added, "It has only one minaret, like our mosque."

"Your mosque?"

"In Raqqa."

"I bet your mosque didn't have the same tiles. You should peek inside."

Ahdaf hesitated. "I don't want to go inside. I don't want to feel like a tourist. Not at prayers."

"No, just a peek, and then we'll have our conversation."

They climbed the wide steps leading to a wooden veranda surrounding the mosque. Men left their shoes in a bank of wooden cubbyholes before crossing barefoot on thatched mats to enter the prayer hall. From where they stood, Ahdaf couldn't see enough to appreciate the tiles, so they took off their shoes and stood on the thatched mats closer to the doorway. An old man, mistaking them for strangers unsure if they could enter, bade them to come inside. The more they hesitated, the more he insisted. His sincere, welcoming smile convinced them, and they followed him into the domed mosque. Satisfied, he touched his heart and left them.

The worshippers knelt on the carpeted floor in haphazard lines, bending over their creaky knees to touch their foreheads to the floor before rolling back on their haunches. Their hallowed words rippling through the room sounded like a gurgling fountain. Blue tiles, rich in color and design, covered the walls some five meters high, atop which ran a band of windows carved into the thick plaster walls. Midday light flooded the room.

"You're right ... it's beautiful," Ahdaf murmured.

Selim smiled, glad for the affirmation, but he couldn't know that it was beautiful to Ahdaf for another reason. Absent the blue tiles, it could have been his mosque – rather, his father's mosque – in Raqqa. Same size, same plaster walls and carved windows, same unadorned dome, same prayer room for women behind a screen. Many of the men in their ubiquitous beige kaftans, clutching a string of prayer beads, resembled his father – or at least, what his father looked like on Fridays. The other days, he wore a collared shirt and slacks, the Western clothes expected of dentists, occasionally forgetting to leave his white coat at the office. At that very moment, in his faraway home-town, Ahdaf's father would also be at noon prayers, kneeling beside his friends in a ragged line and no doubt worrying about his son in Istanbul who, in other circumstances, would have been shoulder-to-shoulder with him in their mosque. Ahdaf suddenly had an overwhelming urge to feel spiritually connected to his father, and asked Selim, "Is it okay if I take five minutes to pray?"

"May I join you?"

"Of course."

They found a space where they could kneel together. Both sat upright on their heels, hands cupped and pressed to their chests. Ahdaf, mouthing verses, repeatedly leaned forward to touch his head to the floor. When he finally stopped and sat back up, Selim's posture had relaxed, his eyes closed and hands loose in his lap. Ahdaf took the moment to study him. He had broader shoulders than Ahdaf, and his shadow of black whiskers, shaven that morning, still evidenced a heavy beard.

Selim's eyes flickered open. "Are you ready to go?" he asked.

They went outside and collected their shoes. The benches, where they could have had a conversation, were occupied by men chatting in the bright sun.

"Do you like hammams?" Selim asked. "There's one next door. It's also a good place to talk."

A few steps down the road they turned into a yard yielding an ochre, two-story building typical of Istanbul's neighborhood hammams. They entered a spacious common area surrounded by narrow changing rooms with the top halves of their doors made of glass. The attendants, slouching against the walls, stood a little straighter.

A man in a booth at the entrance greeted them. "Welcome, Mr. Wilson, and your friend."

Selim asked, "How are you, Adem?"

"*Elhamdülillah*," Adem replied. Holding up keys, he called two attendants: "Berat! Deniz!" The attendants took the keys and escorted the men to changing rooms on opposite sides of the large room.

Ahdaf stepped into his cubicle and dropped his daypack on the bed intended for a short rest to cool down after the hammam's enervating steam. As he closed his door, he watched Selim through his cubicle's window pull off his shirt, revealing a chest of thick, wiry hair. Ahdaf undressed too, hanging his clothes on hooks on the walls, never sure where to hide anything valuable but knowing it wouldn't do much good anyway: obviously the staff had spare keys, and what customer was likely to break down a door? Just for precaution's sake, he hid his wallet in a sock and stuffed it into a shoe. Then he took the threadbare cotton towel folded at the foot of the bed and wrapped it around his bare waist. He locked his door and wrapped the key, knotted to a thick rubber band, around his wrist. He joined Selim at a door leaking steam that led into the actual hammam.

"Will you want a scrub, Mr. Wilson?" Deniz asked.

"We'll scrub each other," he answered. Switching into English, he asked Ahdaf, "Is that okay with you? That way we can talk."

"Sure," replied Ahdaf, who'd begun to wonder why Selim had summoned him that morning. Not a word had been said.

Deniz handed them blocks of soap and loofahs as they entered a hot, wet labyrinth of short passages. "They all seem to know you," Ahdaf commented.

"I tip them well. They remember that."

They arrived at a grand domed room with a circular marble platform in the middle. In the corners were bathing cubicles only partially concealed by marble latticework.

They peered into the washrooms. In one, an old man soaped up his stringy body. In two others, men rinsed suds off each other. The fourth was empty, so they took it and sat on the marble bench on either side of a deep basin. Though already sweating in the sluggish air, they used shallow metal bowls to douse themselves with hot water, opening their pores more and softening their skin. "You never answered whether or not you like hammams," Selim said. "Some people can't bear the heat."

"I like the heat. I grew up in a desert, remember?"

"Syria wasn't steamy heat, like this."

"It doesn't bother me. I like hammams. I like the whole atmosphere."

Selim began in earnest to soap up everywhere he could reach while sitting down. Ahdaf took his lead, and soon both were spilling suds into the runnels that carried the suds away. He couldn't help but steal glances at Selim; skin the color of hazelnuts, a chest of thick black hair, a silkier fuzz on his arms and legs, and a smooth, completely hairless back.

"Do you hear what they're saying in the other washrooms?" Selim asked.

He listened a few moments. "I hear voices, but not the words."

"That's the point. The splashing water muffles and distorts everything. The Ottomans knew that trick. That's why they held their private meetings in harems, which usually had fountains."

75

"How do you know that?"

"Spy class," Selim joked.

"Really?"

"No, not really. On a tour of Topkapı Palace. I thought it was a great idea, true or not. I've used it."

Selim stood and faced the washbasin. Unknotting his towel, he grasped the two loose ends with one hand and stretched them out, concealing himself while creating space to suds everything up. Ahdaf was tempted to wash himself in such a way that he'd lean a few centimeters in Selim's direction, glimpsing him. He restrained himself. He worried that anything he did might be unwanted. Kalam's caution about hammams haunted him again. He was curious, though, what Selim was thinking. Was he flirting? Was his whole routine a come-on to get Ahdaf to act first? Selim's balls, outlined by his thin wet towel, would've been so easy to cup in his hand. He was about ready to dare it when Selim, reknotting his towel, said, "I'll scrub your back first."

"My back?" Ahdaf blurted at the unexpected offer.

"Well, you can't scrub your own. I learned that without a tour of the Topkapı."

"I'll do yours."

"Yours first," Selim insisted, and, leaning closer, added: "That way, I can ask some questions and nobody will notice." He stepped over to be directly in front of Ahdaf. "Bend forward," he said, and when Ahdaf did, Selim nudged his head still lower until it butted against the knot in his towel. It gave Selim leverage as he ran a block of soap in long strokes to the small of Ahdaf's back. He pressed his mouth close to Ahdaf's ear and asked, "Have you ever smuggled anybody trying to escape?"

Ahdaf wondered what he meant. "Escape? From where?"

"From Turkey. From the police or security forces."

"Turks can travel."

"Not if there's a warrant for their arrest."

Ahdaf was stumped. He'd never thought about that possibility. "They wouldn't have told me."

"Did you ever suspect that might be the situation?"

Ahdaf shook his head. "No. They'd be odd in some way, and my clients aren't odd. They're just refugees."

"Don't move," Selim said, reaching for a loofah.

As he stretched for it, Ahdaf confirmed what he had suspected: the knot in Selim's towel had thickened. The clinging wet cloth revealed his upright erection. When Selim resumed the long strokes down his back with the rough sponge, Ahdaf pressed his head against his cock, trying to signal that he was okay with it and hoping he might dislodge the towel altogether.

Selim still had questions, and again used his long strokes as an excuse to press his mouth close to Ahdaf's ear and whisper: "If you were to organize the crossing for somebody like that, what would be the biggest risk?"

"That's easy. The roadblocks. The Turks like to use them, they're always random, and they always look at IDs."

"So, my person needs a fake ID."

"And a burqa," Ahdaf replied, referring to the full-body robe that left only a woman's eyes visible.

"A *hijab*'s not enough?"

"Only women in burqas are truly untouchable."

"What if my person is a man?"

"He should wear a burqa, too, have a woman's ID, and not speak."

"What if he's asked a question?"

"Have a male travel with your person. He can pretend to be a relative and speak for her. Or him, if that's the case."

"Can you arrange a private boat?"

"No one's ever asked me before, but I know it's sometimes done. I'd have to ask around. How soon?"

"Possibly in a day or two."

"A day or two!"

Ahdaf tried to lift his head, but Selim pressed one hand to keep him bent over while dousing him with water so cold that his sides heaved, and he finally managed to sit up. "Now it's your turn!"

"Another time," Selim replied.

"What do you mean?"

"You don't need to wash my back."

"Why not?"

"I think we should leave separately. You go first."

Ahdaf couldn't understand the abrupt dismissal. Selim had obviously been attracted to him. He thought something might happen, but apparently he'd misread the situation. Perhaps Selim's dousing him with cold water had been intended to bring him to his senses; but if anything had, it was Selim's rejection. Was it *really* rejection, or simply wariness?

"You sure?" Ahdaf asked.

"I'm sure. I have a passenger who wants to go to Greece as soon as you can arrange it. So go arrange it," Selim added, with a generous smile – a gesture Ahdaf knew was intended to allay his confusion, but succeeded only in adding to it.

He ducked out of the washroom and was tempted to join a couple of men resting on the circular platform, knowing how its heat relaxed their muscles and relieved stress; but at that moment, he was too tense to contemplate a relaxed moment. He was looking around, trying to remember his way back to the changing rooms, when Deniz appeared and indicated the way before joining Selim in the washroom.

No doubt to scrub his back, Ahdaf thought. Contemplating what else might happen, he felt a pang of jealousy. If that were the case, he felt the rejection more keenly, felt that something about himself ultimately caused Selim to dismiss him. Ahdaf dressed quickly and, upon leaving his room, discreetly gave Berat a small tip. When he tried to pay for the hammam, Adem waved him away saying, "Mr. Wilson always pays."

He walked out of the humid hammam into the dry, cool air of an autumn afternoon. He decided to walk back to the ferry dock. It would give him a chance to sort out the task that had just befallen him: helping a fugitive escape the country. The road to the dock was all downhill, and took him past shops and markets that were a throwback to an earlier era – cobblers, welders, and candymakers, a far cry from the carpet merchants and souvenir shops in European Istanbul across the narrow Bosporus.

His mind, though, quickly drifted from the day's beauty to his new and complex assignment. The first task, he supposed, was renting a car to transport Selim's mystery passenger to the coast – an easy enough task for most people, but Ahdaf didn't have a driver's license and barely even knew how to drive. The very thought that he might need to drive someone to the coast made him queasy. Even more daunting was the challenge of arranging for a private crossing to Greece. How to handle that in a cloak of secrecy? He'd have to ask around, and of course, as soon as he did, rumors would start. Who was the special passenger who needed – and could afford – that type of luxury?

Those were the questions that chased him down the hill and through the turnstile to board the ferry. He went up onto the deck as usual, which reminded him: the man in the beige kaftan had seen him with Selim and had, in fact, obviously been ditched by them. He would report everything to Malik, who would expect his new spy to report what the CIA man had wanted. What *were* the circumstances and consequences of his meeting with Selim? Ahdaf wasn't sure himself.

79

An hour later he was splashing water again, this time with his feet stuck under a spigot at the mosque while speakers on the minaret broadcast the afternoon call to prayer. He stuffed his sandals into his shoulder pack and, barefoot, crossed the courtyard's paving stones, mentally crafting what he would reveal to Malik and what he wouldn't.

As he reached to pull back the heavy curtain to enter the mosque, Malik, coming out, bumped into him. They yelped in surprise, but neither found the moment amusing, and flashed tense smiles.

"We will meet after you pray," Malik said.

"Let's meet now," Ahdaf suggested. "That way, later, I can concentrate on my prayers, not on what I have to tell you."

"As you wish. Shall we walk in the garden?"

On the side of the mosque, stone walkways crisscrossed a lush garden crowded with pines and cypresses towering over beds of lavender, ferns and tulips. Remarkable among the plants were the roses, trained to grow upright on stalks a meter tall. "I met again with Selim Wilson," Ahdaf said. "You probably already know that."

"I do."

"I've seen someone following me. I assume he's working for you."

Malik smiled. "Now you know that you can keep no secrets from me. What did Selim Wilson want?"

"What he said before. To move someone."

"Who?"

"He didn't say. But he must be important. Selim wants it all arranged privately."

"What's that mean?"

"All he specified was: no public buses."

"When?"

"He's not sure. In the next few days, or maybe a week."

"But not tomorrow?"

"Not tomorrow. Apparently, the situation is complicated," Ahdaf adlibbed, beginning to have fun spinning his own story.

"Good, because I have an assignment for you," Malik told him.

Ahdaf gulped. "Tomorrow?"

"I want you to move some people in reverse. Some people coming from Greece."

"I have no contacts in Greece."

"They'll make their own way to Assos. You bring them back to Istanbul."

"How many?"

"Three men. One of them is injured."

"Injured? Injured how?"

"In a fire. Apparently seriously."

"He might die?" Ahdaf asked, alarmed.

"Allah will decide. You only need to pick them up."

"Pick them up? How? I can't put them on a bus, especially someone injured!" Ahdaf's panic was rising. He'd reported enough of his conversation with Selim, intending to appear useful and reliable, and in return, he'd been dealt a dangerous assignment – for the following day!

"You'll take our school bus," Malik answered.

"The mosque's van? I've never driven such a vehicle."

"Have you driven a car?"

"Not much."

"Allah will instruct you."

Inshallah." Ahdaf took a deep breath. He had to appear willing to do what was asked, even as he prayed harder for something to make it not happen at all. "What's the plan?"

Malik's plan was sketchy. Three men – Turks, he offered only that much – needed to leave Greece. Unnoticed.

"Why?"

"You don't need to know. You just need to bring them to Istanbul."

The three Turks would launch from Lesvos at sunset. It had been complicated to arrange transportation in reverse from Greece to Turkey, but local supporters had found a fisherman willing to bring them. They planned to come ashore just north of Assos, where Ahdaf would pick them up.

"When do I pick up the van?"

"It's a five-hour drive to Assos. You need to be there by sunset, so leave at noon to account for delays."

"I'm a slow driver," Ahdaf replied. "I'll come at ten, if that's okay."

"Ten is fine," Malik said.

They both forced weak smiles as they touched their hearts and bid farewell. Once back on the street and away from the mosque's small courtyard, Ahdaf stumbled as anxiety swept over him. He leaned against a wall to steady himself and bring some order to his worrisome thoughts. People passing him on the sidewalk gave him concerned looks; one man asked if he needed help. He didn't. He just needed a moment, and in that moment, he realized an opportunity had been handed to him; unfortunately, it was also a juggling act with life-or-death consequences.

He dialed Selim. When his recorder beeped, he left the message, "It's urgent. I'm not in physical danger, but it's urgent. I'll meet you at Eminönü. I'm going there now."

Ahdaf decided to walk. Why not save the fare and avoid pickpockets at the same time? Besides, at rush hour it would take Selim at least 60 minutes. He left the heavily trafficked road and cut up over a hill busy with shops selling practical clothes and household essentials: mattresses, plumbing equipment, furniture. It was lively, with delivery trucks, men pushing handcarts, and shop owners cajoling passersby to come inside. Soon a gradual downhill brought him to the vast square across the tram tracks from the docks. He joined the crowds crossing the rails to reach the commuter ferries, and was surprised to find Selim already at the news kiosk perusing the headlines. "How'd you get here so fast?" he asked.

"I had an appointment nearby."

It dawned on Ahdaf. "I'm not your only spy, am I?"

"It's an industry in Istanbul. What's urgent?"

Ahdaf outlined Malik's plan: a reverse crossing for three men on a Greek fishing boat. "It's happening tomorrow; that's what makes it urgent."

"Who are they?"

"I don't know, but apparently one is badly injured. From a fire. The Greek fisherman will drop Malik's guys off and go back to Greece. I'm thinking he might take your person."

Ahdaf could see the possibility of a two-way transfer dawn on Selim. "Why would he take my person?" he asked.

"For enough money. Can your person be ready to go tomorrow?"

"My person is ready to go now. What time do you pick up the van?"

"At 10."

"That means you'll get to the American consulate around 11."

"Is that where you work?" Ahdaf asked.

"It's where I'll be," Selim answered. "Do you know where it is?"

"I have GPS."

"Pull up with the passenger door facing the consulate," Selim instructed. "That would be coming up the hill. It'll be more discreet that way."

By the time he'd arrived at Leyla's, it was already dusk. Through the window he could see that the place was abuzz with young men wanting entertainment other than the soaps playing at home, both real and on TV. As Ahdaf was about to go in, Munir came outside.

"*Salaam alaikum*," they exchanged.

"How are things?" Ahdaf asked. "Better, I hope."

Munir frowned. "Yasmin still makes almost no milk for the baby," he said. "She's starving, too."

Ahdaf pulled out his wallet and pressed money into his friend's hand.

"I wasn't asking for money," Munir protested, and tried to give it back.

"Let me buy some food for your family. Yasmin needs it. She can't make milk if she's so hungry."

"How can I thank you?"

Ahdaf, ignoring his question, asked, "Do you still want to leave for Europe?"

"Of course, yes."

"There's a chance you can go tomorrow."

Munir paled. "Tomorrow?"

"It's on a fishing boat, not a raft, so it's safer. A lot safer. The fisherman is a real captain, not a refugee with five minutes of training on how to steer a raft on a rough sea."

"I need to discuss it with Yasmin," his friend replied.

"Of course."

"I mean, we've discussed it, only I expected to have more notice. More time to get used to it."

"I might need help tomorrow, whether you cross or not. You can thank me by going with me. I'll bring you back if you're not ready to cross."

"Help how?"

"Whatever's needed. Dragging suitcases. I don't know. I'm picking up three guys. They're special somehow, that's all I know."

"Will I have another chance?"

"To cross? Sure. It usually takes two or three days to arrange, depending on weather. You should go soon. The seas are already heavy."

"What's the chance of taking the fishing boat another time?"

Ahdaf shook his head. "It's not my contact and not my operation, but I'm sure the boat's expensive."

Munir expelled a troubled breath. "Yasmin and I are always debating. Should I go ahead and my family follows me? Or do we go together?"

"Why leave Istanbul?" Ahdaf asked. "It's safe enough."

Munir's whole body sagged under the weight of his worries. "I can't stay here. The Turks helped to make us refugees, and now they don't want us here. The only reason we *are* here is that it's on the way to Europe. I'm an economist. An agricultural economist. I was a professor in Damascus. Here, I'm not allowed to work."

"I know." Ahdaf sighed.

"In Europe, I can find a job." His voice quivering, Munir added, "In Europe, my son won't have to eat cockroaches because his body is telling him he needs protein."

"So tomorrow, be outside my apartment at ten," Ahdaf said. "I'll pick you up a few minutes later. Just wait for me. If you decide not to cross tomorrow, tell Yasmin not to worry if you come home late. We won't get back until the middle of the night."

"She'll worry anyway."

Ahdaf watched Munir shuffle off and took a moment to regain his own composure. He knew the whole emotional gamut from fear to fearlessness – hopeless to hopeful – that played out in every one of his clients. In himself, too, though he hadn't quite let himself become hopeful. No one was immune to hard choices. Choosing between life and death was sometimes easier than the actual choices confronting someone. Abandoning a wife and infant children, gambling on the family reuniting in a better future? How to calculate the risks? Or the odds of success? It was an unconscionable choice that no person should have to make, yet that was the battle playing itself out in his friend's slumped shoulders as he dragged himself off down the street.

Ahdaf pushed the café's door open and went inside.

Leyla was passing between tables, delivering orders for tea, sodas, and a couple of beers. Someone was sitting at the cowboy bar. It took him a moment before he recognized Kalam because his phone concealed most of his face as he took a video of the room. Ahdaf looked around, wondering what merited a video, and realized he'd grown inured to the animated scene, while to Kalam, recently arrived from beleaguered Raqqa, this was all new. He'd probably forgotten seeing men freely argue politics. Certainly he'd never seen a table of women in a café before. Not everyone, of course, felt as uninhibited as Ahdaf. No one, for instance, had ever joined him for a beer at the bar.

He took the barstool next to Kalam. "I see you found your way back to Leyla's okay."

"No thanks to you. Your hotel man –"

"Fatih."

"– said you would drop breadcrumbs."

"I did. The birds always eat them."

"Fortunately, I have a good sense of direction. Do you want a tea?"

"I want a beer," Ahdaf corrected him, "but you can still buy it."

They glanced at Leyla, who was entertaining a couple of tables with a story. Ahdaf couldn't hear her, but it didn't matter; he could see how she enthralled the men with her confident style and bold gestures.

"Looks like she's busy," Kalam said.

"That's okay. We can talk privately. I've made some progress. You might be able to make the crossing tomorrow."

Kalam's eyes widened with excitement. "Really? You found a raft so fast?"

"Even better. It's on a fishing boat. It's not definite and it's a little complicated, but if it happens, it's safer."

Once more, Ahdaf outlined the plan to pick up three men coming from Greece. He didn't mention Malik other than to call him a "client," nor that one of the three pick-ups was gravely injured. "I don't know more than it's a reverse operation," he made clear. "I'm only the driver back to Istanbul. But why *wouldn't* the Greek fisherman take back passengers? You have some money, don't you?"

Kalam shrugged. "Sure, but not for a whole boat!"

"For the fisherman, whatever you pay is better than nothing. Decide how much you can pay, and I'll negotiate with him."

Kalam beamed. "I can't believe this. In 24 hours, I'll be in Europe! Is it possible? It's been my –"

"Hey! Turn up the TV!" someone shouted.

They whirled around to see CNN Türk's BREAKING NEWS logo on the overhead television. A reporter stood expectantly in front of a large blank screen. Ahdaf caught Leyla's eye. She nodded, and he reached for the remote to raise the volume.

"We are on standby," the reporter said, his hand cupped over an earpiece, "waiting for a report from our special correspondent, Derya Thomas, who's been covering the Assos events. We've not heard from her for many hours. Apparently, she has gone into hiding. I'm told we have a transmission and … here she is!" On-screen, Derya appeared, standing in front of a bare wall. There was no way to know where she was, except that it was indoors. "Hello, Derya, can you hear me?"

"Yes, I can hear you."

The room had fallen quiet, but someone still called, "Louder!"

Ahdaf turned up the volume further.

"Two nights ago, a raft with 64 refugees capsized 20 minutes after launching, and not because of weather. They'd been rammed by the Turkish Coast Guard. I'll let this witness tell his story first."

The image switched to a video of a man, his face blurred so as to be unrecognizable, on a dock with fishing boats tied up to it.

87

The names of the moored boats were also blurred. "I'm a fisherman, and was coming home with one running light. It's enough
unless something big's approaching, and then I turn on more.
As things turned out, it was *me* approaching something big. The
Coast Guard boat without a single light on it. I didn't see it until
I couldn't stop .... I ran into its side ... right in the middle of it!
Suddenly its lights came on, and the engine started. I thought it
was because I'd hit it, but I tossed in its wake, almost capsizing as
it shot forward. It hadn't gone 50 meters before it hit the raft and
flipped it over. I heard screams ... people were thrashing about in
the sea ... yelling and calling .... It was ... horrible!"

Offscreen, Derya asked, "Are you sure it was the Coast Guard?"

"I'm sure. It was painted on the side of the boat. Besides, what
other boats have radar? If I hadn't seen it myself, it would just
be another story about the refugee situation, but to witness it ..."
The fisherman's voice cracked. He had to pause before he could
say, "I saw children falling into the water. I'll never forget."

The camera cut from the fisherman to Derya in her hideout. "I was able to corroborate with some of the survivors that a
boat struck the raft," she said. "To those who saw it coming, it
seemed intentional. Sixty-four passengers on a raft built for 30,
18 dead, a dozen still missing. The government has blamed the
incident on the Islamic State, but ISIS hasn't claimed responsibility, and it's usually quick to take credit. Where was the Coast
Guard the night of the incident? Now we know. It was the cause
of the tragedy. An incident staged by the government. Why? We
don't know yet with certainty, but my hunch is that the president
hopes he'll get international support for an expanded military
campaign against the Islamic State in northern Syria. This is
Derya Thomas, reporting from a secret location."

A sullen mood settled on the room. Probably every smuggler
present had had a client on a raft in distress who'd been rescued
by the Coast Guard. Its ready help unavailable in emergencies

– it *causing* them instead – was a sobering notion. It changed the whole equation by creating risk where before there had been a fragile sense of security.

Profound remorse swept over Ahdaf. It must have showed, because Kalam touched his shoulder and said, "You had clients on that raft, didn't you?"

Ahdaf could only nod. Trying to say anything would have flooded him with tears.

"Do you want to leave?" Kalam asked.

He did, and they stood and headed for the door. Outside, they walked in silence to the corner where they'd parted the night before. They paused; neither wanted to part that night. "I hate the idea of your sleeping at the Tropicana," Ahdaf finally said. "I know it's got bugs. All the refugee hotels have bugs. If you want, you can stay with me tonight. Your choice, bed or floor, and I really don't mind sleeping on the floor."

Kalam smiled. "I'm sure I've slept on worse floors."

"Then let's keep going," Ahdaf suggested, and led them up the hill another two blocks. He felt nervous. He'd never invited anyone to his apartment, let alone a man who shared his sexual desires. Is longing what had made him invite Kalam? Subconsciously hoping the evening might be headed that way?

They turned at a restaurant and walked to the next intersection. "I live there," Ahdaf said, pointing to the corner building across the street. Like the whole street, it needed sprucing up, but it wasn't as rundown as most. Ahdaf had made sure of that. He'd lugged broken furniture and appliances abandoned on the sidewalk into the alley, from which someone would eventually take them or proper garbage collectors would haul them away. He'd tried planting flowers in the narrow band of earth along the sidewalk, but most were stolen before taking root; so he'd limited his caretaking to pulling out the few weeds that grew there.

89

Ahdaf let them in, and Kalam followed him up the stairs. As he fitted the key into his lock, Madame Darton swung her door open, holding a watering can. "Oh, Ahdaf!" she cried, feigning surprise. "You startled me!" He knew he hadn't. He also knew that the watering can and two plants she kept on the landing were props she used as an excuse to cross paths with him. A yapping miniature poodle on a leash ran circles around her legs, effectively tying her feet together. "Fifi! Stop!" she cried, and unsuccessfully tried to shake her ankles free.

"Wait, let me help," Ahdaf said, and to Kalam added: "Go on in." He crouched down to catch the dog and unhook its leash to untangle it.

"I'm glad you're finding friends," Madame Darton said.

"It's true that I don't have many," he agreed.

"You don't need many, if they are all so handsome!"

"I hadn't noticed," he lied. Standing, he handed her the leash. "You're free to walk again."

She laughed and said, "You're such a gentleman!"

"My pleasure," he said, and it was. He didn't mind running an occasional errand for her or taking Fifi for a walk. She was matronly, old to Ahdaf, and was always primly dressed. A headscarf on the street was her one concession to Muslim fashion. "Goodnight, Madame," he said.

He closed the door and turned to Kalam. "She always times her appearances to coincide with mine. She's coming or going when I'm going or coming."

"Is she married?"

"Widowed. I don't know the details, except her husband was a visiting professor in archaeology and dropped dead of a heart attack in class. She says she can't bear to go back to France without him."

"I bet she's in love with you."

"A bit old for me, don't you think?"

90

"It's a matter of what *she* thinks."

"She said *you* were handsome, not me."

"She's not my type either," Kalam said.

Ahdaf heard his confession and impulsively took the risk of leaning closer to kiss him. It turned out to be no risk at all; Kalam's lips were soft and ready, and opened slightly with mutual desire. Then it was over; that's as far as they wanted to go. They pulled apart, certain they'd come back together as the evening took a slower course.

"So this is your room," Kalam remarked.

"It's home for now."

"It's nicer than I expected. It's so clean."

"It was filthy when I moved in. Painting made a big difference."

"It looks a lot cleaner than any place I've slept in the last few months."

Ahdaf pursed his lips knowingly. "How long did you walk exactly?"

"Ninety-one days."

"Eighty-seven for me," Ahdaf told him. "We probably fed the same bedbugs! Are you hungry?"

"I'll always be hungry! But you don't need to feed me."

"Don't worry, I don't have much. First, I need to piss."

Ahdaf ducked into the bathroom. He used the toilet, washed his hands and rinsed off his face. He tried to smell his breath, but couldn't, and swished toothpaste in his mouth to be sure it was fresh. When he went back into the room, Kalam was bent over, examining the bookstacks raising the mattress off the floor.

"Why the books?" Kalam asked. "To keep bugs off?"

"How'd you guess?"

Kalam shrugged. "It's because of the cockroaches at the Tropicana that I'm sleeping on your floor tonight."

"I offered you the bed."

Kalam gave the bed another look. "Do the bookstacks work?"

"If you sprinkle baking soda between their pages. I mix it in the glue between the books, too. They eat that, and boom, they're dead."

"Did your mother teach you that?"

"No. Google."

"Google?" Kalam chuckled, which made Ahdaf laugh, too. The banter fueled each other's need for levity. Ahdaf realized they both were fraught with paranoia. How could they not be, after what had happened to Sadiq? Someone had denounced him. Ahdaf wondered if it might have been Kalam, and no doubt Kalam wondered the same about him. Their laughter urged them to trust each other; yet when it subsided, neither made a denounceable move. What now? How would they go forward? The situation was awkward until Ahdaf remembered, "I promised you something to eat."

"Don't worry about it."

"It's no big worry. All I have is *helva*, olives, and chickpeas. Oh, and some dates." He took them out of the refrigerator and set them on the counter. "Unfortunately, no bread, but I do have a beer."

Kalam chuckled. "Did Sadiq teach you to like beer, too?"

"He did," Ahdaf replied.

"He *was* a bad influence. That's what he was afraid of, that if your families found out about you and him, he'd be accused of being the bad influence because he was older."

"He was only two years older."

"It wouldn't matter. They'd want an excuse, and he'd be it. They can't understand that some people are gay. Depraved, yes, because they've been 'turned' somehow, but naturally gay?" Kalam shook his head. "Naturally gay doesn't exist. Are you going to pour that beer?"

"Sorry." Ahdaf took his only two glasses out of a cupboard. He had just one of almost everything else, including only one chair at his table; why buy two when he was only going to eat alone? But a glass could easily be broken, so he had a second one as a backup. As he poured the beer, he said, "I always wanted to know: how did Sadiq get beer? Even when ISIS was controlling things, sometimes he managed to get it."

Kalam shrugged. "Your cousin had many secrets."

Ahdaf handed Kalam a glass. "Apparently, we were two of them."

"To Sadiq's secrets!" Kalam laughed, and they clinked glasses. "Though I wish," he added, "that *we* hadn't been a secret from each other."

"Sadiq told you about me," Ahdaf reminded him.

"But he never let us meet. Maybe he wanted to keep it a secret that you were so handsome. I don't know how he resisted you, because I can't …" Kalam pulled him into a kiss.

Ahdaf had hoped for a sexual overture, but never had he imagined such a kiss. All he'd known to expect were his cousin's pursed lips, not Kalam's inviting mouth – not his flavor and roving tongue. They set their glasses on the counter and, arms around each other, moved toward the bed. On the way, Ahdaf flicked off the light, leaving a streetlamp's chalky glow to illuminate the room. While kissing again, they fiddled with each other's buttons and pulled their shirts off. Ahdaf wrapped his arms around fair Kalam, pressing their chests together, experiencing the skin-to-skin contact he'd always wanted with another man. Kalam fiddled with Ahdaf's belt buckle, and soon both young men kicked off their shoes and stripped. They embraced again, their hard cocks raking each other's belly before lowering themselves onto the bed.

Ahdaf rolled on his side to press the full length of his body against Kalam. He ran his hand through his fair chest hair, marveling at Kalam's beauty, almost disbelieving of the moment. He closed his mouth over a nipple while reaching for his cock.

Kalam said, "Not yet," and rolled on top of him. He became their lovemaking guide. He'd had more experience, or at least had a better sense of what to do. Ahdaf had never watched a man take him in his mouth before, or touch him in places he would have thought off-limits but, as soon as they were touched, were no longer. It was one long rumpus, hands and mouths everywhere, twisting upside down for some pleasures before twisting back around for others. During one of those twists, the bed's supporting bookstacks all gave way at once, and they found themselves in a lumpy trough. After the initial shock, it was funny, and they laughed – but only briefly, so driven were both by desire. Despite the shifting terrain, they grunted and sweated their way to coming a couple of times before pausing, Ahdaf's head on Kalam's shoulder, again running his hand through his now damp chest hair. "I thought blonds only came from Sweden and California," he said.

"My hair's light brown, not blond."

"Blonder than me and everyone else."

"My mother blames it on Alexander the Great and his soldiers' contribution to our collective gene pool."

"Really?"

"What can't be explained *can* be explained by a regressive gene. That, or a tourist fling, and who confesses to that?"

Ahdaf lifted his head. "Are you saying your mother had a fling?"

"My mother, have a fling?" Kalam laughed at the notion of it. "Not a chance! Besides, I look just like my dad. No tourist involved. Should we move the mattress off the books?"

"First we need to move the books to have enough floor space."

Working together, they stacked the books against the wall. Fortunately, most had survived the bed's collapse still glued together, making it easy to put them out of the way. Ahdaf, who'd rarely seen a naked man, was suddenly laboring next to one. As he watched Kalam, he admired his body: his tawny skin, his flexed muscles, his sex swinging with every move.

"You're staring at me again," Kalam said.

"I've never seen a naked man do more than wrap a towel around his waist."

Kalam tossed a couple of pillows onto the mattress. "Now you have. And now we have a bed."

"I'm not really tired," Ahdaf admitted.

"You will be tomorrow. It's going to be a long day. Do you want to use the bathroom first?"

"You go ahead."

"Do you mind if I use some of your toothpaste?"

"Of course not. You can shower if you want. My towel should be dry."

"Let's save the towel for the morning. Maybe I can finally convince you to shower together." Kalam raised his eyebrows in a smile and shut the bathroom door.

Ahdaf pulled on his boxers and reached for the curtain to block the outside light. As he did so, he surprised a man staring up at his window. The man appeared to take his picture, and quickly walked off. Ahdaf was being watched. But by whom? He shivered, reminded of the dangerous world he found himself navigating.

DAY 5

They awoke the next morning with the same playful intentions, and ended up in the shower with Kalam wanting Ahdaf to wash his back. "It's not had a good scrubbing for months," he said, and turned around. "So scrub away."

Ahdaf wet a bar of soap and turned off the water. "Lean against the wall so I can rub hard," he said.

Kalam straddled the tub's faucet and braced his forearms on the wall. Ahdaf lathered up his back, then rubbed him with his flat palms, using them like loofahs to scrape away the ingrained dirt. He sudsed him up again and, more gently, ran his hands all over Kalam's back, eventually reaching under his arms, his knuckles tangling with his tufts of hair before his hands drifted down his sides to follow the groin lines below his flat belly.

"That's not my back," Kalam murmured.

Ahdaf pressed against him. "I know where your back is," he said. What he did next, he'd never done before, but his body certainly knew what it wanted. Kalam gasped at the initial pain and reached back to stop him until he got used to him, then drew him in deeper when he was ready for more. Both young men, excited and experiencing something new, finished in a few thrusts but remained where they stood, not wanting to separate quite yet. When they did slip apart, Kalam turned in his arms, and they embraced while water splashed over them for a last rinse.

"We need to leave soon," Ahdaf murmured. "I'll make coffee. I hope Turkish is okay. It's all I have."

"In that case, it's what I want. Two sugars."

"The third one's free."

Kalam laughed. "Then why not?"

Ahdaf found his undershorts in a tangle of clothes, not remembering the sequence of how everything got mixed up but glad they had; he would never forget the night's dénouement. He dressed, went to the kitchen end of his long room, and turned on the hotplate. A school bell one street over reminded him that the news headlines would start in one minute. He retrieved his phone from his daypack and stood it on the counter, where he could watch CNN Türk while making coffee. The lead story: during the night, there had been a bungled raid in Istanbul on an ISIS cell thought to be planning a series of terrorist attacks. In an exchange of gunfire, a butane cooking bottle had started a fire on the ground floor, trapping everyone in the building. "Officials estimate at least a dozen people perished," a reporter said.

"Shit," Ahdaf muttered as he filled a copper *ibrik* with water and stirred in two heaping teaspoons of finely ground coffee and sugar. He placed it on the hotplate to heat up. "In another developing story," the reporter continued, "we can now confirm that an arrest warrant has been issued for one of our special correspondents, Derya Thomas, who yesterday accused the Turkish Coast Guard of purposefully capsizing a raft full of refugees." A photo of Derya appeared on the screen behind him. "Derya has been accused of sedition under laws passed after the attempted coup, which define 'sedition' to include the undermining of confidence in government institutions." The reporter looked straight at his viewers when he added, "In journalism, that's often what we do. It's called 'reporting the news.' All of us here at CNN hope this situation will end with restraint and the safety of our colleague."

Ahdaf switched off his phone after the news summary ended. When the water started foaming, he stirred it and turned off the heat. Kalam came out of the bathroom, raking his fingers through his light brown curls. "What's the news?" he asked as he started dressing. "My Turkish isn't good enough to follow what's said on television."

"How's your Greek?"

"Nonexistent."

"Your English?"

"'Hi! My name is Kalam. I am not going to hurt you. Can you help me?' I can say that and a few other things."

Ahdaf handed him a coffee.

"Thanks."

They took sips, and Ahdaf asked, "If you don't speak English, how will you know what's happening?"

"Like what?"

"What areas to avoid. Where it's safe and not safe." He grinned. "The best routes to Hollywood … things like that."

"I'll meet people who can tell me." Kalam grinned. "Or better yet, you come with me!"

Ahdaf briefly considered it and felt disappointed at his own decision. "I can't. I'm not ready yet."

Kalam smiled, his eyes twinkling. "You know we'd be good together. We already are!"

"I know. I'm just not ready."

"I still have a whole day to convince you. What's the news?"

"A government raid on an ISIS cell went badly, and a lot of people were killed."

"Where?"

"Here in Istanbul." To himself, Ahdaf quietly wondered if it might have been Malik's cell, and maybe the weaselly man was dead. "Also, the Turkish government has issued an arrest warrant for a journalist for reporting a story that my guess is true. Remember the female journalist who reported that the Coast Guard rammed the raft? It's her."

"I thought that only happened everywhere," Kalam remarked in a sarcastic tone.

"Yeah, you're right, I shouldn't be surprised. She's a good reporter. I hope she's okay." Ahdaf opened the refrigerator. "We need to eat something and get out of here." He pulled out the few provisions he had and dumped everything on the counter. "Dates, hummus, some pita, cheese."

"Coffee and a couple of dates will do me," Kalam said.

"Me, too." Ahdaf ate three on the spot and threw the pits into a covered bin under the sink. As he did, he thought about what he needed for the round trip to Assos. *Not much,* he decided. From what he could tell, it was nothing more than a long road trip with service stations along the way. At the end of it, they'd be at the sea. He'd never seen a real sea. He'd known the muddy Euphrates and the clogged Bosporus, but never an open body of blue water. It excited him to think about it, and he wished he'd taken a pair of swim trunks from the Tropicana. He went into the bathroom to collect his dental floss and toothbrush, items his father-the-dentist had always exhorted everyone to carry with them after the war started, once getting back home became perilous.

Kalam ducked into the bathroom to use the toilet, and Ahdaf finished dressing. When Kalam finished, it was Ahdaf's turn. After washing his hands, he opened the door and held up the soap. "Want to take it with you?"

"Sure," Kalam said and tucked it into his pack. "Thanks. Obviously, you know how hard it is to find soap on the road." He zipped up his pack. "Ready."

They paused, looking at each other. They were only a couple

of steps apart, but the distance already felt as if it were widening. The sadness showed in their unsmiling faces. They'd both experienced an exceptional night that had rekindled in the morning. They knew, too, that if circumstances were different, they'd likely pair up in some way.

"Let's say our real goodbye here," Kalam suggested, and they clutched each other in an embrace, not wanting to let go.

"Last night was special," Ahdaf murmured.

"So was this morning," replied Kalam. "It was my first time. I'm glad it was you."

Ahdaf laughed softly. "It was the first time for me, too. I didn't know anything could feel so amazing. I'm getting hard just thinking about it."

Kalam grinned. "Me too!"

"Stay a week," Ahdaf urged him. "I promise a spot on a raft if you still want to go."

"After a week with you, I'd never leave, and I don't want to stop," Kalam said. "I'm only at the start of my journey."

A short last kiss, a final hug, and they were out the door carrying their daypacks. From across the landing wafted the buttery smell of something freshly baked.

Kalam breathed it in. "Yum yum!"

"You wait. Madame Darton has something for us."

As if summoned, the older woman swung open her door, her yappy dog at her feet. "Oh good, I didn't miss you!"

"*Bonjour, Madame*," Ahdaf said.

"*Bonjour*. I decided I wanted a real croissant this morning, not what passes for croissants around here. A *French* croissant, but it seemed silly to bake only one, so I made extras for you." She held out a plate with two of the flaky pastries on it.

"That wasn't necessary."

"Of course it wasn't necessary. I wanted to bake them."

"They smell wonderful!" Kalam exclaimed.

"Take them."

Kalam bit into one. "It's delicious. And still warm! Thank you."

"You're welcome. Now you young men go and profit from your day. Come inside, Fifi!" She closed her door after the dog.

"'Profit from our day'?" Kalam asked, following Ahdaf down the stairs. "What does that mean?"

Ahdaf shrugged. "I have no idea, and she always says it. I just smile and try to be nice. You're right, she's lonely."

"And she feeds you."

"She says she misses cooking for someone, and I'm the lucky beneficiary."

As they left the building, Ahdaf put a hand on Kalam's back, but let it drop once in public view. As they finished their croissants on the sidewalk, he said, "I wish you weren't leaving. At least not so soon."

"You organized it!"

"That was before last night. Besides, all I've organized is hoping the Greek fisherman will take you back with him. I can't promise that he will."

Kalam grinned. "Then we'll have more nights together. Or maybe you can arrange for him to come back in a few days?"

Ahdaf saw the emotions that played across Kalam's face. Debating whether to go or to submit to an unexpected friendship that felt shamelessly sincere. Weighing what he might gain by staying or leaving. Assessing his original goals from a different perspective. "Turkey's not a country for men like us," he ultimately replied.

"It's better than in Syria. Here they aren't throwing men like us off rooftops."

"Not yet, but how long before it happens? You said yourself, things are becoming more fundamentalist."

Ahdaf, too, didn't doubt it could happen. He'd seen how his own country, relatively liberal, had been hijacked by ISIS and its fundamentalism. In Istanbul, he knew gays were more open; they were mentioned in the news instead of the news pretending they didn't exist. Even so, conservative Islam's growing influence had encouraged an increase in violence against them – violence that remained largely unreported because, by reporting it, the victims would be outing themselves, in turn risking more violence and, even worse, the insurmountable shame of their families. In the darkest hours of his three-month trek from Raqqa, when overwhelmed by his own sense of guilt and shame, Ahdaf often pondered suicide, and wondered how many gays would ultimately prefer to let ISIS throw them off rooftops than throw themselves off. Sometimes death felt like the only bearable option for men like him.

"There's a better alternative," Kalam said.

"What's that?"

"You come with me."

"To Greece?"

"Think about it, and just in case you want to do it at the last minute, go upstairs now and put a kit together. It'll take you five minutes. A toothbrush and any warm clothes you have because we'll be going north in winter. What else do you need to take?"

"My mother's letter," Ahdaf answered.

"That's easy to pack."

"It's not about packing it. It's about never seeing my parents again. If I go to Greece, I'm sure I won't. From here, I can walk home if I have to. I can't from Europe."

"You can't go back. ISIS has informants everywhere."

"I know, but that's not an excuse to go to Europe, either. I'm surviving okay here, but of course I'd like a few more days with you. The weather should still be okay for crossing for another couple of weeks. I can almost always find you a spot on a raft."

"On an overcrowded raft in a winter storm?" Kalam shrugged off the suggestion. "I'd rather take my chances tonight."

Ahdaf nodded. "I understand. I would, too, if going to Greece is what I wanted to do."

"We'll stay in touch, okay?" Kalam said. "In case you change your mind. And I still think you should pack a kit." He smiled wistfully. "I wish we could kiss."

"I wish we had never stopped!" Ahdaf exclaimed. "Never!"

In lieu of a kiss, they touched their hearts and looked at each other longingly.

"I didn't mention, but another friend is joining us," Ahdaf said. "His name's Munir. He won't be expecting you either."

"Who is he?"

"Another refugee who wants to go to Greece. He's a smuggler like me. Sometimes we help each other with contacts, logistics, stuff like that."

"Why does he want to cross? You say you're doing okay with a toilet, shower, and hotplate." Kalam grinned. "What more could a man want?"

"In Munir's case, he has a wife and kids. His three-year-old son is eating cockroaches and his new baby is probably going to die because his wife is too hungry to produce milk. He's convinced that life will be better in Europe."

"You don't think it will be?"

"For him, it could only be better," Ahdaf agreed. "I'm in a different situation. I don't have a starving family. We should get moving. You need to go collect your stuff and be back here in an hour."

"No problem. Remind me, what's the guy's name at the hotel?"

"Fatih," Ahdaf answered. "Munir will be meeting us here, too. Introduce yourselves to each other. He's dark, a little fat, and has really big ears."

Ahdaf watched him walk off and already yearned for him. He wished he could fall asleep every night running his fingers through Kalam's chest hair, and wake up legs entwined every morning. So strong was his desire that he was tempted to run upstairs, grab what little he owned, and be off to Greece with Kalam that night; but he wouldn't do it. He also knew that the chance of seeing his parents again was becoming slimmer as the war dragged on, especially if going home meant risking his own life. A push off the same rooftop from which Sadiq "fell" would befit ISIS's warped sense of justice.

His thoughts recycled themselves as he walked to the mosque. The commercial street teemed with people, many of them recognizable as refugees by their clothing, skin color, or simple gestures that discerned them from Turks. It was with relief that he stepped through the mosque's gate and left the busy street. A few men sat chatting on benches, enjoying the courtyard's generous space and the greenery of its garden. Ahdaf headed for the spigots, performed his ablutions, and went inside to pray. He knelt, and after the perfunctory verses praising Allah, spoke to his father, believing whatever he said would be heard, or sensed, if not exactly audibly. He had no doubt that his father heard him in the same way that he heard his father. While praying, they had always shared breaths.

Afterward, he left pulling back the heavy curtain at the entrance and stepped into blinding light. The morning sun had edged above the neighboring buildings to make its brightest appearance of the day. Ahdaf shielded his eyes as he retrieved his shoes and sat on a bench to put them on. Usually he wore slip-on sandals everywhere, but sturdier sneakers seemed more appropriate for the coming night's clandestine operation. While bent over tying his shoes, he was suddenly in someone's shadow. He looked up at Malik.

"I thought today you might be here for *fajr*," said the *medrese's* director, referring to dawn prayers.

"The trip to Assos and back is going to take all day and most of the night. I wanted the extra sleep."

"How much did you sleep?"

Ahdaf paused. It was an odd question. "How much did I sleep?"

"You had a man in your room. All night."

"He's a client," Ahdaf replied, shrugging off his innuendo. "Sometimes I rent floor space to clients. Men only, of course, and I only have room for one. It's cheaper for the guy, and I make some money. I use earplugs if he snores, but last night he didn't."

"Did he miss *fajr* too?"

"I don't know. He was gone before I woke up."

"You came to your window naked before you closed the curtain."

"I'm never naked except in the shower. I had underwear on, because that's how I sleep. Besides, the window's set too high to see me naked unless you're on the roof on the building across the street. Maybe at that angle, you could."

Malik held his phone out of Ahdaf's reach but close enough for him to watch a video. He recognized his apartment's window. He couldn't see Kalam or himself, but he saw their shadows on the walls and ceiling as they kissed and undressed each other. The last few seconds showed Ahdaf, shirtless, closing the curtain.

"Why are you spying on me?" he asked.

"Because of rumors about you and your cousin. Now I have proof."

"Proof of what? That I close curtains while not wearing a shirt?"

"Be careful, Ahdaf. For the time being, only I know the truth. If you are useful to me, I'll protect you."

"Then let me be useful and take the van," Ahdaf replied. "That's why I'm here."

"You'll need money for tolls and gasoline," Malik said, and from a deep pocket pulled out a wad of bills that he handed to him.

"And for me?" Ahdaf asked.

"For you?"

"For driving to Assos and bringing your passengers back. How much are you paying me?"

"What's your life worth?"

It took Ahdaf a moment to interpret the trick question.

"Is my payment that you won't throw me off a rooftop?"

"You will have atoned for your sins."

"What if I sin again?"

"Then you must answer to Allah again."

"Answer to Allah, or answer to you?"

"I'm an intermediary. Shall we go to the van?"

Ahdaf followed the miserable little man, hoping his every limp was painful, out a gate in a tall hedge into an alley that ran behind the mosque. A van, originally bright red, had been painted the obligatory yellow to permit it to operate as a school bus. The streaky paint job left the vehicle more orange than yellow, with the *medrese's* name stenciled in black on its sides. The *medrese's* students had been given free rein to paint the van's interior before it was retrofitted with six rows of short, wooden benches along a central aisle. Using only their open palms, they'd covered every square centimeter with handprints in a dozen colors; a few had been allowed on the vehicle's exterior as well. Everybody in the neighborhood knew the clownish school bus, and smiled when they saw it on the street: a bright spot on sometimes grim days.

That morning, though, Ahdaf wasn't smiling when Malik unlocked the van and handed him the key. Noticing his expression, Malik asked, "You do know how to drive a stick shift, right?"

"Of course," Ahdaf told him without much conviction. In fact, his driving experience consisted of three lessons that his uncle had given him in a manual pickup truck, in the event that the family decided to flee Raqqa. The week after his last driving lesson, his uncle's pickup was destroyed in a bombing raid. He took the key from Malik and asked, "How is the injured guy?"

Malik shrugged. "I don't know. Serhan, the team leader, has your mobile number. He'll call me only if he can't reach you, and then I'll call you."

"Shouldn't I have his number in an emergency?"

"It's too dangerous."

"Dangerous?"

"If you're stopped at a roadblock, they'll check your contacts and your recent calls."

"Oh, right," Ahdaf replied, as if he understood, when he had no idea why he'd be stopped at a roadblock or why his recent calls would be suspect.

"They'll start from Lesvos at sunset and land north of Assos … but where, exactly, he'll call to tell you."

"Sounds easy. Let me see if I can start this!" Ahdaf, feigning confidence, stepped on the van's running board and hoisted himself into the driver seat. He shut the door and cranked open the window. Pressing on the clutch, he turned the key, and the engine turned over. Reaching for the gear handle, he noticed their positions weren't marked on it. "Where's 'reverse'?" he asked.

"A hard right and down."

Ahdaf found reverse, but let the clutch out without giving it enough gas, and the van lurched backward. Malik leaped out of the way. "Don't worry, just practicing!" Ahdaf laughed. "I'll get used to it!" On his second try, he managed to back up to the main road, and then swore at whoever had last driven the van into the alley – because now Ahdaf had to back out into heavy traffic. When he realized he had no choice but just dare to do it, he was greeted by an orchestra of horns, which continued to blare at him as he made his slow and jerky way down the road. He wished there were someplace he could practice shifting gears, but in the few blocks to his apartment there was nowhere spacious enough.

He mulled over the fact that he was under constant surveillance.

Malik had a video of him bare chested at the window the previous night, and another, more worrying one of the shadows of
Kalam and him coming together in an obvious kiss. He had no
doubt that the man he'd startled on the sidewalk that night was
another of Malik's spies. Perhaps a neighbor was an informant,
too. The thought made him anxious. He didn't want to pull up to
his apartment in the *medrese's* school bus and pick up two guys
instead of only Kalam when word might get back to Malik. As
soon as he could, he pulled into a side street to telephone Kalam.

"It's Ahdaf," he said when he answered. "Are you outside my
apartment?"

"Of course. With Munir."

"I'll pick you up at the Tropicana."

"Not here?"

"Not there. The Tropicana. I'll be there in 10 minutes." He
hung up.

His next challenge was to return to the main road through
a spiderweb of backstreets, which gave him all the refresher he
needed on clutching and changing gears. He managed to pull
into traffic without a single blast of a horn before turning a
few minutes later to find his way to the fleabag hotel. A block
before reaching it, he came up on Kalam and Munir, chatting
and laughing. He pulled over. Munir slid open the side door
to get in the back while Kalam reached for the front passenger
door.

Ahdaf, recalling Selim's admonition to make the pickup as
discreet as possible, said, "Both of you, get in the back. We have
another passenger to pick up at the American consulate and I
want to make it fast without a lot of changing seats."

"No problem," Kalam said, and got in the back.

"What other passenger?" Munir asked.

Ahdaf, fiddling with his phone, said, "A third passenger who's
going to Greece." He propped his phone where he could see the

GPS map and tried to find first gear. Forgetting to clutch, he ground the gears instead. "Sorry about that," he said. "I'm still learning how to drive this thing!"

"And you're driving us to Assos?" Munir griped. "Besides, I thought you were picking somebody up in Assos, not taking somebody there."

"There are two things happening, which is why there's a chance to get you on a boat tonight." He explained the situation, how his main task was to pick up three guys coming from Greece on a fishing boat. He was gambling that he could convince the Greek boatman to take Kalam and Munir back with him. But first, they had to pick up a third passenger, who also wanted to get to Greece by boat to avoid the risk of a raft.

"Who is it?" Munir asked.

"I don't know."

"He works for the Americans?"

"I'm guessing yes."

"You don't know for sure?"

"The arrangement is that I'll pick him up at the consulate. Who he is, or why he's at the consulate, I don't know."

"It sounds risky."

"What's risky? We drive to Assos. Some people get off a boat, and you get on it."

"Are you sure you can trust them?"

Looking at Munir in the mirror, he tried to make light of his worries and replied, "You're a smuggler. You know the answer to that!"

"That's why I'm nervous. It's also why I brought this." Munir pulled a gun out of his shoulder pack and held it up for Ahdaf to see in the mirror.

"What the fuck!"

"I've heard Europe can be dangerous. Thieves, and worse."

"Put it away!" Ahdaf snapped as he turned a corner to start up a hill, accidentally downshifting into first gear instead of second.

When the van jerked, Munir dropped his gun. It ricocheted between the seat posts before tumbling to a stop at the back. Munir scrambled to get it and returned to his seat. He stuffed it into his shoulder pack and looked at Ahdaf in the mirror. "At least we have it if we need it."

Ahdaf slowed as he approached the American consulate. At the curb, Selim was waiting for him and waved him over. As soon as Ahdaf braked, the Marine guards flanking the consulate's entrance lifted their weapons, ready to fire. Selim whirled around to signal that all was well. One guard yelled back, "You said only a driver! Nothing about two passengers!"

Again, Selim motioned for restraint as he came up to the passenger window. "Who are they?" he asked Ahdaf in English.

"Friends. I asked them to come along in case I need help. They also want to go to Greece. If I can get your passenger on the Greek's boat, maybe I can get them on it, too."

Selim looked hard at the two men who'd suddenly been inserted into his operation. He had to be wondering if he'd misread Ahdaf. Was a team of suicide bombers now parked on the consulate's curb? Reverting to Turkish, he snapped, "No one gets out of the vehicle. No one even moves."

They all watched Selim disappear into the consulate, wondering what would come next. They didn't have long to wait. Moments later, he reappeared, followed by a woman in a black burqa with a matching black daypack over her shoulder. *Or is it a woman?* Ahdaf wondered. Had Selim decided to use Arafat's rumored disguise to steal out a man? He looked for clues, a giveaway of the person's gender. Nothing was obvious, nothing especially mannish or womanish about the person hastening to keep up with the CIA man.

The cafés across the street from the consulate fell silent; everybody was increasingly aware that something out of the ordinary was happening. Why had a *medrese's* clapped-out school bus been allowed to pull onto the curb in front of the consulate? Why were the Marine guards noticeably agitated? Why was a woman in a burqa being escorted to the van?

Selim opened the passenger door and the mystery passenger got in, tugging at the burqa's clinging material in a way that looked practiced. She had to be a woman.

Once she was settled, Selim walked around to the driver's side. He handed Ahdaf a bank card. "Use this to pay for tolls and gas. Food, too – you'll need some. It's contactless, so it should be easy. There's usually only one lane if you're paying with a card or cash. It's marked. If you have a problem, call me."

"There's already a problem," Ahdaf replied.

"What's that?"

"I can't pay the fisherman with a debit card."

Selim whispered, "She has 10,000 euros."

"Is that enough for three people?" Ahdaf worried aloud.

"If it's not, she goes alone. That's always been the plan, anyway."

Ahdaf pulled off the sidewalk and drove them to the top of the hill, where he stopped to set his GPS. "Assos," he muttered to himself.

"You don't need that," the woman said in Turkish. "Do you prefer to speak in Turkish or English?"

"English," he replied.

"Do you know how to get on the road to Ankara?"

"This is the first time I've driven in Istanbul."

"Okay, then go straight," the woman instructed. "When you come to a stop sign, turn right and then right again to get back down to the main road."

Ahdaf followed her directions, wondering where she was from; more specifically, he was curious about her English. She spoke it flawlessly, and he detected a hint of a British accent without any

Turkish influence. By her hands, he could see the stranger was a young woman: 20s, maybe 30? The absence of a ring or telltale white band suggested she was unmarried. Other than that, all Ahdaf could be certain of was that she wasn't a man disguised in a burqa.

Ahdaf made the two right turns that dumped him back into Istanbul's heavy traffic. "You're going to stay on this road a couple of kilometers," the woman said, "until we merge onto the national road. Then you must make a decision."

"What's that?"

"Going west, which is shorter and more scenic, but has a ferry ride and we'd need to get out of the car. Or going east, then turning south. It's a little longer, but there's a road the whole way."

"The second makes more sense. Are you from Assos?"

"I've been many times," the woman replied. "Do you have a battery charger for your phone?"

"Hey! If you're expecting us to hear you, you've got to talk louder," Munir let them know.

"We're just talking directions," Ahdaf said loudly. "Does one of you have a battery charger for phones?"

No one did. Only cables, and the ancient van didn't have USB ports.

The woman twisted to face the back. "You should turn off your phones to save your batteries, because you won't have a chance to recharge them," she said.

"The back windows don't open!" Munir complained. "I want to smoke. Can you open yours?"

"Sure," Ahdaf said, and thought to ask the woman, "You won't be too cold?"

"Do you have any idea how hot a burqa is?" she scoffed.

"I've never worn one."

"No man who's worn one would force women to wear them unless he truly hated women. Except for the rich, who can afford cotton burqas. The others are all made from synthetic fabrics that don't breathe. Eventually even your hands sweat, and you can't wipe them dry because the cloth is too slick. Too plasticized."

Ahdaf was surprised by her frankness. Women who wore burqas were essentially forbidden to speak to unrelated men, let alone complain about how men treated them. "Who are you?"

"It's safer that nobody knows, especially you."

"Safer?"

"In case we get stopped. You're a driver hired to take someone to Assos. You weren't told who."

"Okay, don't tell me who you are. Why do you speak English and Turkish?"

"My father is English. He came to Turkey on a holiday and met my mother."

"And lived happily ever after," Ahdaf said flatly, as if ending a fairy tale.

"They'd say so." She glanced at her watch. "It's almost noon. Can we listen to the news?"

"If the radio works. I haven't tried it."

The woman switched on the radio pre-set to a station playing traditional Turkish music. She switched the channel to CNN Türk, where the news had started.

"... using roadside bombs to stop a convoy in northern Syria, then gunning down the Turkish soldiers as they fled the burning vehicles. At least 10 were killed. ISIS has already claimed responsibility. In another story, authorities in Assos have called off their search efforts for the last four people, including an infant girl, still missing when a raft capsized three nights ago. Wanted for questioning in that incident is one of our own special correspondents, Derya Thomas, whom the government has accused of sedition for her report accusing the Coast Guard of purposefully capsizing a raft filled with refugees. The government has accused

ISIS of the tragedy, but ISIS, usually quick to claim responsibility, has denied any involvement in the incident. Those are our top stories."

The woman switched off the radio.

Ahdaf glanced in the rearview mirror. Kalam and Munir were both lost in thought, looking out the windows. He lowered his voice. "You're Derya Thomas, aren't you?"

She hesitated before answering, "Yes."

"I've often seen you on television. Especially recently."

"I'm not on every day. I do special reports."

"I saw your report two days ago about the raft capsizing."

"It didn't exactly capsize. It had some help."

"Last night, you were hiding somewhere. At the consulate?" he asked.

"It was a hiding place," she answered.

"You're very brave, what you do. I've seen some of your other stories about the refugees."

She turned her shrouded eyes to him. "Selim said you were a smuggler."

He shrugged. "I don't like that word, but there isn't any good word for what I do. Smuggler, gang member, racketeer, trafficker: they all imply being a cheat, and I'm not. Most of us aren't. I help people who want to be helped, and if I'm lucky, I earn enough for rent and a couple of meals a day. Sometimes I try to help and something goes wrong. This week, I helped a family, and ..." He couldn't continue. Instead, he reached into his daypack, felt around in it, and handed her a newspaper clipping.

She unfolded it and looked up, surprised. "Meryem?"

Ahdaf glanced in the mirror to be sure the others weren't listening. But they were engrossed in exchanging their own stories about how they'd ended up in the back of that van on the last leg of their journey to Europe.

"Were you her smuggler?" Derya asked.

"Yes."

"You bought the lifejackets that drowned her family?"

Ahdaf hadn't expected the blunt question. He nodded miserably. "It never happened before."

"That you know. Or want to admit."

"You're right; it could've happened and I wouldn't necessarily know. I'm not lying when I say I never heard about such a ramming. Or such lifejackets. I know the rafts are overloaded, but that's the situation. Clients always want to keep moving, not get stuck in a camp or try to be invisible in Istanbul. Your story about the Coast Guard was the first I'd heard about a deliberate capsizing. I hate ISIS because it's something they would do; it's hard to believe the Coast Guard would."

"I hate ISIS, too, but in this case, they didn't do it. The Coast Guard was following orders, and in this political environment, you follow orders or you're hanged. Look at me. I reported the truth, and now I have to leave my own country. Otherwise they'll arrest me, and I'll disappear into their system. Into their mock courtrooms. Into their prisons. They won't kill me, not at first, but I'll never see the world again."

For an hour they drove along the national highway, stopping at the occasional toll stations; Ahdaf was always nervous that the bank card Selim had given him wouldn't work, but it did. As their route took them south, the road passed through rolling hills with alternating stretches of heavy forest and working farms. The trees were just turning autumn colors, the occasional one already bright red or orange. In the distance, Ahdaf caught glimpses of towers poking up over the trees and asked, "What's that?"

"The Osmangazi Bridge," Derya replied. "We'll cross it in

about 15 minutes."

As they drove toward it, Ahdaf marveled at its engineering. He'd never seen a bridge so tall or long, and couldn't quite make out how it stayed aloft with so few pylons. "Hey, guys," he said to Kalam and Munir, "I think you're going to want your cameras."

Crossing the bridge itself was its own surprise: the vast waterway on both sides had fewer boats but no less variety than Istanbul's Bosporus. While the other men snapped pictures of the water views, Ahdaf twisted his neck to look up and try to understand the bridge's construction. "So those ropes hold up the bridge?" he asked Derya.

"They're called cables, and yes, they hold up the bridge."

"You aren't afraid the road will collapse without support?"

"There is support – but it's from the top, not below. Turkey is a modern country with modern architecture. It surprises many people."

"Turkey doesn't surprise me," Ahdaf remarked, "but this bridge does!"

"That's one reason I love my country," Derya said. "I like surprises – they make interesting stories – and I belong here. It's where I know how to make things happen."

"You'll come back," Ahdaf said.

"Not until the government changes, and how many years will that take? The more authoritarian it becomes, the harder it will be to change it. In the meantime, I'm exiled, and I don't want to be in exile. I want to resist from here. I was able to do that until the second coup succeeded."

"The second coup?"

"The government's coup against democracy, when it redefined 'treason' to include reporting or acting in any way critical of the government."

"And in Greece? What will you do?"

"I'm not too worried about that. CNN will take care of me. I'll have a job and a visa, and everything I need, except my friends. Can you imagine leaving all your friends without one goodbye? It's only been hours, and I already miss them."

"I didn't have time for goodbyes either," Ahdaf said. "I only had a minute with my parents, which I'm sure left them confused."

"Then you know how I feel. We've experienced the same thing."

Only in that one respect, he thought. A job, a visa, and everything else he needed weren't waiting for him in Greece as they were for her.

As they came off the bridge, Kalam whooped and waved his phone in the air. "That is going to be great in my movie! And without needing special effects, because it's already special!"

Derya let Ahdaf know there was a service station in one kilometer.

He checked his fuel gauge. "I don't need gas yet."

"I need a toilet," she replied.

"Oh, sure. No problem. You know this road that well?"

"This is probably my tenth trip to Assos in three months. Here's the exit."

Ahdaf slowed and downshifted, cringing when he briefly ground the gears.

"What's happening?" Munir asked.

"Toilet stop."

"Good! I need one!"

Ahdaf took the exit and pulled into a parking space. As soon as he cut the motor, Munir slid open the side door and jumped out. Kalam followed him, and Ahdaf asked, "Will you open the door for her?"

Derya adjusted her burqa's long skirt. "I don't need help," she said.

"Let him help you. It's expected. Otherwise, we might draw

attention to ourselves."

Kalam swung the door open and Derya scooted off the van's high seat. He offered his arm, but she ignored it and led them into the building. At the Y-junction for the toilets, Derya headed for the women's room, which made Ahdaf wonder: what if Derya had turned out to be a man in disguise? Of course, he'd have to keep up the charade. Ahdaf didn't want to imagine what might be done to such a person if discovered.

Munir stood at the last urinal in a short bank of them. Kalam took the closest, leaving the middle one for Ahdaf's use. For a long moment, they all concentrated on the wall in front of them.

Zipping up first, Munir turned sideways and used his elbow to flush. "Who is she?"

"A journalist," Ahdaf answered.

"She must be important."

"Why?"

"To start with, we picked her up at the consulate," Kalam said.

As they moved to the sinks, Ahdaf told them, "She broke the news story about the Coast Guard sinking a raft a couple of days ago."

"That's *her*. Fuck!" Munir exclaimed. "Everybody's looking for her."

Ahdaf paled. "What do you mean, 'Everybody is looking for her'?"

"The president has ordered a national manhunt," Munir told them. "He's making a big deal out of the case. You didn't know about this?"

"I saw her report yesterday, but I didn't see the news this morning." He exchanged glances with Kalam. Both men knew why they were so uninformed about an unfolding story so crucial to them. The situation unnerved Ahdaf. He anticipated manageable problems that could be resolved with a phone call or two, but not the risk of being caught aiding a fugitive in a high-profile political case. If they were stopped and Derya arrested, what would happen to them? Arrested too? Never to see the world again? The injustice he felt in Derya's case – that she was probably reporting the truth, and now there was a manhunt for her – already angered him. He wanted the truth told about the incident for the sakes of Yusuf, Meryem, and Issa. The probability that he and his friends would likely be arrested if discovered aiding her escape only fueled Ahdaf's determination to protect her. "What should we do?" he asked. "I'm asking you first."

When Munir didn't respond, Kalam spoke up. "Aren't we already halfway to Assos?"

"Probably only a third of the way."

"Okay, a third of the way. I say we keep going. Just don't speed. Why not?"

Ahdaf thought through the why-nots. The likelihood of a checkpoint at Assos topped his list. Just as likely, if they turned around, was a roadblock into Istanbul, though all day, they hadn't seen anything to suggest a heightened police presence.

"What about her?" Munir asked. "They're not looking for us. They're looking for her."

The truth dawned on Ahdaf. "Now we're her bodyguards," he said.

Literally, her life savers, they all realized at the same time. They could empathize with her plight. Their lives had all been upended by the same politicians pursuing the same wars. If she convinced the Greek fisherman to take her to Greece, he'd probably take them all.

"Let's keep going," Munir said. "I might change my mind at the last minute, but she can't. She needs to escape or she'll be arrested and raped. Plus, we can always turn around if we want."

"Thank you, Munir. I'm good with that. You?" he shot at Kalam.

The golden-haired youth smiled. "I told you, let's keep going.

Just don't speed."

Ahdaf shook his hands dry and shouldered his way out the men's room door, holding it open with his foot for the others. He couldn't help himself. "Sanitary practices" was one of his father's favorite subjects. Following them into the food section of the service stop, he said, "You should buy stuff to eat. I brought a few things, but not enough for everybody, and I don't know what's ahead."

The three young men went in different directions, checking out the shelves and food coolers, and pretty much bought the same things: bottles of water, sandwiches (two apiece), and fistfuls of sesame bars. Ahdaf, seeing Derya waiting at the door, purchased enough for both of them. When the men joined her, he said, "I bought food for you, too."

"Thank you."

Kalam held the door open for Derya to climb back into the passenger seat. He followed Munir into the back, sliding the door shut as Ahdaf took his place behind the steering wheel. Checking all were in their places, he nudged the van into reverse without a complaint from the clutch. When he pulled out of the service station, turning right to Assos instead of left in retreat to Istanbul, he felt the decisiveness of that moment.

By the time Derya told him to take the turnoff to Assos, it was already mid-afternoon. The shadows of the olive trees stretched over hills parched from summer and still waiting for their first good autumnal soak. The road, only two lanes wide, dipped and twisted and brought them to a rise, where they could see the columns of ancient Assos perched over the azure sea. In the distance rose the outlines of the closest Greek islands. It was idyllic – until they came around the next bend to discover a roadblock.

"Fuck," Ahdaf said, braking.

"What's wrong?" Munir worried.

"A checkpoint. I'll need your IDs."

Ahdaf braked further, and they came to a stop at the sawhorse barrier. A couple of soldiers peered into their windows while a third one, reading what was painted on the van's side, reported, "It's a mosque's van." He stepped up to Ahdaf's window. *"Se-lamün aleykum,"* he said, sizing up who was in the van.

"Wa aleyküm selam," everyone murmured, and touched their hearts.

"Your IDs."

They handed them to Ahdaf, who didn't know what he held in terms of authentic or counterfeit documents. He and Munir had refugee IDs issued by the Turkish authorities, which should pass, he thought. Kalam had only a Syrian passport, but it was still valid ID in Turkey. What made Ahdaf nervous was Derya's Turkish passport. Once they read her name, he expected they'd all be arrested. The soldier, frowning, twice went through all the IDs before he asked her, "Is one of these men your husband?"

"My husband is dead," she replied.

"I'm sorry."

"He was a soldier, like you."

"May he be at peace. I asked because usually women travel with their husband or another relative, and your name matches none of theirs."

"He's my cousin," she said about Ahdaf.

"But he's Syrian."

"I was, too, before I married a Turk and applied for citizenship."

"I see," the soldier said, still pondering their IDs. "Why does your cousin have a refugee card?"

"I invited him to Istanbul. Since he's been here, his house has been bombed. I want him to stay. He's been a big help to me, and

121

has nothing to go back to. To be legal, he registered as a refugee."

"And you?" the soldier asked Kalam. "Why don't you have a refugee card?"

Kalam grinned. "I'm not a refugee. I'm a tourist!"

"Funny guy," the soldier replied.

"He's making a joke," Ahdaf spoke up. "He just showed up yesterday, slept at the mosque, and this morning, hearing me talk about coming to the coast, asked for a ride. He wants to cross."

"I should arrest you," the soldier told Kalam.

"I'm on the first raft to Greece," Kalam promised.

"Good," the soldier said. "The fewer rats the better. And you?" he asked Munir.

"Me?"

"Yeah, you. Why are you coming to Assos?"

"He's another volunteer like me at the mosque," Ahdaf answered for his friend. "He asked if he could come along because he's never seen the sea. I haven't, either!"

"And you," the soldier said, coming back to Derya. "Why are you coming to Assos?"

"My husband and I used to holiday here. It's a place where I have happy memories. Old memories."

"You're not old enough to have 'old memories,'" the soldier said.

"A woman becomes old when she loses her husband."

He gave them all one last hard look. Ahdaf held his breath. Would one of them do something to give themselves away? Away as *what*? Someone suspicious? What did that mean? The soldier didn't know; he returned their IDs to Ahdaf. "Enjoy the sea," he said and stepped back from the vehicle. A second soldier pulled the sawhorse out of the way.

For the next few minutes, they rode in silence, all contemplating the near miss of being discovered. Had the soldier insisted that Derya reveal her face, no doubt she'd have been recognized, and they all would have been arrested. As it was, Ahdaf wondered, "If they're looking for you, why didn't they recognize your name?"

"I have a fake passport for situations like this when I don't want to be recognized, or I'm investigating something undercover. Also, for the record, my 'husband' never existed. No one ever bothers a widow in a burqa – especially a soldier's widow – so I've made it my cover story if anybody asks, and they always ask. It's their moral perspective. He thinks I should be traveling with my husband and not three unrelated males. That's the shift in tone that's becoming more common. He wasn't enforcing the law; he was moralizing."

"You convinced me," Ahdaf replied, "and apparently him, too."

"It helped to be in the mosque's van. No one expects a mosque to be aiding a traitor. That's what the pro-government news stations started calling me as soon as my arrest warrant was issued. They literally reported everything about me in the past tense. I was listening to my own obituary. They'd written it before I died, like newspapers do for famous old people. The only thing missing was my body."

They crested a hill, where Ahdaf pulled into a turnout and stopped. Below them lay Assos, not much more than a village, its stone houses spilling down to a harbor full of colorful fishing boats. Out to sea, the water could not have been bluer or more beckoning.

"Hey boss, aren't we two or three hours early?" Munir asked.

"I wanted to give us plenty of time in case we had a problem," Ahdaf replied.

"Like shifting gears?" Kalam joked.

"I was thinking serious things like roadblocks. I'm sorry about my driving."

"Hey boss, don't be sorry!" Munir said. "Now we have time for a swim. In my whole life, I swam only in the Bosporus, where the water is never clean. I never even swam in a swimming pool!"

"Hey boss!" Kalam mimicked Munir.

"Yeah?"

"Let's all take a swim in the sea! Do you see how blue it is?"

Ahdaf grinned at him in the mirror. "Sounds fun."

He pulled back onto the road and followed its zigzagging route down the hill, soon passing simple plastered homes with a few stone mansions among them. Eventually he reached a thread of asphalt skirting the shore that gave him a choice: left to the village, or right, north along the coast. He turned right. The shoreline was a shelf of shale and rough limestone broken up by shallow coves with smooth-pebble beaches. "Our boat will probably land somewhere close to here," Ahdaf said. "I'm told it's along here where the rafts launch."

"Maybe not," Derya suggested. "If it's a motorboat, there's no place to tie up, and it risks ripping out its hull unless the exchange is made offshore."

"What's 'offshore' mean?" Ahdaf asked.

"In the water. Everybody gets wet. Hopefully no more than knee deep, but higher is possible."

"Is that why rafts are usually used? For smuggling, I mean."

"Rafts can be inflated on a beach anywhere and pulled into shallow water for boarding. To put 70 refugees on a motorboat, you'd have to do it in the harbor, where everybody's watching you."

"How do you know so much?"

"I've covered the refugee crisis since it started."

Ahdaf turned left into a parking area overlooking a cove that looked especially good for swimming. The whole coast was a ridge of black limestone shrapnel punctuated by long, shallow coves with pebbly beaches worn smooth over millions of years. "How about here, guys?"

"Perfect!" Munir answered, and slid open the van door. He jumped out and ran for the sea, where he stripped down to his boxers and dived into the water.

"Me, too," said Kalam, climbing out. "How about you?"

"I'll join you later. I have something to do in town. How about you?" Ahdaf asked Derya.

"Do you mind if I go with you?"

"Not at all," Ahdaf replied. In fact, he had a hunch she might be able to help him. For the moment, though, he didn't say anything as they watched Kalam scramble down the incline and strip to his undershorts before jumping into the water. "Yahoo!" he cried when he breached the surface a moment later. "Come on, Ahdaf, join us for five minutes! It feels great!"

"When I come back!"

"Don't forget to come back!" Munir shouted.

"I won't!" Ahdaf made a U-turn to head back to the village. As he did, he watched the shirtless young men splash water on each other and felt a pang of jealousy. He wanted to be in Munir's place, splashing Kalam. If things were different, he was certain they'd be lovers. But things were as they were, and that was why he could only wish to be the one splashing Kalam, hoping they'd find a way for a second goodbye.

Derya interrupted his thoughts to ask, "What do you have to do in town?"

"I want to find Meryem."

"Why?"

"To help her."

"Help her how?"

"Maybe she can go with you on the boat tonight if she still wants to go. I'll help her however I can, but I need to find her first."

"I know where she is," Derya told him. "I made sure she was safe before I returned to Istanbul."

"How'd you find a place so fast?"

"I'm not sharing my contacts."

"I'm not a spy."

125

"If you're working for Selim, you are."

"It's an accident that I'm working for him. I never asked for the job, and I don't plan to do it again. My job's pretty simple, really. I coordinate three things, and take care of everything else that comes up: getting phone cards, replacing lost crutches, replacing medicine that gets ruined. Something almost always goes wrong, and the villagers here aren't helpful. Sometimes they're even hostile. That's why I asked how you found Meryem a room so fast."

"There are still some sympathizers," Derya replied. "Very few, but they exist. Most people are simply exhausted by the situation, and want it to go away."

"Me too," Ahdaf admitted, and he braked as he approached the turnoff to the road back to Istanbul. "Left or straight?" he asked.

"Straight through the village," she answered.

They passed the harbor a street in from it, glimpsing its turquoise water and the bright fishing boats between the stone buildings. Ahdaf had a hard time reconciling its perfect serenity with the chaos of Derya's broadcast only a couple of nights earlier. "What's she going to do?" he asked.

"Meryem? How can she know? She can't travel alone; it's too dangerous for a woman. She can't go home – I mean, Syria, home – because it no longer exists; and even if it did, the chances are she'd be killed in an airstrike. A camp is probably her only option if she can get to one safely, but a single refugee woman handed over to Turkish soldiers to transport her to a distant camp? What do you think is going to happen?"

Ahdaf's body sank under the weight of his remorse. "I feel responsible."

"You're not responsible, unless it wasn't the first time with the same supplier."

"I've worked with the same supplier many times. There's never been a problem."

"Then you were trying to help. Most people don't try. In fact, most people try not to see what's really happening. That's why I became a news reporter. To make them notice."

"You've certainly succeeded, with your last story."

"I hope it's *not* my last story. Pull over here. That's where she's staying." Derya pointed to a stone cottage set back from the road, with a cobblestone path to its door. Ahdaf parked and cut the van's motor.

"I should go talk to her first and explain why you're here," Derya said.

"What if she refuses to see me?" he asked.

"Don't you think *she* should decide?"

Derya got out of the car and walked up to the door. She knocked, and a woman opened it. Derya spoke to her, and a couple of times the woman glanced in Ahdaf's direction before stepping out of sight. A moment later, Meryem appeared. He wondered what Derya would say to her. How would she couch the situation? Why was he there, and should she trust him again? How would she calibrate the unexpected chance to make the crossing to Greece, presumably safely, if that was still her intention? He shook his head at the thought of it. How could Meryem know what her intention was? Or what she should do? Losing her whole family was not only incredibly sorrowful; it also left her in circumstances completely unpredictable and dangerous.

The women ended their conversation, and Derya came back to the van.

"What did you tell her?" Ahdaf asked.

"She'll talk to you," she replied.

Derya got in the van as Ahdaf got out and trudged up the stone path. His shoulders couldn't have drooped more than they already did with the weight of Meryem's many tragedies. Her life had inalterably changed. She might survive, but would never recover. In his head, he knew he wasn't responsible, but his heart couldn't *not* bear some responsibility.

The woman who'd opened the door for Derya now stood in it, eyeing him as he approached. She turned aside to ask, "You still sure you want to talk to him?"

Meryem did, and she replaced the woman in the open door. As soon as she saw Ahdaf, she launched her fists, beating on his chest, hitting as hard as she could; and he let her, only deflecting, not always successfully, her punches to his face. Her tears splashed his hands.

"Why?" she moaned. "Why did it happen?" She started to crumple. The woman who'd opened the door had stayed nearby, and caught her before she hit the floor. In the same moment, Derya pushed past him and helped the woman move Meryem into a bedroom. Ahdaf could see them tending to her, taking off her shoes and adjusting the pillow, and decided to wait in the van.

It wasn't long before Derya joined him.

"Will she be okay?"

"How can she be okay?"

"I meant –"

"Yes, she'll recover from this." She handed him a tissue. "You have a bloody nose."

"Thanks." He dabbed it, checking himself in the mirror. "I assume she's not crossing tonight."

"She's not ready."

Ahdaf started the engine and made a U-turn in a couple of maneuvers. "What about you? Are you still going tonight?"

"I had never planned to travel with Meryem. It was your idea to find her and have us make the crossing together."

"It's true. I've been thinking about it the whole trip."

"It's too soon for her," Derya repeated.

"Not for you?"

"I don't have the option to stay. I'll be arrested, and don't want to imagine what they'll do to me."

Minutes later, Ahdaf turned into a service station and pulled up to a gas pump. While he filled up, Derya went inside to use the facilities. When the tank was full, Ahdaf hung up the hose and pulled into a space in front of the store. He got out and leaned against the van until Derya emerged. "My turn," he said. "Do you want something to drink or eat?"

"Both," she replied. "Especially water."

He made quick use of the men's room before touring the two aisles with shelves of snacks. All he wanted to do was fill his empty stomach, and discovered a shelf of doughy-looking muffins in cellophane pouches. He took two, along with a couple of large bags of potato chips, water, and enough sandwiches for Kalam and Munir, too. He carried his full sack back to the van and fit it into the gully between the front seats.

Ahdaf started the engine, and with minimal crunching gears, backed up to turn onto the road. He had a good sense of direction but thought, as a novice driver in unknown territory, he should ask, "Am I going the right way?"

"You're fine," Derya said. "This becomes the coastal road. Did you remember to buy water?"

He rummaged in the sack and handed her a bottle.

It disappeared under her veil. As she drank, he heard the plastic bottle dimple. She sighed, saying, "You can't imagine how thirsty these horrible polyester robes make you. I'm starving, too. What food did you buy?"

"Sandwiches and potato chips."

"Potato chips! I was hoping you'd get some."

"You like them?"

"They're an occupational addiction. Journalists have a lot of cocktail parties. I used to go to them for news and contacts; now, I go for the potato chips!"

Ahdaf laughed. "Honestly? You go to parties for the potato chips?"

"I don't allow them in my house. If I did, I'd become a potato chip blimp."

"So I'm guessing it's potato chips before sandwich." He reached into his sack and passed her a bag.

"And it's a large one!" Derya attacked the crinkly paper, splitting open its sealed top, and in a second, the first potato chip disappeared under her veil.

Crunch!

Then another, another, and another.

Crunch! Crunch! Crunch!

Ahdaf burst into laughter.

"What's so funny?" Derya asked.

"That crunching sound coming from under your veil! It wouldn't be so funny if I could see you."

"That's the whole point of a burqa: to make a woman invisible," Derya replied. "Only the man who owns you is allowed to see you."

"Well, I don't own you, but if you're waiting for permission to take off your veil, go ahead." He shrugged. "Who's going to see you? There's no one around, and we're almost out of the village."

"You're right." Derya removed her headpiece and shook out her hair. "That feels better!"

"Now I recognize you from TV," Ahdaf said.

"I hope no one else does. I probably should eat something healthier than potato chips. You also bought sandwiches?"

He pulled one out of his sack. "Here."

She bit into it, and more bites followed. "I didn't realize how hungry I was."

"When was the last time you had a real meal?"

"Last night, if food from vending machines counts."

"At the American consulate?" Ahdaf asked, realizing when he and Selim had watched her broadcast from a secret location the night before, the CIA man knew exactly where she was. He suddenly felt wary of Selim. What else hadn't he told him?

"Yes, that's where I was," she answered.

"How do you know Selim?"

"We're useful to each other. Until I met him, I automatically thought spies were evil, but Selim's a good man. He'd save humanity from itself if he could."

Crunch!

Ahdaf chuckled, and in response, Derya crunched through a whole handful of chips. That made them both laugh, and they were still laughing when he pulled into the turnout for the cove where they'd left Kalam and Munir swimming an hour earlier. Now the two young men were face down on the pebbly beach, with their wet underwear spread next to them to dry.

Hearing the van, Kalam flashed them a bright smile. Lifting an arm, he pointed to his watch and shouted, "How much longer?"

Ahdaf checked the sun already dipping to the horizon. A thunderstorm hovered over distant Lesvos. He figured the Greek would launch soon, if he hadn't already. Maybe they had an hour, maybe 30 minutes. "I don't know!" Ahdaf shouted back.

"Come swimming! You've never been in water like this!"

At that moment, his telephone rang. "Wait!" he shouted to Kalam and answered it. "*Merhaba.*"

"No Turkish," the Greek fisherman replied. "You speak Greek?"

"No Greek. Do you speak English?"

"Sometimes enough English."

"Good. What's happening?"

"The weather is difficult. It's pushing me east and north. Do you know Big Rocks Beach?"

Derya, overhearing the conversation, whispered, "It's about five kilometers north of here."

"Yes, I know it," Ahdaf said.

"I am there in one hour. Flash your lights. Try again until I flash back. Maybe I won't see you the first time in the rain."

"It's clear here."

"Don't worry, I will bring the rain with me. We go in the same direction. Do you know that one man is injured?"

"I know."

"I wasn't told," the Greek complained. "He needs a hospital."

Fuck, Ahdaf thought.

"Okay, one hour," the Greek said.

"Wait!" Ahdaf cried before the fisherman cut the connection. "I have three return passengers for you."

"That's not the plan."

"They'll pay, and nobody's a problem," Ahdaf replied.

"Everybody's a problem, and I don't like surprises. The injured man, he's big enough surprise." The Greek hung up.

"Fuck," Ahdaf said.

"Ahdaf, come on!" Kalam called from the beach. Munir had stood up, too. They were both naked, forgetting – or maybe not caring – that Derya could see them.

"Do you mind if I join them?"

"I wish I could," she replied.

"You might want to avert your eyes."

"Are you kidding?"

"Answer my phone if it rings." He jumped out of the van and ran clumsily across the smooth pebbles, unbuttoning his shirt, and finished dropping his clothes in a pile while his two friends waited. Naked, they ran into the water together, whooping and hollering and splashing around. Kalam was right; he'd never been in such clear water, and despite the salt sting, he ducked under and opened his eyes, something he never could have done in the muddy Euphrates where he'd learned to swim. To Ahdaf's amazement, an arm's length away was an enormous school of small fish, a pronounced gold stripe on their sides flashing in the late day's long light. As he swam toward them, they stayed just out of reach, drawing him close enough to the end of the cove to feel licks of the cold currents bringing in the approaching storm.

Kalam and Munir were already ashore, brushing off water, when he swam back and joined them. He shook off what water he could before using his shirt to dry where he didn't want to feel wet all night. He figured his shirt would dry on its own. They all started to dress.

"Do you think she's watching us?" Munir asked.

"Wouldn't you be watching us?" Ahdaf replied.

"How could I, if I'm one of us?"

"Yeah, yeah. Very funny."

Ahdaf fastened his pants and sat on the pebbles to put on his shoes. He told them, "The Greek doesn't like the idea of taking anyone back with him."

"How do you know?" Munir asked.

"That's who called before I went swimming. When I told him about you two, he said he doesn't like surprises and hung up."

"He'll do it," Kalam predicted. "He's going back to Lesvos anyway. Whatever you pay is better than nothing, and I'm sure the consulate made certain she has plenty of money."

They returned to the van and climbed inside. Ahdaf started the engine and checked the odometer.

"I'll tell you when we get there," Derya said.

He waited for three speeding police cars to pass before backing onto the road and following them north. The rain lashing the Greek at sea abruptly reached them on shore, the thunderous clouds blackening the sky and gusting winds threatening to push the high-sided van off the road. Ahdaf crept along, unworried

133

about the time; even in that weather he could make five kilometers in 30 minutes.

"We're crossing in this storm?" Munir fretted aloud.

"The Greek's got a boat, not a raft," Ahdaf reminded him. "You should be safer than on any raft on any day. One person shifts his weight, and a raft can be swamped – storm or no storm."

"We don't have lifejackets," Kalam worried aloud.

Ahdaf grinned at him in the rearview mirror. "I thought you said you could swim."

"In this weather?"

"The Greek should have them. But don't worry, even in this weather, on a real boat you shouldn't need them."

"Inshallah," Munir said.

They rode in silence until Derya said, "It's coming up. There. Park there," she pointed to a turnout on the sea side of the road. Ahdaf turned left into it and cut the motor. In the dark, he could make out a pile of huge boulders perched on the craggy shore with a thicket of pine trees next to them.

He flashed his lights out to sea.

No response.

Gusts of wind and rain rocked the van.

"Flash your lights again," Kalam suggested.

Ahdaf did. Again, no response.

"I've got to do something," Munir said. Sliding open the door, he jumped out. Moments later they heard him pissing behind the van. Ahdaf glanced in the mirror at Kalam who, with a slight nod at Derya, grinned that she was hearing him, too.

Munir got back in, but before he could close the door Kalam said, "My turn."

"I'll join you," Ahdaf said.

They got out and met behind the van.

"Wait a minute," Ahdaf said, "I saw headlights coming."

A moment later, a car appeared around a bend and passed them. As soon as it did, they turned their backs to the van and unzipped. Kalam asked, "Are you nervous about tonight?"

Ahdaf snorted. "Why wouldn't I be?"

"I'm more nervous about what comes next," Kalam admitted. "The crossing had been my biggest worry. How to arrange it? Okay, I had your name, but it took me three months to walk here – would you still be doing what you're doing? Then the stories of capsized rafts, drownings, boats turned back … you know the stories. How many are true?"

"Probably most of them," Ahdaf admitted. "Though I'd never heard about lifejackets being filled with shredded newspaper before."

Kalam shook his head. "That's a bum situation. No one ever says what happens to the people forced back to Turkey. That makes me nervous, too."

"They cross again."

"I don't know where I'm going after Greece," Kalam said. "Come with me. The three of us – you, me, Munir – we start out together, but eventually it would be just you and me. We'll go north together."

They zipped up. Ahdaf said, "I don't have anything with me except my ID and a toothbrush."

"What else do you need? I really like you, Ahdaf."

"I like you, too."

"We should have a last kiss, though I hope it's not the last."

"We can't. They might see us."

"They can't see me do this." Kalam reached over and touched him seductively. "We'll have this, too."

Ahdaf was tempted. Kalam was more than handsome and completely likable; and the journey would be safer with a friend. But did he need to take the risk at all? He was set up in Istanbul. He spoke the language. He'd felt safe – not entirely satisfied, but safe

135

– until both the CIA and ISIS made their moves on him. Would he be any safer crossing countries openly hostile to refugees?

"Hurry up!" Munir shouted from inside the van. "A boat's flashing a light!"

A last glance between them, conveying a shared affection but encumbered by Ahdaf's indecision: would he join Kalam and make the crossing or not?

Then they were back in the van. A light flickered from out at sea. Was it the Greek fisherman, or a splash of the moon breaking through the departing clouds? When Ahdaf flashed back, his telephone rang. It was the Greek.

"I'm 10 minutes away," the fisherman said. "I can't pull up to shore and my passengers are going to need some help disembarking the injured one."

"And my passengers?" When the Greek didn't reply, Ahdaf added, "The woman will have a payment for you."

"How much?"

"A lot more than nothing if you go back with an empty boat."

"It better be a lot more than nothing."

"It is."

The Greek blinked his lights, which Ahdaf interpreted as agreement. He hung up.

Inside the van, nobody said anything, each envisioning a host of scenarios, knowing their guesses all had one thing in common: none would play out as envisioned. There were too many variables.

"You *do* have money for him, right?" Ahdaf asked.

Derya nodded. "Of course."

"You don't even know if she's got the money to pay the guy?" Munir said from the back seat.

"I was just double-checking."

"Double-checking? What the fuck else don't you know? Don't you think it's a little late to be double-checking? What if she didn't? What were we going to do, steal his boat and sail to Greece ourselves?"

"Hey, calm down," Kalam said. "Ahdaf's been straight with us. We knew he had to convince the Greek to take us back."

"It feels too iffy to me."

"Three people get off the boat, and three people get on it. What's iffy about that?"

"That nothing else has been planned," Munir said. "I don't like it. I'll help you tonight, but I'm going back to Istanbul with you."

Ahdaf looked at Derya. "Do you still want to cross?"

"I have no choice."

"I'm still going," Kalam spoke up. "Come with us, Ahdaf. It'll work out. Munir can drive them to Istanbul, or they can drive themselves. It's your life, not theirs, that you should worry about."

"I'm leaving my gear on board, except for this." Munir stuck his gun into his belt.

"You won't need that," Ahdaf said.

"How do you know?" The van rocked as Munir got out. "Besides, I've been thinking." He tapped his wedding ring. "This means something. I've got to go back and help my family. I can't run away." He turned up his collar, a futile effort in the drenching rain, and headed for the water.

"I think he just wants an excuse not to go," Kalam said.

"He has a family," Ahdaf replied. "For their sakes, I'd want things to be planned right, too, because if something happens to him, they'll be much worse off."

Munir reached the waterline, standing back so as not to be splashed by the surf; though it hardly mattered, given the wind-driven rain that soaked his shoes. "He makes me saddest of all of you," Derya said. "Maybe because I overheard some of the things he said today."

"And me?" Kalam asked.

137

"You're too handsome not to survive," she replied. "And also, too clever."

"I see the boat," Ahdaf said. "Let's go."

Kalam and Derya gathered their few possessions. Ahdaf wondered if he should take Munir's things to him in case he had another last-minute change of heart. He decided against it, not wanting to encourage him; he wanted his friend to go back to his family and make the crossing when better prepared. They shared the same daily struggles, but Ahdaf had to make decisions only for himself. Munir had a family, and that changed the whole equation for him, especially contemplating where they might reasonably expect to have a future. It wouldn't be Istanbul unless a lot changed for the refugees. Families needed services – schools, for instance. Refugee children couldn't attend school until a sluggish bureaucracy processed the family's paperwork, and then the rules could change, closing the school doors to them again. Finding legal employment was confounded by the same sluggishness and changing rules, which is why Munir, like Ahdaf, worked for the smuggling rackets. How could Munir promise his family a future in a place where they had no present?

Derya, blinded by her veil flapping in the wind and hindered by two shoulder packs, clung to Ahdaf's arm as they crossed a patch of rough stone to reach the smoother beach pebbles. She let go of his arm, freeing her hand to hold the veil in place. The clouds broke open long enough for the waxing moon to silhouette Munir pacing at the waterline. He could not have been a more wretched figure on that beach, where everything, even the water, was a shade of black. His stout shadow puddled on the smooth stones; he wrapped his arms around himself for warmth. He was shaking – and crying, they all realized. When Ahdaf touched his shoulder, he clung to him and sobbed, "I wish I were braver!"

"Munir, look at your situation. Every decision you make is a brave one. Deciding to stay is as brave as deciding to leave. You want things to be clearer. I don't blame you."

"Are you sure?"

"I'm sure."

They fell into a friends' embrace. "I'll help you when you're ready to cross," Ahdaf promised.

"Thank you."

"The Greek's here," Derya told them.

"I need the money," Ahdaf said.

She handed him a pouch from her daypack, which he opened to see packets of euros. "How much?" he asked.

"Ten thousand."

Kalam put his camera strap around his neck to videotape the boat's arrival. It was sleek and modern, with a high bow; not at all the putt-putt fishing boat Ahdaf had imagined. The captain cut his engine, intending to glide to a stop, when a double swell threatened to ram the boat into the pebbles hard enough to damage it. Kalam and Munir instinctively ran into the water to hold it back. The captain dropped them lines to anchor it with their weight. Ahdaf stood at the edge of the water and shouted at the captain, "Where are your passengers?"

"Down below, to stay out of the rain."

"And the injured guy?"

"You'll see."

The captain took a moment to look around. Ahdaf sensed he was looking for something, but decided he was only making sure it was safe before he dropped a rope ladder off the bow and climbed down it. Knee-deep in water, he sloshed the few steps to join Ahdaf on the beach. "Who are your return passengers?"

"Only two of them. The blondish guy," Ahdaf said, pointing to Kalam, "and her."

"Fuck. They don't want to see burqas in Greece."

"It's a disguise. She'll take it off."

"Who is she?"

"A journalist."

"No pictures. If she takes one picture, her camera goes overboard."

"Hey!" Ahdaf shouted to get the others' attention. "The captain says no photos or your camera goes overboard! That includes videos!" he added, so Kalam wouldn't be tempted.

"Here's your money." Ahdaf handed him Derya's money pouch. The captain unzipped it to see the stacks of euros.

"How much?" the Greek asked.

"Ten thousand."

The Greek looked sullen and said, "For *two* persons? Only 10,000 euros?"

Ahdaf had expected him to bargain, and replied, "I'm only the driver delivering and picking up the goods. I didn't decide the amount to pay you."

The Greek thought it over and pointed to Kalam. "I'll take him."

"It's both or no one," Ahdaf replied. "You choose: 10,000 euros or go home dragging your net to catch what you can. I bet you'll be lucky if it's as many as three red snappers and a kilo of sardines."

The Greek instinctively wanted to bargain for more, but as quickly dismissed the futile thought. How would Ahdaf come up with more money on that deserted beach? "Okay," he said, and zipped up the pouch, slinging it across his chest. He yelled toward the boat, "Serhan! Let's go!" To Ahdaf, he said, "I'm going to need your help."

Two men appeared at the stern, carrying an inert man by his arms and legs. The burlier of the two had an automatic rifle securely strapped around his neck and shoulder. The rain had passed as quickly as it came, leaving a bright moon to illuminate their macabre dance as they lurched to the bow, struggling to keep their balance as choppy water rocked the boat.

"Let him down feet first and we'll grab him," the Greek captain shouted.

"Özan!" Serhan barked. "Get his feet over the side, but don't let go until they have hold of him!"

"Kalam, can you handle the boat by yourself?" Ahdaf called.

"No problem!"

"Then Munir, we need your help!"

He joined them alongside the boat.

By then, Ahdaf could make out that the wounded man was stocky, and obviously difficult to carry as the two struggled to maneuver his feet over the boat rail. As his body followed, the three men in the water grabbed for his legs, belt, whatever hold was possible to carry him onto the beach. He reeked of decaying flesh. Ahdaf felt sure he was dead; he smelled like the corpses he'd collected in Raqqa. When they lowered him onto the pebbles, Ahdaf saw why: half his face had been melted by a recent fire, and holes in his clothes revealed other festering wounds. Ahdaf turned aside and gagged.

"You okay, boss?" Munir asked.

Ahdaf spat and wiped his mouth. "Yeah, I'll be okay."

Serhan jumped into the water and splashed ashore. "Is that our ride?" he asked, pointing to the van.

"Yeah."

"Come on, Özan," he called. "Let's get him into it."

Özan, a little guy, scampered down the rope ladder.

"Is there a hospital near here?" Serhan asked. "We just have to drop him off."

"I'll check GPS," Ahdaf replied.

Serhan bent down to say into the unconscious man's ear, "Do you hear that, Taner? You're going to a hospital. Hang on, brother. Hang on just a little bit longer. Let's go."

He and Özan, carrying the unconscious man, headed for the van. Munir straggled behind, prepared to help them. As they approached the stand of pine trees, suddenly the headlights of three hidden cars illuminated the cove.

Five policemen ran out, silhouetted by the blinding lights. "Stop! Police!" one shouted.

Munir, clutching his gun, whirled around. The policemen saw it illuminated in the headlights and, in a spurt of heavy gunfire, dropped him to the ground.

Derya, standing apart from the men on the beach, ran for the van. "Police! Stop!" the police yelled again, but she kept running as best she could in her burqa, her vision impaired by its mesh veil. She distracted the police before they realized that Serhan had unshouldered his rifle to unleash a merciless stream of bullets, taking down every cop backlit on the beach, and likely anyone remaining in the cars, given the sound of crashing windshields. When the last headlight exploded, the scene plunged into its original darkness. Only the moon remained to reveal Derya's scramble into the van.

In the shocked silence that followed, the Greek ran for his boat and climbed up the rope ladder. Crouching, he ran for the helm and put the engine in reverse. Kalam, hearing it, glanced between the bodies on the beach and the boat inching away. He abandoned his shoulder pack and raced after it, splashing in the shallow water and grabbing for his own abandoned line as it snaked across the surface, teasingly out of reach. The water, already at his knees, was becoming too deep to run in. Realizing he probably had just one last chance, he threw himself forward and swam so hard that he caught the line and pulled himself to the rope ladder. He climbed up enough to be out of the water, and hung there. As the Greek towed him out to sea, he and Ahdaf exchanged forlorn looks. Then there was the moment that Kalam remembered his video work and lifted his phone-cum-camera to his eye to shoot the escaping moments.

Ahdaf retrieved Kalam's pack and ran to Munir, stooping next to his body. His face wounds were so savage, he was unrecognizable. He began to take the gun from Munir's hand but stopped, realizing he'd probably end up just as dead as his friend if he ever tried to use it. He twisted Munir's wedding ring off and slipped it onto his own finger to safeguard it. Then he sprinted for the van and arrived just as Serhan and Özan were approaching it with Taner, the injured man. Again, Ahdaf threw up as soon as he smelled the putrid flesh. Wiping his mouth on his sleeve, he said, "He's dead. You can smell he's dead."

"He's not dead!" insisted Serhan. "He makes noises!"

"What, he farts? Bodies get bloated, and they fart."

"What if he's not dead? How do you know for sure?"

"If he is or not, the same thing's going to happen. A lot of policemen are going to descend on this spot, and they'll call an ambulance. That's his best chance. Not us using GPS to find a hospital where all we can do is drop him at the front door and run away."

"I'm not abandoning him!" Serhan pleaded. "He's my twin!"

Ahdaf, working hard at restraining his rebellious stomach, managed to put a sympathetic hand on Serhan's shoulder. "Twins continue to live through each other if one dies. That's what I've always been told. Now get in the van or you'll be dead, too. And take off that stinking shirt before I throw up again."

He gagged anyway.

Serhan fumbled with the shirt buttons until he finally just ripped it off and threw it aside. Kneeling, he kissed his fingers and touched them to his brother's forehead. "I'm sorry, Taner," he said and stood up. "Let's go." He threw open the van's passenger door and jumped back when he saw Derya hiding in the seat. "Who is she?" he asked.

Ahdaf hadn't thought how to explain Derya's presence because he'd never expected that he'd have to, at least not to the passengers he was picking up. At that moment, the journalist should've been on the Greek's boat, which was still motoring in reverse out of the long cove. He glanced at it again just as Kalam managed to pitch himself onto the deck. Ahdaf wished he were right behind him, and sensed that he'd just made the worst mistake of his life. "She's his wife," he finally answered Serhan, and pointed to Munir's body on the beach.

"His wife? But he's dead."

"Yeah, he's dead."

"She's his widow?"

"I hadn't thought of her in that way, but yeah you're right, now she's his widow."

Serhan shook his head. "She can't come with us. Widows bring death. Get out!"

"She can ride in the back," Ahdaf said.

"She's not coming with us! Nobody told me about her. It's supposed to be you, me, Özan, and my brother. Get out!"

Derya, clutching her remaining daypack, got out of the car.

"Where's she supposed to go?" Ahdaf asked.

"It won't matter if I shoot her." Serhan brandished his rifle to make his point.

Ahdaf grabbed the barrel of his rifle and pointed it at the sky. "In your brother's memory, don't do that."

"I should fucking shoot you, too," Serhan growled.

"Don't do that, either," Ahdaf said calmly, wanting to defuse the situation. "Now get in and sit in the back. The very back. We need to get out of here."

Özan climbed into the back and closed the sliding door behind him. Serhan took the passenger seat, and as soon as Ahdaf opened his door, he gagged again. "You've got to get rid of your clothes. Both of you. Pants and everything."

"You get used to the smell," Özan told him.

"Not me. Never. It's how we found bodies after bombing raids. We could smell them after a week. I've got clean clothes for both of you. So get out and strip. Fast!"

"Fuck it," Serhan said, and got out. Özan joined him. They both started stripping while Ahdaf reached behind his seat to retrieve Munir's shoulder pack. The men stripped down to their briefs. "Everything," he said. "You still stink."

Özan indicated Derya, who stood with her back to them. "What about her?"

"She's not looking this way." He thrust Kalam's pack into Özan's arms. "Everything in here should fit you, though you'll need to roll up the cuffs." He felt sickened by the thought that the repulsive little man would touch Kalam's clothes, much less wear them. "And anything in here should fit you," he said, handing Munir's pack to Serhan.

"Is he the guy on the beach?"

"Yeah."

"I can see from here he was big like me. I feel sorry for his widow."

"Sorry enough to give her a ride to Istanbul?"

Serhan shook his head. "I don't want to risk my luck with his unlucky widow." He pulled a pair of pants from Munir's pack. "Yeah, these should fit."

"That's a superstition about widows," Ahdaf said, hoping to change his mind.

"Superstition or not, we're not taking her."

Ahdaf's mind reeled as he reassessed his situation. There was Derya, a step away, her back to them. What could she be thinking? He wished he had taken Munir's pistol, but outside of pulling a trigger a couple of times to experience a gun's kick, he'd never held one. If anything more than pulling the trigger was necessary, he'd be dead before he figured it out.

145

When the two men had changed into fresh clothes, Ahdaf said, "You still stink. You both get in the back."

"No fucking way," Serhan said.

"Yes fucking way. I can't drive you to Istanbul if I'm vomiting every five minutes."

Frowning, Serhan followed Özan into the van, and Ahdaf slid the door shut. Derya hadn't moved from her spot. "I tried," he said to her back.

"I heard you. I understand. Ahdaf?"

"What?"

She turned to say to his face, "Don't give him a reason. Don't argue. Don't do anything."

"Let's go!" Serhan shouted from inside the van. "We're suffocating in here! LET'S FUCKING GO!"

"I won't forget you," Ahdaf promised, as he climbed into the driver's seat. He started the engine and backed onto the road, the headlights bouncing off Derya, who seemed frozen to her spot. He watched her in the mirror as he drove away. The moonlight helped, reflecting white off the black water and silhouetting her. Defeated, her body sagged; then, she lifted her burqa's skirt to navigate the rough black stones and ran toward the next cove.

"How do you open the windows back here?" Serhan wanted to know.

"They don't open. It's a school bus," Ahdaf reported, wishing they *did* open, to make the rank air more bearable.

"Close your eyes!" Serhan shouted and let loose a couple of spurts of gunfire, which were followed by crashing glass. "Now two of them don't close!"

Ahdaf strained to find Derya again in the mirror, but she had disappeared, no longer backlit by the moon.

146

Ahdaf pulled onto the coastal road with his unsavory passengers in the back rows of the van. He assumed the massacred policemen had been in radio communication with someone at their station who would've heard Serhan's savage blitz. A minute later, his assumption was confirmed when a police car, sirens blaring and blue lights flashing, sped past them, headed for Big Rocks Beach. Özan cowered on the floor while Serhan put a hand on his rifle.

Three joyriders, speeding up behind them, blew their horns to signal that they wanted to pass. Ahdaf slowed to let them. Five minutes later, at the turnoff for Istanbul, the same cars had been pulled over at a makeshift checkpoint. Two policemen, interrogating the drivers, waved Ahdaf along when they saw the *medrese's* name stenciled on the side of the van.

As much as he could, Ahdaf stayed off the main road, relying on his GPS to find older side roads. They took advantage of passing olive groves, pissing there instead of at funky truck stops, and taking an extra couple of minutes to appreciate not being in the putrid van. The moon traveled with them, spilling a liquid light that reflected on the trees still wet from the earlier rain.

Eventually they rejoined the national road to buy gasoline. While Ahdaf filled the tank, Serhan and Özan went inside to use the toilets. He paid at the pump and pulled the van into a space in front of the minimarket. When the other two came back out, Ahdaf sensed something was wrong. It didn't matter. Whatever it was would have to wait; he was suddenly struck with a desperate need for a real toilet. He got out of the van as they started to get into it. "My turn," he said.

"Let's go," Serhan grumbled. "We'll pull over somewhere."

"Sorry, but I need one now, a proper one."

He closed his door just as a police car parked alongside the passenger side of the van.

"Fuck," Serhan hissed, and slid the side door shut.

Ahdaf pushed his way through the double-glass doors of the shop. It was a sizable room with a coffee counter, pastry area, sandwich bar, and a couple of grocery aisles stocked with snack foods. Naturally, the WC was in the far corner. He was ready to sprint for it until the large TV mounted over the door caught his eye. With the word LIVE tucked into the corner of its screen, a cluster of headlights illuminated two men carrying a body on a stretcher to a waiting ambulance. Ahdaf instantly recognized Big Rocks Beach.

He dived into the men's room and closed himself in a stall. A moment later, the restroom door slammed open, and two men entered the room. They passed close enough to Ahdaf's stall that he could glimpse, under the door, that they wore the same style shoes and creased trousers. He guessed they were the policemen who'd pulled up outside. With their backs to him at the urinals, he peeked through the crack caused by the stall door's hinges and saw their uniforms. One of them, as big as a bear, complained, "Can you believe this shit? I have a fucking date tonight!"

"The situation's a big deal," the second one said.

"So's my date."

"I thought you were married."

"I am. That's why it's a big deal! Do you know how hard it is to organize cheating on your wife?"

Chuckling, they went to the sinks to wash their hands. "It's crazy, though," the bearish man said. "Who are we looking for? We don't have a single clue. The whole country's on alert – for what? White, black, brown, or yellow, we don't even know that much. What are we supposed to do, check everybody's ID and then ask if they've just shot six cops on a beach?"

They dried their hands with paper towels.

"If it's the guys who did the Athens job, I'm not sure I want to catch them," the bearish one continued. "In some ways, they did us a favor."

"How do you mean?"

"I've got a teenage son. You too, right?"

"Yeah. Sixteen."

"You want faggots trying to seduce him?"

The policemen walked out before Ahdaf had a chance to hear the second guy's answer. He took his time washing his hands, not wanting to run into them and risk a spot-check. When he finally returned to the main room, they were walking outside, carrying paper espresso cups.

Caffeine was exactly what he needed for the night ahead. He ordered a double espresso and sipped it with his back against the counter to watch an ambulance on the television news pull onto the coastal road, its blue lights flashing, but no siren; it was the same coastal road he'd pulled onto some three hours earlier. In a voiceover, a male reporter said, "That's the ambulance's last trip tonight, taking away the body of a man who'd been severely burned. Who he is, and why his body was on this beach, is only one of the mysteries surrounding what happened tonight on Big Rocks Beach. Stay tuned for updates on this unfolding story."

The broadcast cut to a commercial break. Ahdaf drained his cup of its last drop, not minding the fine grounds that made his tongue gritty; he needed every molecule of coffee to ward off the day's encroaching exhaustion. Had it only been that morning that he'd picked up the van, picked up Kalam and Munir, picked up Derya, survived a shootout, and picked up two passengers about whom he knew nothing except that they were cop killers? Or at least the big guy was. He hadn't sorted out the little guy, except to know he didn't amount to much, and was fidgety, always scratching something or biting a fingernail or cowering when other vehicles sped past them.

The policemen pulled away as Ahdaf approached the van. He watched them head south on the main road as he climbed into the driver's seat.

"Where the fuck have you been?" Serhan asked.

"Waiting for them to leave. I heard them talking about random ID checks. I didn't want to be one of them, because they might've wanted to look in my car. I wouldn't even be able to tell them your names."

"They would've found this," Serhan said, and brandished his rifle in Ahdaf's mirror.

"That's what I wanted to avoid," he said. Serhan had already killed enough policemen to be hanged, he wanted to add, but thought better of it. He didn't want to antagonize either of the edgy men sitting behind him.

Ahdaf decided to stay on the national road. It was easier driving, and he kept to the speed limit, not wanting to give a policeman any excuse for pulling him over. It made him the slowest vehicle on the road. Annoyed drivers tooted their horns as they passed, but he didn't care. The van's inherent clumsiness gave him an excuse to drive carefully. Besides, who would think to search a *medrese* van for fugitive terrorists? When his nerves had calmed a bit, it gave him a chance to tell Serhan, "On TV, I saw them take your brother away by ambulance."

"Just now? Back at the stop? And you fucking said it would be faster for them to call an ambulance! That was three hours ago! I should kill you for leaving him behind." In the rearview mirror, Ahdaf saw how tempted Serhan was to reach for his rifle. "I should fucking kill you," he muttered and faced the window.

"It wasn't live TV," Ahdaf lied. "It was taped when the ambulances first arrived."

"Did they say if he's still alive?"

"They didn't say."

"He is, *inshallah*," Serhan said, his voice cracking.

Ahdaf had no siblings, and though many of his friends had lost a brother or sister, none had lost a twin. He couldn't imagine, really, that sense of losing a whole other *you*, or half of yourself, depending how you looked at it; in either case, part of you would be mortally wounded.

Nothing more was said, and the tension dissipated. Nor did anyone gripe about the air quality. Shooting out the two windows had definitely improved it: better breezy than bloated. Soon the rhythm, the motor, and the humdrumness had Ahdaf's two passengers nodding off. Their heads rested against the windows, unconsciously adjusting to the van's shifting angles, until its rickety shock absorbers met a pothole and knocked them awake to their uncomfortable reality. It happened frequently enough that they both tried stretching out on the seats, but they were intended for two upright skinny kids, not grown men using them as beds that were barely long enough to accommodate their bums. They only managed to stay in place by wedging their knees against the seat across the narrow aisle.

As soon as they both started snoring, Ahdaf fleetingly wished that he had taken Munir's gun out of his hand back on Big Rocks Beach. That way, he could've shot the two men in their sleep and been a hero.

DAY 6

Over distant treetops, Ahdaf caught glimpses of the illuminated towers of the approaching Osmangazi Bridge. He recalled the thrill of driving across it for the first time – *what, only 10 hours earlier?* – Kalam exclaiming over what he videotaped; Munir sharing the pictures he'd send to his wife; Derya remarking on the bridge's many engineering feats; Ahdaf marveling at the sensation of flying over water that stretched forever on both sides.

The return ride was much different. He didn't have to look in the mirror to know that Serhan and Özan were in the back; he smelled them and heard their snores. With every bump or turn, they unconsciously clung to their precarious perches on the van's short benches. Just looking at them, Ahdaf knew things weren't going to end well.

He braked as he approached the impressive suspension bridge. That roused Serhan, who automatically reached for his rifle. "It's just a toll station," Ahdaf reassured him. "Hide your rifle and go back to sleep."

As he crossed the long bridge, even the clunky van's tires hummed on its smooth surface. He balanced his cell phone on the steering wheel to send Malik a message: CROSSING OSMAN-GAZI BRIDGE.

He decided to let Malik calculate how long it might take him to arrive at the mosque. He couldn't predict rush hour, accidents, or anything that might influence his driving time. One hour or three? Ahdaf had no real idea.

The city's towering skyscrapers soon came into view. Many had long strings of lights outlining their corners or elaborate spotlighted roofs, which, building by building, switched off as dawn dispatched the night. Traffic quickly became heavy, and eventually came to a standstill. That woke the two men in the back.

"What's happening?" Serhan asked.

"Traffic," Ahdaf replied.

Özan said, "I gotta take a piss."

"You're going to have to hold it."

"Fuck, man, I just woke up. I always gotta piss when I wake up."

"Where am I going to pull over?"

Özan slid open the side door.

"What are you doing?" Ahdaf demanded.

"I can't wait or I'll piss myself!" Gripping the top of the open door, Özan used his free hand to unzip and pee.

The driver in the next car swore at him and rolled up his window. Other drivers, realizing what he was doing, honked their horns in complaint.

"I'm sorry," he shouted back. "I have a small bladder!"

"A small fucking brain! That's your problem!" Serhan complained as he slid the side door shut. A couple of final blasts of horns registered everyone's disgust.

"Özan, can you put on your GPS?"

"Where do you want to go?"

"Aksaray. What are the options for side roads with less traffic?"

Özan studied the map on his phone's screen. "No good option. Only small roads through neighborhoods that turn here and there constantly. It'll take longer."

"Than staying in this traffic?"

"That's my guess."

They drove in silence for a while before Ahdaf asked, "I assume you two are Turkish because you speak Turkish with each other. Are you from Istanbul?"

"I grew up in Aksaray," Özan replied. "Serhan, too."

"You went to Raqqa together?"

"With his brother, Taner."

"Shut up, Özan," Serhan barked.

"To fight for ISIS," Özan continued.

"I said shut up!"

"He wanted to prove to Allah that he wasn't a faggot."

"Who? Taner?" Ahdaf asked.

"SHUT UP!"

"We joined Malik's old cell because they liked to kill faggots."

Serhan lunged at Özan, shouting, "I'LL FUCKING KILL YOU!"

"Calm down!" Ahdaf cried. "You're going to cause an accident, and then what happens to us? Özan, how far now?"

Studying his GPS, Özan replied, "The time has just doubled if we stay on this route."

"Is that usual?" Ahdaf asked.

"No, it's strange. There must have been an accident. Do you want to try the smaller roads?"

Accident or roadblock? Ahdaf wondered, and said, "Tell me where to turn."

An hour later, Ahdaf realized too late that he should have gone around the block to make a right turn into the mosque's alley instead of blocking traffic waiting to turn left. Finally, there was a break, and he gunned the clumsy van to make his turn. A chorus of horns roused behind him. He wondered why they were complaining until he realized that they were cheering that he'd gotten out of the way. He wasn't so cheerful himself as he bounced along the alley's broken asphalt, glimpsing Malik behind a clump of dusty oleanders before he limped into the open. Ahdaf was tempted to pretend he hadn't seen him and run him over, but he braked as Malik's body tensed, ready to spring out of the way. Through a swirl of dust, the look they exchanged made it clear they despised each other for the same reason: each had put the other in a detestable situation. Malik had sent Ahdaf off to bring back a team of fugitive terrorists. He'd returned with cop killers who were the target of a national manhunt.

"You two stay in the van until I know what's going on," Ahdaf said.

"We need air," Özan complained.

"Open the side door. Then stay seated where no one can see you. You don't know who's watching." He shouldered the three daypacks he'd piled on the passenger seat – Munir's, Kalam's and his own – and joined Malik in front of the van.

"Who survived?" he asked.

"Serhan and Özan."

"So Taner died," Malik said.

"You know them?"

"Yes. What happened?"

"You mean on the beach? With the policemen?"

"Why did Serhan shoot them? I assume it was Serhan, and not Özan."

Ahdaf hesitated, debating if he should mention Munir's presence and the role his gun played in setting off the savage shootout. He decided Malik would learn of it sooner or later, so better to tell him. "After you told me that someone was badly injured, I worried I might need help. I didn't know what to expect, and wanted to be ready. So I asked a friend to come along and help me. He agreed and was hoping the fisherman would take him back to Greece with him. When the police suddenly showed up, he pulled out a gun. I knew he had it, but it was for his own protection in Europe. It was stupid of him. What was he going to do, shoot all of them with a pistol when they had automatic weapons? They saw it in their headlights and shot him, and then Serhan mowed them down with his rifle. I saw five policemen, but the news says six were killed. My guess is that the sixth guy stayed back with the cars to be in radio contact with someone. Serhan's bullets found him anyway."

"They shot at your group first," Malik pointed out, "so what Serhan did was self-defense."

"It wasn't self-defense. It was a massacre."

"They're still heroes," Malik said.

Ahdaf snorted. "Heroes?"

"For what they did in Athens."

"Yeah, heroes, for killing people who were dancing. Is dancing *haram*, too?"

"It's a special sin for men to dance with men who act like women. That's why they were killed."

"The six policemen in Assos who've left behind families now without husbands and fathers, what was their sin?"

"Whatever happens is Allah's will," Malik said.

"Obviously we pray to different Allahs," Ahdaf replied. "The key is in the ignition. Your two men – if monsters can be called that – are waiting to get out."

Ahdaf started to walk off.

"You can't walk away from this now," Malik said to his back. "There's certain to be witnesses. People, especially in the countryside, remember things like a *medrese's* orange bus from Istanbul."

Ahdaf turned back to ask, "What's your point?"

"Your fingerprints are all over that bus. So are Serhan's and Özan's."

"Aren't yours, too?" Ahdaf's question intentionally underscored their complicity in the same crimes.

That time he did walk off, the three daypacks slung over one shoulder.

Malik, of course, would have known in advance who the special passengers were, but he had no way to predict the outcome of the attack on the Spartacus Club, nor by what route the terrorists, if any survived, might ultimately try to escape. Of course there were backup plans for an operation of that scale, unless it was intended to be a suicide mission – and nothing suggested that to Ahdaf.

All that was in the back of his mind as he navigated the few blocks to his apartment, detouring through the morning market still setting up and already filled with picky shoppers wanting the day's freshest of everything. He needed nourishment, not junk food, and went for his usual dates, hummus, and flat bread. It took too much effort to think past a survival diet, and he'd survived on it for many weeks, though he'd walked off thousands more calories than he consumed until he arrived, emaciated, in Istanbul, barely recognizing himself despite having looked in windows and mirrors at selfies of his wasting away.

He knew he should appreciate the bright afternoon imbued with autumn's freshness, but, veiled in exhaustion, he couldn't. He'd been awake more than 24 hours, most of that pumping with adrenaline. He staggered, barely able to place one foot in front of the other. He so craved sleep that he was tempted to join the occasional other refugees stretched out on the sidewalk or patch of ground.

He turned onto his block and aimed for his building on the next corner. After the insanity he'd experienced, the mundane click of turning a key in his building's front door seemed surreal. So did the sound of his plodding footsteps climbing the single flight of stairs. Every moment since the murderous firefight on Big Rocks Beach, he'd expected to be killed on a whim. Going through the motions of his daily life brought home to Ahdaf that he'd survived. By the time he reached his apartment door, he was trembling, overwhelmed by the unexpected reprieve.

He went inside and leaned against the door to steady himself. He was tempted to slide down it and fall asleep on the spot, but his growling stomach reminded him that he needed to eat. He carried his survival provisions to his small kitchen table, washed his hands, and popped a date in his mouth. He kept eating them while he plugged in his phone and brought up the news. He scanned the current topics, saw ASSOS AMBUSH, and clicked on the latest report:

"Some breaking news on the story we are following in Assos. In addition to the six slain police officers, and a seventh man who died from burn wounds from an undetermined source, officials now report that an eighth body was found at the site. He had no ID papers but appears to be Turkish or Middle Eastern, around 30 years old. He died of multiple gunshot wounds."

"He was 32," Ahdaf corrected the reporter as he opened the container of hummus. "The fucking police shot him, and he was guilty of nothing."

"Police are launching a national effort to apprehend whoever shot the policemen, but they are stymied by one important detail: they have no idea who that person is. Stay tuned to

CNN for updates as this tragic and increasingly bizarre story unfolds."

"It's not so bizarre," Ahdaf again talked back to the reporter. "It's only another botched police operation." He called Selim and left the message: "It's urgent we talk about your passenger."

He hung up and opened the plastic container of humus to drag a corner of pita through it, with a second piece of the leathery bread trailing close behind. Partly satisfying his hunger only made him feel his exhaustion more. He couldn't wait to crawl onto the mattress, now on the floor surrounded by the mounds of books that had once kept it aloft until his rowdy lovemaking with Kalam had caused the carefully engineered stacks to collapse; but he wouldn't let himself sleep until he heard from Selim. He didn't want to miss a message, and the ping of an SMS wouldn't be enough to wake him. Besides, as inviting as his bed was, he could smell, on himself, the scorched flesh and endless cigarettes he'd had to endure. He needed a shower.

He went into the bathroom and perched his phone on the sink, where he could easily reach it if Selim called. He ran the water, wanting it to be as hot as he could stand it to melt away his grime. When the water was hot enough, he remembered to take off his belt so as not to ruin its leather, and otherwise stepped fully dressed under the shower. He stripped naked, dropping his clothes to the bottom of the tub to mash them with his feet while sudsing them up with the soap running off his body.

His telephone pinged. He picked it up and read: MY PASSENGER IS SAFE. YOUR PASSENGERS ARE UNDER SURVEILLANCE AT THE MOSQUE. MEET 21H AT LEYLA'S. GET SOME SLEEP.

He dried off and hung his wet clothes on the shower faucets and towel rack and the back of his only chair. The shower had revived him enough that he decided to take care of a dreaded chore before allowing himself to sleep. While donning his spare shirt and pants, he accidentally knocked his phone and sent it sliding across the floor. "Shit!" he muttered, always fearful of breaking it – his lifeline to the world – but it was fine when he tested it by turning on the news again, just as a reporter said: "We have a video from a source who claims to have witnessed what happened at Big Rocks Beach."

The screen filled with a bouncy video taken by someone running over jagged black stones. It was night, with barely enough starlight to distinguish where the rocks ended and the dark sea began. A digital clock in the corner of the video registered the date and time, coinciding with the events of the previous night. Ahdaf guessed it was Derya, fleeing, and then he recognized her voice when she said: "I'm not going to describe exactly what I saw happen because the regular news will be full of the gory details – and it *was* gory. The police were there waiting for the boat from Greece. How did they know about it? It had to be a trap, but set up by whom and why? That's the question –"

Suddenly her phone hit the ground. She had tripped. "Shit, I'm bleeding," she said offscreen, and her report stopped.

The reporter reappeared. "I want to reassure our viewers that our contributor survived her fall, or of course we wouldn't have her video, which we've just broadcast for the first time. There's certain to be an official response to allegations of some sort of trap. Who trapped whom? We'll keep you posted as this intriguing story develops."

Ahdaf stuffed his phone into his pocket. He felt he'd abandoned Derya and betrayed Meryem, and wanted to help them both; but even more pressing was the need to visit Munir's wife, who was surely tortured by her husband's unexplained silence.

There wasn't much left in Munir's daypack after Serhan had put on the extra clothes he'd packed. There was only his phone, identity card, and toothbrush. He took a picture of the ID card, knowing it was something Selim would want. He checked the contents of his own daypack and pulled out the newspaper photo of Meryem. He flattened it on the table, asking her forgiveness as he did so, and then slung his and Munir's packs over his shoulder and walked out.

The landing was filled with the buttery smell of baked goods. He knew it emanated from Madame Darton's flat. His stomach growled, hungry for whatever she was baking. As if she'd heard it, the matronly woman swung open her door holding a plate. "Sugar cookies!" she exclaimed. "Fresh out of the oven!" Fifi, of course, yapped incessantly while running in circles. "Fifi! Stop that!" she scolded.

The way the older woman doted on him reminded Ahdaf of how his grandmother always had something freshly baked waiting for him when he came home from school, though Madame Darton was nowhere near as old. Taking two of the sugary cookies, he said, "Thank you. How'd you know I'm starving?"

"You must take them all," she insisted.

"No, I couldn't possibly."

"You said you're starving!"

"It was an exaggeration."

"Please, I baked them for you," she said, and forced the plate into his hands. "I have no one else to cook for."

He smiled. "I'm glad to be a beneficiary of your cooking. It's delicious! But please, not too often. I'll get fat! Excuse me while I take these inside."

He put most of the cookies in a plastic bag, which he concealed in his daypack and transferred the rest to his own plate, which he put in the refrigerator so they wouldn't attract bugs. He *was* starving, and chomped into one, which soon became two cookies when he returned to the landing where Madame Darton expected a report. Wiping powdered sugar off his mouth, he exclaimed, "Delicious! Thank you!" She took back her plate and held it like a trophy as he bounded down the stairs.

On his way to Munir's apartment, only a few blocks away, he stopped at a grocery store, mulling over what food to buy that would be the most nourishing when he smelled it: rotisserie chickens in front of the butcher shop next door. "I'll take one on my way out," he said to the vendor, and went into the grocery to buy fruit, baby formula, a tub of yogurt, and a handful of chocolate bars. He collected his chicken and headed for Munir's street. He agonized for the next 10 minutes how to tell Yasmin that her husband was dead. He practiced some lines of explanation and condolences as he walked, not caring that he drew attention by talking to himself or wiping away stray tears.

Soon he arrived at Munir's building and rang the bell. A moment later, Yasmin asked over the scratchy intercom, "Who is it?"

"Ahdaf Jalil. Munir's friend."

She buzzed him in.

He knew Munir's apartment was two flights up and, clasping his bundles tighter, started climbing the stairs. The news he carried grew heavier with each step. When he reached the first landing, he heard a door open on the next floor. As he continued up the stairs, he could see Yasmin peering past him, in search, of course, of Munir, her face painfully sad. "Munir's not with you?" she needed to ask, though obviously he wasn't. "The one they can't identify – it's him, isn't it?" She shrank into her grief and he barely caught her before she toppled over. It felt awkward, touching her, but she needed comforting, and he let her anguish weep into his shoulder. "Why don't they show his face if they want him identified?" she continued. "They blur it. I recognized him by his ears."

"It's him," Ahdaf confirmed. He almost told her that Munir had been shot in the face but couldn't bring himself to conjure that image for her.

"Mama?" a child called from inside.

"I'm out here, Samir. Talking to a friend."

"Is Baba home?"

"It's not Baba, sweetheart. I'm talking to a friend. Maybe Baba comes tomorrow." She looked pleadingly at Ahdaf. "How do I explain his *baba* is dead to a three-year-old?"

"I don't know. I'm so sorry."

"Mama?"

"What is it, honey?"

"I'm hungry."

"I brought you a chicken," Ahdaf told her. "He must smell it. I have other things for you, too. May I come in?"

"Of course."

He followed her into the apartment. When Samir saw him, he asked again, "Is it Baba?"

"It's Baba's friend, sweetheart," she answered, and to Ahdaf explained, "When he hears a man or sees one, he thinks maybe it's his father. He doesn't see well."

"Munir told me."

"I'm hungry," the boy whined.

"Here, start with these," Ahdaf said and handed him a couple of Madame Darton's cookies. He noticed animated images flickering on a cell phone propped on the windowsill and told the boy, "Go watch your cartoons. I'll bring you more food in five minutes."

The boy trailed cookie crumbs back to the bed where he leaned close to the small screen to see his program. "I have some things for you," he told Yasmin, and unzipped Munir's daypack.

A baby's irritated squeal distracted them. Ahdaf glanced around the corner of the counter and saw a newborn infant swaddled in a kaftan, lying in a cardboard box. He bent down to tickle her belly and she squirmed, almost smiling. "Is she any stronger?" he asked.

"I have more milk, but she doesn't try to nurse. I'm worried she's learned it's a wasted effort. Maybe her body says, after so many tries when I was dry, not to waste her energy trying again."

"She'll try again," he reassured her.

He opened a cupboard, found a plate, and slid the roasted chicken onto it.

"What are you doing?" Yasmin asked.

"I'm fixing you and Samir some lunch."

She jumped up. "I can do that! And you must stay and eat with us."

"I can't, and you, *please* sit down. You look exhausted."

In reality, Ahdaf would gladly have stayed and eaten the whole chicken himself, which is exactly why he had said no. Once started, he couldn't have stopped himself from devouring it – yet it was Munir's family who needed every bit of nourishment they could get if they were going to survive. Despite all the war orphans he'd seen, he'd never met a child with cheeks as sallow as Samir's, and from what he could see of the newborn daughter, she was a twig. He piled pieces of chicken on two plates along with roasted potatoes and a large spoonful of yogurt. He set one plate with cutlery in front of Yasmin and took the other one to the boy, who ignored the offer of a fork and immediately started eating with his fingers. Ahdaf put the fork away, glancing at Yasmin, who was scarfing down her food with equal relish. "Please, you must eat something too," she said between bites.

"I have other food at home. Until you have enough milk, I also bought this." He displayed the round carton of baby formula. "You add water. It's not real milk, and of course natural is better when you can. How are you doing, Samir? You want more to eat?"

The boy shook his head and set the plate on the bed next to him. Ahdaf wasn't surprised; he'd eaten a huge portion for a kid his size. He was probably a kilo heavier. "I'm sure you have room for something else," he said, and reached into his daypack for a chocolate bar.

Yasmin smiled when she saw it. "He will have room for that," she said.

Ahdaf picked up the boy's plate. "You sure? No more?"

"No more."

"Not even this?"

The boy grabbed the chocolate and immediately peeled back its waxy wrapping.

"I thought so," Ahdaf said, and sat back across from Yasmin at the small table. "I have more things for you, too."

She shook her head. "No, Ahdaf, you have done enough already."

From his daypack, he pulled the rest of the chocolate bars he'd purchased. "Hide them from the boy," he advised her. "In fact, I'm going to put them on the top shelf of the cupboard with more cookies, too. Don't let him see where they're hidden, or he'll try to get them and might hurt himself. I have more things for you."

"You've done too much already," she protested again.

"They're Munir's things. I have his daypack."

"He carried that from Damascus. I carried Samir. That's all we had."

Ahdaf opened a zipper and pulled out a wallet. "Here's his ID and some money. Did he leave you with some money, too?"

"What money? I was already begging on the street."

Ahdaf sighed hard. "Munir never said."

"He was too ashamed," she choked out, barely able to speak as her new reality sank in. Her husband was confirmed dead. She had two infant children. Only a thin wallet separated them from starvation. "Why was he killed?"

"I saw what happened, but I don't know why it happened," he replied. Sensing her mounting panic, he added, "I'll do my best to help."

"Thank you," she murmured.

"One last thing." He worked Munir's wedding ring off his finger and handed it to her. "He changed his mind. He wasn't going to go to Greece. He was coming back to you. It's the truth. He left his pack in the van, and as he got out, he pointed to his ring. *'This means something!'* he said. It was the last thing he said to me. The last thing he said to anyone. He was coming home."

Yasmin closed her hand on the ring.

Ahdaf squeezed her fist with both his hands. Then he was gone, down the steps and outside, out of the stagnant air his murdered friend had once breathed.

Back in his own apartment, Ahdaf pulled his drape closed, set his alarm, tied a bandana around his eyes to keep out the daylight, stripped to his boxers, and crawled onto the mattress. He woke up six hours later, wanting to sleep six more. He'd set the alarm early enough to have time for another shower, not certain where his late rendezvous with Selim might lead. He puzzled over why the CIA man hadn't wanted to meet him during the day. Why wait until nine at night? Wouldn't debriefing him about the Spartacus terrorists be a priority? It was almost as if he didn't know what had happened – or what Ahdaf had been through – but of course he knew if he had reported that Derya was safe.

Thirty minutes later, Ahdaf sat next to the CIA man at Leyla's cowboy bar. There was a full glass of foamy beer already on the counter – and cold, based on the condensation running down its sides. "Is somebody sitting here?" he asked.

"You are," Selim answered. "Leyla said you'd be on time, and the beer'd still be cold enough."

Ahdaf scowled at his beer. "Maybe cold enough by *her* definition."

"Let's test it," Selim suggested.

They clinked glasses and sipped.

"Was she right?" Selim asked.

Ahdaf ignored him, instead asking, "Did you know what was going to happen in Assos?"

"No, I didn't. I swear I didn't."

"But you know what happened?"

"I've pieced it together."

Ahdaf wrapped his hands around his glass and stared at it when he said, "I've been thinking about this all the way back. You set me up, Selim."

"You're forgetting that *you* suggested the operation to *me*. Malik wanted you to make a pick-up in Assos. I wanted you to make a drop-off in Assos. *You* proposed coordinating the two."

Ahdaf snickered in disbelief. "You're blaming me? You set me up the first time you came looking for me. You were baiting Malik. I was the bait, and he took it."

Selim pursed his lips. "You're right," he admitted.

"You must have guessed who Malik wanted me to pick up," Ahdaf continued. "They were three members of his cell. They went to Raqqa to 'kill faggots.' Now they're coming back from Greece following an attack on a gay nightclub. How many attackers were there?"

"Three."

"Three," Ahdaf spat out. "Who else would Malik be trying to bring back from Greece, or did you think it was just a coincidence?"

"I had a hunch, that's all, and if I shared it with you, you wouldn't have done the job."

"You're right, and my friend wouldn't be dead either."

"You friend's dead because he pulled out a gun."

"So now it's Munir's fault? Fuck."

"I wasn't expecting the local police to show up. If they hadn't, it would have been a ride back to Istanbul and no one would be dead."

"Why were the police there?"

167

Selim shrugged. "They must have been tipped off – but by whom, we'll probably never know. All of Assos's policemen are dead."

Ahdaf looked accusingly at Selim when he asked, "Was there any point when you thought about rescuing me? Or letting me know that you knew what was happening? One word would've let me know I wasn't forgotten."

"Any message might have made Serhan suspicious. That would've made it more dangerous for you." Selim put a hand on Ahdaf's shoulder. "I'm sorry."

Ahdaf shook his hand off. "Fuck your 'sorry.' How do you know about Munir's gun, anyway?"

"Derya saw it."

"Where is she?"

"I can't tell you, but she's safe."

"You can't tell me much, can you?"

"The operation isn't over."

Ahdaf looked puzzled. "What do you mean it's not over? They're at the mosque."

"The ÖKK doesn't want to launch an assault at the mosque. They want to find a way to lure them out."

Ahdaf asked, "What's the ÖKK?"

"It stands for *Special Forces Command* in Turkish. It's an elite unit for tactical strikes."

Ahdaf, completely baffled, said, "I don't understand. They're Special Forces. They know what they're doing, and they're armed. Serhan has one assault rifle and I doubt that Malik has an arsenal. They should go in, arrest or kill them, or do whatever they do." Ahdaf thumped his fist on the bar. "But go get them!"

"They don't want to launch a military operation at a mosque. That's why we still need your help."

"Forget it."

"We need to know what Malik plans to do with them as soon as he plans it."

"I said forget it."

"Go to morning prayers. Malik will have a plan by then."

"Forget it!" Ahdaf repeated, loud enough to draw a startled glance from Leyla from across the café. "Don't you have an informant in Malik's cell?"

"*Had*," Selim replied. "He disappeared. We don't know how or where."

Ahdaf genuinely laughed. "And I'm supposed to replace your disappeared guy! What kind of job description is that?"

"Not if we manage to break up the cell first."

"I'm not helping," Ahdaf said, shaking his head. "Before I'm pushed off a tall building, I'm disappearing on my own."

When he got off the barstool, Selim placed a hand on his shoulder. "Before you go," he said, "I want you to know that everybody who knows what you've done thinks you're a hero."

"Have you asked my dead friend's wife? I think she'd disagree with you."

"I need his name. And her name."

"She's going to need help."

"She'll get some. I promise."

"You expect me to trust you?"

"I need his personal info before I can."

"He has a name. Munir Mahmoud. I took a picture of his ID card." Ahdaf showed it to Selim on his phone.

Selim pulled out a pen. "Let me take down his info."

"I can AirDrop it to you." After a couple of taps, Selim's phone pinged.

He checked his screen. "Got it."

"If I'm such a hero," Ahdaf started, "and I'm so important to the operation, why'd you wait 12 hours to meet me? Or were you done with me until the ÖKK balked at attacking the mosque, and now you need me to spy on Malik again?"

"The mosque has been under constant surveillance. Our two

guys aren't going anywhere, and if they tried, I figured you needed some time to recover from your experience. I can and can't
imagine all you endured, but I know it was terrible. I also know
even heroes need sleep."

"This one still does," Ahdaf said. He drained his beer and
headed for the door.

Leyla, walking among the tables taking orders, caught his eye
and cocked her head as if to ask, *Is everything okay?* He tipped his
head in his hand to indicate sleep, and went outside.

The cool evening refreshed Ahdaf after the stuffy café. Walking the few blocks to his apartment, he tried not to think of anything. He didn't want to rerun his conversation with Selim nor
revisit his anger at him. He was finished with the whole affair.

As he entered the building, his nostrils twitched; instead of
rancid, the air smelled of fresh-baked bread. The smell alone
brightened his mood, and when he reached his door, he was only
mildly surprised to find a baguette in a plastic bag hanging from
his doorknob. He put the still-warm loaf to his nose and closed
his eyes with pleasure. He guessed Madame Darton had watched
for him to come down the street and quickly dashed across the
landing to leave it for him. After the harshness of the last two
days, he almost cried at the thoughtfulness. He broke off an end
to eat as soon as he closed the door behind him.

Looking around his room, taking in the jumble of his mattress
and books, his one chair and tiny table, he felt glad he'd survived
to be able to come home. Despite his afternoon nap, sleep was all
he wanted – but first he had one thing to do. Meryem's photo still
lay on the table; he picked it up and tacked it back on the wall.
She'd become an icon with the power to protect him, and imbued
his current tribulations with a purpose. He prayed for her safety
as he stripped to his boxers and fell onto the mattress.

DAY 7

The call to prayer woke Ahdaf the following morning. He'd been half-awake, listening for it. He knew he should get moving but lingered in bed, letting the *muezzin's* sonorous chant seduce him even as he sorted through the day's potential perils – and there were many.

He'd had a change of heart. He blamed it on Meryem. While he was sleeping, she'd put into his head the notion that Munir's death would only mean something when Serhan and Özan were captured. He knew it was dangerous to act on a dream, but he also felt Meryem was right; and as a result of his dream, what he had hoped to avoid entirely was his first stop: the mosque, with the intention of meeting Malik to learn his plans for the terrorists.

He took a quick shower and tested the clothes he'd washed with his feet the day before; still damp and reeking despite the perfumed soap he'd used. Ten minutes later, wearing a kaftan, he was on the sidewalk, his feet following a familiar route. After walking away from Malik the day before, he wondered how he would explain his sudden reappearance, when he realized no explanation was necessary. Coming for prayers was excuse enough. Ahdaf had surprised himself once he'd reached Istanbul by maintaining his habit of praying every day, and only at a mosque. He didn't pray five times daily as prescribed by Islam. Neither he nor his father was that religious. While walking the length of Turkey with all the time in the world to think, he'd realized why his father had insisted that they pray together. It was, of course, to introduce Ahdaf to their community, to their neighbors and to the world in which he would grow up. It was also to spend time together – father and son – if rarely more than the few minutes walking to and from the mosque. Ahdaf couldn't remember when he stopped holding his father's hand on that short journey from home to a prayer rug, but he had never wanted to hold his father's hand more than at that moment in Istanbul. He yearned for its promised protection as he turned the corner and the mosque's minaret rose in front of him. Never had a minaret seemed so menacing.

He entered the courtyard and bypassed the men seated at the spigots along the ablutions wall. He considered searching for Malik, assuming he'd find him in the *medrese*, but decided against it. He didn't want to stumble upon Serhan and Özan if they were still there. More than a little nervous, he needed to relieve himself, and he headed for the public WC. No one else was there, though as soon as he stepped up to a urinal, the man in the beige kaftan took the one next to him.

"He moved the two men," the man said quietly.

"What two men?"

"The men you brought to him."

"Where are they?"

"In the van."

"Why in the van?"

"Malik hasn't said anything to me."

Finished, they dropped the fronts of their kaftans and stepped away.

"What's your name?" Ahdaf asked.

"Suleiman."

"I'm Ahdaf."

"I know." With a curt nod, Suleiman walked away.

Ahdaf had had no doubt that one of Malik's spies would inform him of his presence. The headmaster would find him when he wanted. In the meantime, Ahdaf decided to pray, and tucked his shoes into a bank of cubbyholes before climbing the broad steps to the entrance of the mosque. The moment his hand touched the velvet curtain, Malik whipped it open and muttered, under his breath, "Come with me. We'll talk while we walk."

After retrieving their shoes, they walked in silence until they reached the mosque's expansive garden with crisscrossing marble paths. "Why have you come this morning?"

"I'm a man of habit. I came to pray."

"You met with Selim Wilson last night."

"He still wants to smuggle a journalist out of the country, but doesn't yet have a definite plan."

"Who's the journalist?"

"I don't know."

"Why is this journalist important to the Americans?"

"All Selim said is that he's in danger for criticizing the government."

"Did he say anything about what happened in Assos?"

"Selim? Why would he? He didn't know that I was there."

"It's all over the news. He might've said something."

"We only talked about smuggling the journalist. That's all we talked about."

"He doesn't know about Serhan and Özan?"

Ahdaf shrugged. "I don't know what he knows. You said he's an American spy. I assume that means CIA, but of course he hasn't told me that himself. Honestly, though, I don't think he'd

173

be worried about a journalist if he knew Serhan and Özan were in Istanbul."

They reached the wooden door built into the back hedge. Malik, pulling out keys, asked, "Who was the woman?"

"What woman?"

"Serhan said she was someone's widow."

"Oh, Yasmin. She's the wife of the friend I asked to come along and help me."

"You didn't mention him. Or her."

"I told you that he wanted to go back with the fisherman to Greece. Of course his wife would go with him, too. He didn't ask; she just came along with him. What was I going to say?"

"Where is she now?"

"I assume she survived because the news hasn't mentioned finding a woman's body. Where is she specifically? I have no idea. Alive, *inshallah*."

"*Inshallah*," Malik repeated, and opened the garden door. They stepped into the bright alley where the van-cum-school bus was in a patch of shade. Someone had turned it around to make it easier to pull onto the main road, Ahdaf's rational side was thinking, even as his heart raced at the sight of the vehicle in which he'd spent the most frightening hours of his life.

"You'll need these," Malik said, offering him keys.

Ahdaf took them instinctively. "Why?"

Malik slid open the side door.

Ahdaf heard scuffling, and Serhan grabbed his rifle. Then he saw who it was and grumbled, "Knock first next time."

"You're taking them with you," Malik said.

"With *me*?"

"To your apartment."

"*What?*"

"I can't keep them here. They're too visible."

"Excuse me," Serhan said, and stepped out of the van. "I gotta take a dump." He bounded through the hedge door.

Özan followed him out. "Me too," he said.

"What am I supposed to do with them?" Ahdaf asked.

"Hide them," Malik replied.

"Hide them? How can I hide them? I have neighbors. Nosey neighbors!"

"No nosier than the *medrese's* pupils."

"I'm not doing it, Malik. I never agreed to this."

"You'll agree to it now."

"Why should I?"

Malik leaned closer to whisper in his ear, "You'll do it because your cousin confessed you had sexual relations."

"You're lying!"

"Allah's soldiers went looking for you, but you'd already run away."

Ahdaf *had* run away. As soon as the crowd began throwing stones at Sadiq's motionless body to ensure he was dead, he'd sprinted home, slung a daypack over his shoulders, and embraced his parents for the last time. His mother couldn't understand why he was so afraid, and he was too ashamed, too hurried, to explain. Only later did he learn that ISIS soldiers had come for him that same day, no doubt revealing his crude shame to his parents. By then, he was kilometers away, keeping to the Euphrates's muddy trails to avoid the vagabonds and thieves that haunted the roads. Avoiding that danger, he risked another: an encounter with rogue ISIS soldiers. Though officially routed from Raqqa itself, the Islamic State's fighters were never far away in the countryside and often camped along the river. Their attacks were precisely planned, like that day, when they pounced on Sadiq and two others accused of homosexuality and summarily executed them. With every raid, they strove to intimidate civilians into accepting the twisted logic of wanting ISIS back in control if that was the only way the attacks would stop.

"What was your original plan for Serhan and Özan?" Ahdaf asked. "Why can't that still happen?"

"What happened in Assos changed everything."

"They were already on the run."

"But not on the run in Turkey for killing Turkish policemen. We need a new plan."

"A new plan for us?" Serhan asked, coming around the back of the van. "That sounds unplanned. I don't like that."

"Don't worry, we have a plan," Malik reassured him. "First you're going to Ahdaf's apartment."

"After that?"

"Back to Raqqa. You can play your favorite sport there until there's another operation."

"How do we get to Raqqa?"

Malik stared at Ahdaf when he replied, "I'm trying to find a driver."

Özan reappeared, head down, working on freeing the shirttail caught in his pants zipper. "I hope you're finding some food, too," he said.

Ten minutes later, Ahdaf parked in front of his apartment building with his undesired passengers. The whole way, he'd fretted over Malik's last, piercing look, which conveyed the expectation that Ahdaf would drive Serhan and Özan to Raqqa. He mulled over many excuses why he shouldn't. Given some time, he was confident he could find someone with a vehicle willing to take them, if Malik paid enough. Driving the round trip to Raqqa would take a week – and wouldn't the *medrese* need its school bus? Could the van even endure the journey? What if he were stopped for any reason and asked to show his driver license? He didn't even have one. As logical as his arguments sounded, he was unsettled by Malik's allusion to Serhan's "favorite sport," which he guessed was pushing gay men off rooftops. A horrific image flashed across his mind, of his cousin suspended in the air before the ground broke his body.

"I'm getting out," Serhan said, with one hand picking up his rifle and the other sliding open the van's door.

"Wait!" Ahdaf exclaimed. "Let's all walk together to try to hide your rifle." He got out and stepped around the front of the van. At the open side door, he told Serhan, "Keep your rifle pressed against your leg. I'll walk beside it. Özan, you walk behind us to block anyone's view of it."

They took their positions on the curb. As they walked in step to the front door, Ahdaf noticed a curtain ruffle in his neighbor's window and knew Madame Darton would appear on their shared landing on some pretense.

That's exactly what happened as they tromped up the stairs. Ahdaf, in the lead, unlocked his door, and the other men entered just as Madame Darton stepped out holding a watering can. "Time for their daily shower," she said brightly, referring to two plants she kept on their shared landing. They exchanged good mornings, and she said, "It's nice you have more friends visiting."

"They're my cousins."

"You never mentioned you had cousins living in Istanbul."

"They're visiting from Raqqa. All my family lives there except me."

She smiled, a bit of red lipstick staining her teeth. "How nice to see members of your family. You must miss them. Will they stay a long time?"

"No more than a couple of days. I promise, they won't be a bother. Have a nice day, Madame," he added with a smile and went inside.

Serhan was peeing. Özan was checking what was in the kitchen cupboards. "I told her you're my cousins," Ahdaf said. "She asks a lot of questions, so don't talk to her. In fact, don't let anybody see you."

"Don't you have any food?" Özan complained, until he opened the refrigerator and exclaimed, "Cookies!"

"There's also *helva*." Ahdaf took it out of the otherwise empty refrigerator and unwrapped it. "I don't keep food around because of bugs. You two finish this and I'll go to the market after I return the van. Is there anything special you'd like?"

Serhan, zipping up, grinned. "Yeah, two women. Find a short one for Özan!"

It took Ahdaf almost an hour to drive the few short blocks to the alley that led to the mosque. Rush-hour traffic verged on chaotic as everyone competed for every opportunity to edge forward. He turned on the radio news, and after an update on the traffic he was stuck in, the news reporter came back on:

"Welcome back to *News Now*. It's the top of the hour, and we have an update on the events in Assos. Authorities have identified the anonymous man killed there two nights ago. Once his family is notified, they will release his name to the public."

Ahdaf flicked off the radio and turned into the alley. He stopped alongside the door in the hedge. He was about to remove the key from the ignition when he realized he didn't want to hand it to Malik – because he didn't want to see him. Though the two terrorists were camped out in his apartment, he wanted Malik to know they weren't his problem, but *Malik's* problem. To start with, he wasn't driving them to Raqqa. He left the key in the ignition, signaling his non-intention.

He retreated on foot down the alley, thinking of Yasmin, who was soon to be officially told – if she hadn't been already – that her husband was dead. When he reached the sidewalk, he glanced back over his shoulder. Malik stood next to the van, shaking his head disapprovingly. Ahdaf ducked out of sight and turned at the next corner to take less polluted neighborhood streets. He stopped at a juice stand where the vendor had stacked pomegranates into a tall mound and drank a long glass of their tart juice. At a corner, the whiff of sizzling kebabs and fries, as well as his growling stomach, convinced him to stop and eat. How many hours and missed meals had it been since he'd had real food? He ate double portions of everything.

As he was finishing, his telephone pinged. A message from Selim: I KNOW MALIK'S TWO PASSENGERS HAVE MOVED TO YOUR APARTMENT. MEET ME IN ONE HOUR AT EMINÖNÜ.

He decided to walk to the docks instead of taking the tram. It felt good to move, and the morning air was fresh. He tried not to dwell on his circumstances or Malik's unveiled threat. If it were true that Sadiq had confessed to their sexual relationship, no matter how tame, it was tantamount to a death sentence. To make such a confession, Sadiq's torture must have been horrendous. Or perhaps not, Ahdaf thought, because when had there been time to torture him? More likely, on the rooftop, he'd been offered a reprieve to name names and then was executed anyway. Distracted by his thoughts, Ahdaf followed an old woman who was crossing a street. Suddenly a car bounded over the hill, heading for them. He grabbed the woman to pull her out of the way. The driver of the car braked hard, but still sideswiped him and continued without stopping. It took Ahdaf a moment to realize he was unhurt, and so was the woman. She was already shuffling away as if nothing had happened.

Shaken by the close call, Ahdaf stopped at a stall for tea. When he reached for his wallet to pay, it was gone. He patted all his pockets; perhaps he'd misplaced it? But no, it was missing.

179

"Ah fuck!" he exclaimed. "I've been pickpocketed!" The vendor saw his distressed expression. "Happens a lot around here," he said. "Enjoy your tea. It's on me."

Ahdaf took a couple of sips before resting his elbows on the counter to cradle his head in his hands. What was he going to do? He needed his identity card for almost every transaction he made. Without his ID and bank cards, how could he get money? Who else but the old woman could have pickpocketed him? It was only then that he realized that the whole thing had been a setup. She'd seen him coming down the sidewalk, signaled the car driver, and, feigning feebleness, had lured Ahdaf into the road to help her, knowing the car would create a distraction and off she'd go with his wallet. He couldn't even be sure it had in fact been an old woman and not a teenage boy in disguise; he hadn't seen her face.

He was bemoaning his stupidity when he felt a tap, low on his back. He swung around to find a young boy, maybe five years old, looking up at him with solemn brown eyes. The kid held out his wallet. "Mister, you dropped this." As soon as Ahdaf took it, the boy dashed off.

"Hey!" Ahdaf shouted after him.

The kid disappeared into an alley.

He checked his wallet. Only the money was missing. His ID and bank cards were still there.

Ahdaf emerged from the crowded narrow streets draining into Eminönü Square, made even narrower by shopkeepers who appropriated the sidewalks for their display cases, lining up racks of clothes or piling high every sort of household product. He angled across the broad plaza, then waited patiently, along with dozens of others, for a tram to pass before crossing its tracks.

The docks had their own frenzy created by passengers hurrying to catch the ferries and boat taxis serving the neighborhoods strung along the Bosporus. He didn't spot Selim anywhere, and went to the newsstand. Under a photograph of the burning Spartacus Club read the headline: ISIS CLAIMS RESPONSIBILITY FOR ATHENS ATTACK. It was confirmed, then; the men – the butchers – in his apartment *were* ISIS. It had never been stated outright.

He stepped closer to read the finer print: "The American consulate in Istanbul confirms that –" The next line disappeared under the fold. He needed to flip the paper to finish the sentence. That's all he wanted, not more than the end of the sentence. He glanced at the news vendor, who rubbed his thumb and forefinger together. His meaning was clear: reading above the fold was free; reading below it meant he had to buy the paper. That morning, robbed of his money, Ahdaf couldn't have bought the newspaper even if he'd wanted to. He reread what was visible to him and heard over his shoulder, "The American consulate in Istanbul confirms that ISIS has claimed responsibility for the attack on the gay club in Athens."

He turned to Selim. "Do you always memorize the news?"

"I wrote the press release. Come, we have a lot to talk about. I know a place off the square."

Ahdaf shrugged. "Why not? Except I don't have any money. I was pickpocketed."

"Don't worry. Uncle Sam can pay for it."

"Uncle Sam?"

"It's an American expression. Tell me about the pickpocket."

As they crossed back over the tram tracks Ahdaf told Selim about the old woman and the car that nearly rammed them, which he now realized was all one cunning pickpocketing trick. The woman might not have been old, and was probably the mother of the kid who came back with his wallet, minus only the money.

"Sounds like they were refugees to me," Selim said. "So many of them are desperate. They need cash to survive, not your ID or bank card."

"I'm a refugee, too," Ahdaf reminded him.

"You have to admit, the fact he brought it back was a friendly gesture."

"I'll think about that."

"Let's go this way," Selim suggested, and led them to the same café where he'd seen the news broadcast in which Derya first called Meryem "the Syrian *Pietà*." Could that really have been only four days earlier?

The waiter came over, and they ordered Turkish coffees. "Medium sweet," they said at the same time, and the waiter left them.

"What's Malik's plan?" Selim asked.

"He wants them to go to Raqqa, but since you know they're at my place, why not arrest them?"

"I haven't discussed it with my counterparts yet, but I know what they'll say. Only a couple of days ago, the ÖKK botched a raid on an ISIS cell and three buildings burned down, killing 18 people."

"I saw a report about it. Originally, they were estimating a dozen killed."

"Then you understand why they won't risk another raid in an apartment building."

"Can't you tell everybody to leave first?"

"You don't think Serhan and Özan will notice and start shooting everyone and everything?"

"What am I supposed to do?" Ahdaf asked. It was more complaint than question.

"How's Malik planning to send them to Raqqa?"

"He wants me to drive them."

"Then that's what you'll do."

"Are you crazy? I'm finished. I'm not going to Raqqa. ISIS is looking for me."

"They've already found you in Istanbul."

Ahdaf put up his hands, dismissing the whole idea. "I'm not going to Raqqa."

"You won't have to. You'll drive them into a trap."

"What trap?"

"I'm not sure yet. Malik must make his plans first. Killing those policemen made his job harder. There's a massive manhunt, and no one wants to be accidentally exposed, especially when they realize that the Athens terrorists are somewhere loose in Turkey – and they're going to know that today. The forensics on the bullets in Athens and Assos match the same rifle."

Ahdaf snorted. "I could have told you that."

"The authorities need evidence. Listen, I don't want you to be afraid. They're under constant surveillance. They can't take a step outside without being reported."

"Yeah, but I'm going to be *inside* with them."

Selim pulled out his wallet and handed Ahdaf a wad of money. "Buy enough food for them for another day."

"I have to stay with them another day?"

"You only have to take them the food. Are they in direct contact with Malik?"

"They probably could be, but haven't been as far as I know."

"Good, tell them not to be, because it's a given that his line is monitored. Tell them you have another operation and you might be gone all night. Imply it's Malik's operation. Then leave before they have time to think about it."

"Why?"

"Serhan might decide to hold you hostage."

"Why?"

"That's their mentality."

Ahdaf exhaled a long breath. "And I'm not supposed to be scared?"

From the sidewalk, Ahdaf stared up at his apartment window. The reflection of the afternoon sun made it impossible to see anything inside. With a deepening sense of dread, he entered his building and immediately heard a blaring news broadcast in Arabic all the way to the front door. Carrying a bag of food in each hand, he climbed the stairs, hearing the yapping of Madame Darton's dog grow louder. As he suspected, Madame Darton had been watching for him, and she swung open her door as he arrived at precisely the last step leading to their shared landing. Before she could complain about the noise, he said, "Something smells delicious!"

She smiled begrudgingly at the compliment. "Roast chicken," she said.

Ahdaf winced at an especially loud sound coming from his apartment. "I'm sorry for the noise. Unfortunately, one of my cousins is almost deaf. He must be told when something's too loud."

"I knocked and told them it was too loud."

"They didn't turn it down?"

"The big one threatened my Fifi!"

"Why?"

"Because she was barking and he couldn't hear the radio!" She picked up the dog, which fell silent in her arms.

Ahdaf, too, had had menacing thoughts about the annoying dog, but instead of sharing them, he simply said, "Try to keep Fifi quiet, and I'll turn down the volume on their cell phones. They're watching the news, not listening to it."

"Well, not everybody wants to listen to it!" Madame Darton harrumphed, and disappeared into her apartment.

Ahdaf knocked on his door to alert them that he was there. Then he unlocked it, but as soon as he cracked the door open, he heard Serhan leap for his rifle. "It's me! It's Ahdaf!" he shouted and opened the door wider.

Serhan held his rifle, ready to shoot him.

"I brought some food," he told them.

"Food!" Özan cried, and grabbed the sack of groceries. "What is there?"

"And turn this down!" Ahdaf reached for a cell phone perched on the counter and lowered its volume. "You can hear it all over the building!"

"It's because of that bitch's dog across the hall," Serhan said. "We couldn't hear the news because it's barking all the time."

Özan began stacking things on the table. "Hummus and bread! Olives! *Helva!*" He broke off a chunk and scarfed it down.

"You don't want to draw attention to yourselves," Ahdaf reminded them. "Keep the noise down."

Serhan tore off a piece of flat bread and dragged it through the hummus. "Where the fuck have you been?"

"Taking the van back. Shopping for food. I confess, I stopped for a coffee."

"There's even meat!" Özan exclaimed, and broke open a package of sandwich rounds.

"Don't eat everything all at once," Ahdaf cautioned them. "It might have to last another day."

"Why? What's going on?" asked Serhan.

"I'm waiting for instructions from Malik. It's his operation."

Outside, the call to prayer started. Özan continued eating, unfazed, while Serhan took a moment to cup his hands and bow a couple of times while moving his lips in a quick prayer. He finished by whacking Özan on the shoulder. "Don't eat everything!" he said.

Özan grabbed a handful of olives and stepped aside where he could spit the pits into the sink. Serhan, claiming his share of the food, told Ahdaf, "Call Malik. Ask what's the plan."

"I can't use the telephone."

"Why?"

"You don't think every call to a mosque is intercepted by some-one? The CIA or MIT?"

From the cell phone on the counter, they heard the news chan-nel's familiar chime, announcing breaking news.

"We have news that's just come in about the recent events in Assos," a news anchor said.

Ahdaf propped up Özan's phone so they could all watch.

"Forensic experts now confirm that bullet casings retrieved from last week's terrorist attack in Athens match the bullet cas-ings retrieved from Big Rocks Beach, just north of Assos. The same weapon was used in both attacks. The terrorists are as-sumed to be in Turkey."

"Fuck!" Serhan exclaimed.

"The public should be vigilant. These men – probably two of them – are extremely dangerous. Officials expect to be able to confirm their identities soon."

"Fuck! They already know who we are!"

"Shhh …" Ahdaf cautioned. "People might hear you."

"We gotta have a plan."

"I'll go talk to Malik. We usually meet at prayers, and he'll be expecting me."

Ahdaf shouldered his daypack and was ready to leave when Serhan flattened his palm on the door and slammed it shut. "How do we know you're coming back?" he asked.

"Why wouldn't I?"

"You left all day today."

"I was gone three and a half hours, and if Malik offers, I'll sleep at the mosque tonight. How can we all sleep here? I'll call to let you know what's happening. My guess is that he wants me to drive you to Raqqa. What's your mobile number?"

As Ahdaf was tapping Özan's number into his phone, Serhan

moved his body in front of the door. "You're not fucking going anywhere."

Unexpectedly, there came a knock. "*Coucou*," Madame Darton called from the other side. "I have a surprise for you!"

The terrorists glanced from one to the other.

"It might be a roasted chicken," Ahdaf tempted them. "I smelled it coming up the stairs."

"A chicken!" Özan said, rubbing his hands together.

"I have to answer the door, or she'll become suspicious. In fact, you both should go into the bathroom so she doesn't recognize you now that your pictures are all over the news."

"Fucking bitch and her dog," Serhan muttered. "Come on, Özan."

They closed themselves in the bathroom, and Ahdaf opened the door.

"I had an extra chicken, so I roasted both!" Madame Darton exclaimed. "Where are your cousins?"

"In the bathroom."

"Together?"

"The deaf one is afraid to be alone."

She looked puzzled. "Because he's deaf?"

"He had a troubled childhood. Here, let me take that from you."

He set the tray with the perfectly browned, scrumptious chicken on the counter. This was his chance to go, but he couldn't pass such temptation. "Wait! I'll test it," he cried. As fast as he could, he tore off a leg. "Let's go," he said.

"Go?" she said.

"I'll walk you home."

"But I live –"

"I know, but a gentleman always walks a lady home."

"*Quelle gentillesse!*"

"I don't know what that means, but it sounds nice," he said, shuffling her out the door and shutting it. Across the landing, Fifi sniffed under the door and growled.

"You haven't tried my chicken yet!" Madame Darton protested.

"That's easy to fix," Ahdaf said, and he took a big bite. His eyes widened with pleasure.

"Is it good?" she asked.

"*Quelle gentillesse!*" he replied and bounded down the steps.

He'd devoured the drumstick by the time he reached the next corner. All the way there, he felt Serhan's eyes on his back, following him like a moving target. He wanted to run out of sight, but he forced himself to approach the corner nonchalantly, even raising an arm to greet the waiter at the corner restaurant. He noticed Suleiman at a shaded table and was relieved to see a less threatening face. The older man stood up as he passed. As Ahdaf rounded the corner, he glimpsed the beige kaftan following him. With no reason to hurry, he slowed his pace, and Suleiman caught up with him just short of the gate of the mosque. Under his breath, Ahdaf asked, "Why are you following me?"

"If I don't, Malik won't believe anything I tell him. Sometimes I think he might have someone following *me* just to verify what I do tell him."

"Let him know I'm here."

Ahdaf headed for the ablutions wall while Suleiman disappeared into the *medrese*. The long benches were virtually empty. He sat on one and pulled off his shoes. Normally he wore sandals; they were far more convenient than laced shoes, given how many times a day he was obliged to remove them. He'd worn sturdier shoes for the operation in Assos, and was glad he had, though they did make his feet sweaty. Pulling off his socks, he wiggled his toes as the cool water trickled between them. It could have been a meditative moment if he hadn't had so many worries, chief among them meeting with Malik in a few minutes. He expected to be ordered to drive the terrorists to Raqqa, which would be nothing short of a suicide mission. If Serhan didn't kill him on a whim, Ahdaf envisioned being in the crossfire when they were finally caught, because – of course – Serhan would never surrender.

His worries were interrupted when his phone beeped. He pulled it from his daypack. Kalam had sent a message: IF YOU'RE READING THIS, ALHAMDULILLAH YOU SURVIVED THE ATTACK ON THE BEACH. CAPTAIN G NEEDS A MECHANIC. GUESS WHO HE HIRED FOR A WEEK! COME JOIN ME! WE'LL MAKE A HOLIDAY IN GREECE BEFORE WE TRAVEL NORTH TOGETHER. I MISS OUR "SPECIAL" FRIENDSHIP!

Ahdaf choked up at Kalam's desire to be together. He longed for the fair-haired youth, too; and if longing was the same as love, then he supposed he was in love. A holiday in Greece! Would he ever feel that carefree again? When he imagined them side by side on a beach, their hands casually resting on each other's backs, he couldn't hold back tears for the life withheld from them by the mad, unholy holy men prepared to execute them for a different affection. He let the tears run down his face until he glimpsed Malik approaching. He leaned into the spigot and splashed his tears away, listening to the scrawny man coming closer, his lame foot scraping over the paving stones like an errant lisp.

They exchanged the perfunctory greetings before Malik sat on the bench next to him. He didn't bother to kick off his sandals. "What's the situation at your apartment?" he asked.

Ahdaf grunted. "What do you think? They both stink. Özan isn't smart enough to wipe his ass, and Serhan is a lunatic."

"That's why he was chosen for the Athens operation."

"Did you help plan that attack?"

"I knew about it. If they survived, one escape route was to come to Turkey, where I could help them."

"When they got to Istanbul, what was your plan?"

"After what happened in Assos, it doesn't matter. Everyone is

189

too nervous. I had a driver to take them to Raqqa, but now he refuses."

"I'm sure you can find someone else."

"Have you heard the news that now the police know – the whole world knows – that they're responsible for what happened in both Athens and Assos?"

Ahdaf spread his hands in a shrug. "Yeah, I heard it. That doesn't change anything for me."

"Everybody knows they're in Turkey, and every Turk is looking for them," Malik replied, trembling in anger at Ahdaf's indifference. "You must drive them to Raqqa. Tonight! Before they have time to organize roadblocks."

"Tonight?" Ahdaf looked at Malik as if he were crazy. "I've hardly slept in two days."

"You'll do what I want or you know what will happen," Malik threatened.

"How do you expect me to drive three days to Raqqa?"

"You can stop on the way."

"I won't last until tonight. Besides, I can only take them to the border. It's too dangerous to drive in Syria with Turkish plates. And I don't have a driver's license! Someone else needs to take them to the border, and then a second driver from there to Raqqa."

"Can you arrange that?" Malik asked.

"I can try," Ahdaf answered, "but people are going to be suspicious."

"What do you suggest?" Malik asked.

For the first time, it occurred to Ahdaf: "Send them back to Greece."

"Back to Greece?"

"No one's looking for them there," Ahdaf improvised. "Greece is the last place anyone expects them to be, as there's proof they're already in Turkey. Everyone expects them to run back to Raqqa."

"You can arrange this?" Malik asked.

"Serhan and Özan thought the captain who brought them from Greece was reliable, so they're more likely to agree to go back if he takes them. Hopefully they have a contact for him. I'll try for tomorrow night. I'll need money for him, gas and food expenses, maybe some bribes – whatever comes up."

"I'll go to the bank now," Malik said, relieved that his problem might be easily resolved.

"The banks are already closed," Ahdaf reminded him, "and it's more than you can take from a money machine."

"I'll go tomorrow. How much?"

"I know the captain will want 10,000 euros for each man."

Malik paled. "Ten thousand euros for each of them?"

"That's what I've heard quoted for a private crossing," Ahdaf replied. "Why? Is the money going to be a problem?"

"It won't be a problem," Malik answered.

"I'll telephone Serhan to let him know the plan. I won't go back to my apartment except to pick them up."

"Where will you go?"

"Somewhere to sleep. Your man following me will know."

"When will I know what you've arranged?"

"I'm not promising that I *can* arrange anything, but let's plan on it happening and be ready. I'll come at noon tomorrow for the van and money, unless you hear something different from me."

Ahdaf pulled on his socks and shoes, and both men stood up. "Please make sure the van has a full tank of gas," he said.

"Of course."

"And park it so I can pull out without backing out."

"Of course."

The men touched their hearts, and Ahdaf walked off. As he did, he feigned confidence that he didn't feel. His gut was so knotted with tension he wanted to throw up. He had just concocted a scheme, completely clueless as to whether he could pull it off.

Outside the mosque gate, Ahdaf strode down the sidewalk, intent on putting some distance between himself and Malik. He sighed with relief when he turned a corner; it meant the mousy man couldn't summon him back and couldn't change their new plan, no matter how half-baked it sounded. Ahdaf's thoughts turned to what needed to be done to put it into motion. Whom to contact? Selim. Serhan and Özan. But Kalam was first. Nothing was going to happen without Captain G's agreement. He typed a message as he walked: IS CAPTAIN G INTERESTED IN A PRIVATE TRANSFER FROM ASSOS TO GREECE? 2 PASSENGERS. NO PROBLEMS LIKE LAST TIME. TOMORROW AT SUNSET? HOW MUCH?

Next was Serhan. He called Özan's number and Serhan answered. "Who is this?"

"Ahdaf."

"What's the plan?"

"You're going back to Greece."

"What?"

"Malik decided. He says it's the last place they'll be looking for you."

"Fuck him. We're going to Raqqa."

Ahdaf was prepared for his reaction. "And risk roadblocks? Police stopping you, who knows how many times? You'll be caught for sure."

Serhan seemed to be weighing these points. "Once we're in Greece, what then?" he asked.

"Malik has it all worked out. We have sympathizers who'll meet your boat and hide you. In a week or so, your cell in Raqqa will announce that the Athens heroes have returned, and the manhunt will be called off. In the meantime, Malik will have everything arranged for you to go to Raqqa: a boat back to Assos, and from there, drivers, safe places to stop, and a switch of cars at the Syrian border."

"I still don't like it," Serhan said, grumpy.

"Think of it as a holiday where women wear bikinis, not burqas. We're still working out the details, but you should be ready to leave by noon tomorrow. I'll confirm the time later. I'll telephone when I'm approaching the apartment. You come down and get in the van. And hide your rifle!"

"Where are you going?"

"To find a place to sleep."

"You can sleep here."

"No, I can't. I haven't slept in almost two days. I need a whole day of it to catch up."

"We need more food," Serhan complained. "Özan's eaten most of it."

"I'll bring more tomorrow. You don't go outside for any reason."

Ahdaf's hand was shaking when he disconnected, but he also felt a newfound sense of control over the situation. Serhan couldn't threaten him with his rifle over the phone, and he'd overridden Serhan's complaints about the plan he'd concocted on the spot. He could barely believe his own daring lies about the arrangements Malik had already "made" for them to get from Greece to Raqqa.

He'd been walking as he talked on his phone, and hardly noticed when he arrived at the Tropicana Hotel. He needed a room, but hated spending money when he had his own apartment. Though, when he thought about it, he was really spending Selim's money. He ran through his options again for free places to sleep and came up with nothing more feasible than a park bench, which he knew was dangerous. The other option was to curl up in a corner of the mosque, but then he risked encountering Malik, which he wanted to avoid. All in all, the Tropicana was his best choice.

Ahdaf pressed the buzzer and looked up at a surveillance camera, making it easier for Fatih to recognize him. When he was buzzed in, he stepped into the long hallway flanked in swimming trunks. He fingered a silky pair of black trunks and removed them from their hook. When he reached the counter, Fatih flicked the switch on a toy hula doll, dressed in a grass skirt with coconut shells over her breasts, that rotated her hips while singing a tinny *luau* song.

Ahdaf chuckled. "Where the heck did you find that in Istanbul?"

"I didn't. People bring me things. I guess you can say I have a collection."

"Or a reputation!"

Fatih flicked the switch to silence the toy. "Those are for guests," he said, indicating the trunks in Ahdaf's hand. "Most need something that can pass as clean underwear."

"Then I qualify on both counts. That is, if you have a room tonight."

"*You* need a room tonight?"

"Yep. I'm letting my cousins use my apartment."

"Shouldn't they be the ones staying in a hotel room?"

Ahdaf shrugged. "In a fair world, yes. But, you know, family obligations. How much?"

"One night?"

"That's all I need."

"It's free. A bonus for bringing me business. Plus, I have empty rooms."

"Why empty rooms?"

"Ebb and flow." Fatih handed him a key. "3L. Go take a shower. You need one. And here, you need this too." Fatih handed him a cellophane-wrapped toothbrush with a miniature toothpaste tube. "I usually sell these."

"I already have my own."

"Toothpaste too?"

"Always."

"Then go use it and get some sleep."

Ahdaf climbed the stairs to his room, knowing what to expect as soon as he turned on the light: a scramble of cockroaches scurrying into shadows and cracks. Most would stay hidden as long as the light was on. He shut the door and immediately called Selim's message machine. "It's urgent, but I'm not in immediate danger," he said and hung up.

The phone rang a moment later. "Hello," he answered.

"It's Selim. What's urgent?"

Ahdaf told him of Malik's "request" to drive the two men to Raqqa, and how he'd convinced him of the dangers of a full-scale manhunt now that it had been confirmed that the attackers in Athens and Assos were the same men. "Instead, I convinced him to send them back to Greece."

"*Greece?*" Selim sounded incredulous.

Ahdaf explained his thinking: basically, it was the last place anybody would be looking for them, and it relieved him of a dangerous journey into Syria that he doubted he'd survive. "Malik also threatened me again," he concluded.

"Don't worry about Malik. He's under surveillance, too. He'd be stopped if he tried to harm you."

Ahdaf exhaled gratefully. "That's good to know."

"When's the return to Greece going to happen?"

"Arrangements have not been made yet, but in theory we leave tomorrow at noon to arrive in Assos just before sunset."

"Do they agree with the plan?"

"Not exactly. Serhan still wants to go to Raqqa, but understands his lack of options."

"How will they make the crossing?"

"Kalam, the guy who escaped with the Greek fisherman, is still with him. I can contact the Greek through him. If he won't help,

195

I don't know. You mentioned a trap, so maybe we don't actually need a boat."

"Let's keep our options open. The boat might be part of a trap. Let me talk it around. Can you meet later?"

"I need some sleep," Ahdaf replied and checked the time. "Is 11 too late for you?"

When his alarm rang three hours later, Ahdaf jerked awake, disoriented until he recalled why he was at the Tropicana. He quickly ticked off the jumble of things he had to sort out, but a shower was first. The bathtub's plug was missing; he searched for a way to stop the water from running into the open drain, causing the cockroaches to stream out. With nothing else to use, he plugged it with his boxers and kept his foot on them while he showered and brushed his teeth. When the water reached his ankles, he got out, and his underwear stayed in place.

Getting dressed, he pulled on his newly acquired swimsuit for underwear; but its mesh lining was constricting, so he ripped it out, converting the nylon trunks to silky boxers. He'd never worn anything so sensuous, and shook his hips to make his cock slide back and forth across the slick material. He was still partially aroused when he walked out of the slum hotel 10 minutes later.

He longed for Kalam at that moment – not for sex, but for the friendship he knew they could have. Of course, he wanted intimacy, too. Since their night together, he'd thought so many times about running his hand through that silky hair on his chest and legs. Maybe he *should* go to Greece, Ahdaf suddenly thought, and see what might develop between him and the fair-haired Kalam. Get away from Malik and his threats. Stop what had become a crazy life of secrets and danger. He was headed for a rendezvous with a CIA agent, and had terrorists holed up in his apartment!

How insane was that?

Those were his thoughts as he approached the big window of Leyla's Cafe. Inside, it was crowded. She was circulating between tables, delivering orders and taking new ones. Selim sat alone at the cowboy bar. Ahdaf was ready to go in when his phone beeped. It was a message from Kalam: CAPTAIN G IS GOOD FOR JOURNEY BUT FOR PICKUP DAY AFTER TOMORROW AT DAWN. 10K EACH PASSENGER. BRING A TOOTHBRUSH IN CASE YOU CHANGE YOUR MIND!

Whew, Ahdaf thought, relieved that he could report a firm plan to Malik to return the two terrorists to Greece. He went inside and wound through the tables to join Selim at the bar.

"Isn't it kind of crazy that we meet in public?" Ahdaf wondered aloud.

"Why?" Selim asked. "Meeting with informants is an open secret in this town. What *is* secret is what we talk about."

Leyla squeezed her way back behind the bar. "What's also not a secret is that I'm old and fat!" she said.

"Nobody but a pretzel can get behind your bar," Selim replied. "Why don't you widen it 10 centimeters?"

"Because the day I get stuck, I'm retiring, and I don't want to be 10 centimeters thicker when I do."

"And you're not old," Ahdaf muttered.

Leyla pinched his chin. "Someone wants his beer."

She pulled a bottle from the refrigerator, uncapped it, and pushed it toward him. She put another two bottles on a tray and then restocked the cooler.

"You need a bigger refrigerator," Ahdaf said.

"I'll get one when I get bigger tips," she retorted.

They sipped their beers while watching Leyla drop sugar cubes into a dozen small glasses and fill them with tea from a simmering kettle. She left the tray on the bar and retrieved it after squeezing around its end.

When she moved out of earshot, Ahdaf said, "I just received a message. Captain G says okay, except he wants the pickup to be at dawn the day after tomorrow."

"Captain G?"

Ahdaf shrugged. "It's what Kalam calls him. He's the Greek fisherman who brought Serhan and Özan. He wants 10,000 euros for each passenger."

"That can be managed."

"What's your plan?"

"You just made it easier."

"How?"

"You'll leave late at night, not noon. It's easier to set a trap in the dark."

Selim proceeded to describe his plan. Ahdaf would leave Istanbul, crossing the Şehitler Bridge and driving south through Üsküdar, where he'd pick up the national road in the direction of Ankara. "Right after the third toll station, the road splits: Ankara one way, the Osmangazi Bridge and Assos the other."

"What if Serhan puts a gun to my head and forces me to drive them to Raqqa?"

"Agree to it to keep him calm. The trap will be at the toll station before the split."

"Why wait until the third station? Why not the first?"

"Serhan will be edgy when you start," Selim explained. "We want him to get complacent about you and the toll stops. Remember, at all the tollbooths, pull into the far-right lane. It'll be the only one that takes a bank card."

"What's the trap?"

As Selim described it, Ahdaf sensed he was envisioning how everything would play out and felt his confidence growing that his plan would work. As he concluded, he added, "You need to wear a white polo shirt."

"Why?"

"It'll be night, and in white you can be seen. Everyone will have orders not to shoot the guy in the white shirt."

"That's reassuring."

"You'll be fine."

"I don't have a white polo shirt."

"I brought you one." Selim picked up a sack on the floor.

"You bought me a shirt?" Ahdaf asked as he pulled it out.

"The first time we met, didn't you say you needed a third shirt?"

"*You* said I needed a third shirt."

Selim shrugged. "Now you have one."

"Actually, it's now my second shirt. Özan pinched my only clean one. How'd you know my size?"

"I'm a large. I figured you're a medium. Try it on."

"Right here?"

"Go in the back."

Ahdaf disappeared down a grubby hall that ended at a smudged sink with a yellowing mirror over it. To each side were toilets behind sagging doors. He took off his shirt and was looking for a clean spot to put it down when Leyla stepped out of the women's WC.

"I'll hold it," she said in her smokey voice, and took it from him. She surprised him by running her other hand through the hair on his chest. "I like a man with a hairy chest, but not a hairy body."

Ahdaf felt himself blushing. "I don't have a hairy body," he stammered.

"I noticed." She stepped around him to reach the sink and wash her hands.

He pulled on the white polo. Watching him in the mirror, she said, "It looks good on you." Drying her hands with a paper towel, she faced him and asked, "You've never been with a woman, have you?"

He wasn't expecting the question. "Maybe," he responded.

She laughed. "Maybe? You don't remember?"

"I've been with a woman, but not in the circumstances you're suggesting."

"In what circumstances, then?"

"Not with a woman like you, is what I'm trying to say."

"Of course not like me. No one is like Leyla." She brushed the chest hairs sticking out of his new collar and made her way back to the café.

Leyla had often flirted with him, but never so boldly, and never more than jokingly, though what had just transpired wasn't funny. It left him equally flustered and flattered. He looked at himself in the mirror. The spongy cloth of the new shirt clung like a loose glove to his body, but not so loose that it concealed his trim build. He rinsed his face and ran wet fingers through his black curls to separate them. He wanted to look good wearing Selim's new shirt. He balled up his old one and went back to the café.

Selim was squashed into the corner of the short bar. Three young Turks now claimed it, engrossed in their cell phones while charging them. At first, Ahdaf thought they must be playing a game between themselves, because they shouted excitedly or slapped their foreheads at the same time, until he realized they were watching the same soccer match. Someone scored, and they high-fived each other as he squeezed up to the bar beside Selim.

"Looks like the shirt fits nicely," the CIA man remarked.

"It looks okay?"

"White's a good color for you."

"Technically, white's not a color," Ahdaf replied. "I was taught that in school."

"Technically, you're right. It's still a good color for you." Selim tipped his head in the direction of the three guys concentrating on their phones.

"I think we should go someplace else, but first I need about an hour to put some things into motion now that we have a day and time for the transaction. Can we meet at Galata Tower? I'll be in that area."

"Sure."

"I'll leave first," Selim said. "We shouldn't leave together, and you still have some beer." He shook Ahdaf's hand and headed for the door.

Ahdaf decided to walk to Galata Tower to save the tram fare, which was mere *liras*, but in his circumstances, everything added up. Walking gave him time to think, too. Physically, he walked at his normal pace; mentally, he was racing. Kalam's message confirming that Captain G had agreed to his plan had set into motion what had seemed implausible – that the terrorists would return to Greece – though of course, ultimately, they wouldn't.

He walked the last block leading to the square in which Galata Tower stood. Its bright shops selling souvenirs, leather bags, and cheap jewelry distracted him from his worrisome thoughts. He stopped at a window to admire a whole collection of sport shoes with brand names that had only been available in Raqqa on the black market; here, it seemed, every brand was displayed in a single shop window.

The square itself had an altogether different atmosphere from the commercial street. The circular tower was illuminated by hazy lights, not the bright lights of shop windows, which added a touch of romance to everyone's evening. Even noisy tourist groups grew quieter as they approached the tower. Ahdaf had passed it a few times, usually on his way to meet a client, and there was always a rambling line of people waiting to go to the top for its panoramic view of the city.

"Beautiful, isn't it?" Selim said over his shoulder.

Ahdaf turned. "It's very special."

"Have you been to the top?"

"Once. My clients end up all over the city, so I took a map up to try to sort out how the neighborhoods fit together."

"Did you? Sort it out, I mean."

"Are you kidding? Istanbul must have a thousand neighborhoods."

"This is one of the nicer ones. I also happen to live nearby. I have beer and a better view than from here, if you don't mind a short climb."

"Sure," Ahdaf replied, not exactly sure what he'd agreed to. It smacked of the sort of encounter he'd been fantasizing about since their awkward moment in the tiled hammam. He'd wanted something to happen, and perhaps it just had.

The moment Selim turned the key in his door, Ahdaf realized that he'd never been in a Westerner's apartment before. He'd only seen them in movies. He followed the CIA man into an expansive living room, vibrant with a mixture of color photographs and paintings. "Let me show you the view," he said, and slid open a glass door to reveal the city, so vast that its carpet of lights rolled over the horizon in a haze.

"It's amazing," Ahdaf murmured, taking it all in.

"That's true, it's amazing," Selim replied. "I offered you a beer, but I also have wine."

"I haven't had wine since I left home."

"Why not? Wine's sold in the shops."

"Beer is less expensive."

"So then it's wine?"

"Why not? *Haram* is *haram*, right? Forbidden is forbidden, like too many things."

"I agree that too much is forbidden. I'll be right back." Selim disappeared into the kitchen.

Ahdaf returned his gaze to the city displayed before him. It was a wonder that he'd learned to navigate any part of that urban sea to survive. He'd sorted out transportation, walking routes, and where to buy food and sundries. He'd even discovered a special butcher shop for rabbits, feeling like a stone age hunter-gatherer when he carried home their skinned carcasses.

Selim rejoined him on the balcony. "I hope white's okay," he said, and handed him a glass of wine. "You look serious."

"Apparently that's how I look when I'm thinking. So Leyla tells me."

"Want to share your thoughts?"

"I was thinking about how I know a butcher somewhere out there who sells the best rabbit. They're so good, even my mother would approve, and it's her favorite dish. Now that I see just how big Istanbul is, it's a wonder I can find my way back to his shop, or back home from it. It's a wonder anyone manages in such a huge city."

"Most people rarely leave their neighborhoods," Selim said, and raised his glass. "Cheers."

They touched glasses and sipped.

"Hmmm … that's better than I remember," Ahdaf murmured.

"It's a sauvignon blanc from New Zealand. I doubt if they had much of that in Raqqa even before ISIS showed up."

"It's nice."

"Before it gets too nice, let's go over some details of the final plan in case you have any questions. Nothing's really changed from the original idea except the pickup in Assos is at dawn not dusk. The ÖKK's happy with that change. They prefer the operation take place at night."

"In their plan, what happens to me?" asked Ahdaf.

"If all goes well, you'll be the hero of the story. You risked your life driving two international terrorists into a trap."

"And if it doesn't all go well?"

"At least you tried."

"Hero or not, I'd rather not be in the story."

"You're already in it. You might as well be its hero. The fact that it'll be midnight at the toll station, not midday, is good. You can hide a lot in the dark. Soldiers, equipment, props, whatever. If one or two spotlights aren't working, who knows any particular tollbooth well enough to notice? At night, from the back of a van, what are Serhan and Özan going to see? Plus, they don't want to be seen, either. They aren't going to be pressing their noses to the windows for the scenery."

"Okay, I'm convinced," Ahdaf said.

"Convinced of what?"

"That it's going to be dangerous."

"I have all the bases covered," Selim assured him.

"What's that mean?"

"It's an English expression for having a plan for every contingency."

"I'll try to remember that if I ever have a chance to teach English again."

"You'll teach English again."

"I should contact Kalam and tell him the Greek fisherman doesn't need to come."

"Let's keep things as planned, in case something changes," Selim replied.

"Are you covering your bases again?"

Selim smiled. "That's right. Another glass of wine?"

"Yes, please. It's nice. Is it okay if I use your toilet?"

"Of course." Selim waved him down the hall. "It's on the left."

On his way, Ahdaf paused to look at the photographs displayed on the hallway's walls. They were bold, both color and black-and-white, with no particular theme other than capturing moments of great emotion or beauty.

Ahdaf found the bathroom, used the toilet, and at the sink used a dab of Selim's toothpaste to freshen his breath. He wasn't sure where things were headed, but he hoped something might happen between them. Even the possibility of it made him feel bolder, ready to make the first move if Selim didn't – although, he reminded himself, they'd both made first moves in the tiled hammam until Selim stopped them. Would he stop them again?

He opened the bathroom door to find Selim holding their glasses. "I thought I'd come find you," he said and handed him one.

"Thanks. Did you take these photographs?" Ahdaf asked.

"I wish. I'd be famous if I'd shot even one of them. I considered becoming a photographer, but life took me on a different path. I'm only a collector."

"They're great."

"Mine are in the bedroom. Do you want to see them?"

"Sure."

As soon as Ahdaf stepped into the bedroom, he stopped, astonished, craning his neck in every direction to take it all in. A chain hanging from the center of a high cathedral ceiling held aloft a platform bed by ropes tied to its four corners. Hundreds of black-and-white photos of people from around the world, indigenous and contemporary, had been copied onto sheets of wallpaper, which unevenly crept up the walls. The otherwise whitewashed room was monastic and seductive at the same time. "It's incredible," Ahdaf murmured. "Did you really take all these pictures?"

"My mother has the originals. It was her idea to make them into wallpaper. She was right. My idea to tape them to each other would have destroyed them."

"Have you really traveled so much?"

"When I was 12, I discovered a book in a used bookstore called *The Family of Man* that had pictures of people from everywhere in the world. On the spot, I decided I wanted to see my own 'family of man.' I traveled a year after college, and every chance I've had since then. At first, I only thought to see the people, then I wanted to help them. It's why I do what I do."

"How does a spy help people?"

"The big picture? We try to make the world safer. At a personal level? We often end up helping people like Derya Thomas."

"That's good," Ahdaf agreed. Holding onto one of the bed's corner ropes, he leaned back to examine its construction and asked, "Did you design this?"

"I saw a photo of one on the Internet and loved it. I had a local engineer design it. I could only do it because I'm on the top floor and could anchor it to a crossbeam."

"It's incredible," Ahdaf repeated. He nudged it to see how much it moved. "Does it swing a lot when you're in it?"

"It won't make you seasick, if you're worried! Do you want to try it?"

"You mean get on it?"

"If you're ready."

"Ready?"

Selim set their wineglasses aside and pulled Ahdaf into a tender kiss, their lips barely brushing.

"Are you sure you want this?" Ahdaf murmured, even as, lips pressing harder, their hands explored their desire. "You didn't seem interested in me at the hammam."

"I didn't want a quick handjob to be my first time with you …. I haven't stopped thinking about you since we met."

"I thought maybe you found something wrong with me."

Selim chuckled. "What I've seen so far, I don't think I will. Let's get undressed."

They unbuttoned their shirts, kicked off shoes, and pulled off their pants. Embracing again, they tugged at the elastic bands of the other's undershorts until they stepped out of them and rolled onto the bed, wanting to touch each other all over, all at once. Kalam had given him ideas of what was possible, but Selim was even more confident in his moves. Selim was hairier than fair-haired Kalam, and stockier, yet gentle as he dragged his tongue down Ahdaf's body. When his last stretch of kisses brought Ahdaf close to coming, he said, "Not yet," and instead straddled him. "I want you this way." He guided Ahdaf into him, slowly, his expression changing from pinched to pleasure. He pushed hard on him while pulling on the bed's suspending ropes to create a gentle sway until neither could stop himself from coming. Ahdaf moaned as Selim splattered his chest.

DAY 8

The following morning, Selim jostled Ahdaf awake when he climbed back onto the suspended bed.

"What time is it?" Ahdaf mumbled.

"Almost noon."

"Noon? Are you kidding?"

"It's okay. You don't launch until 22 hours."

"You make it sound like a military exercise."

"It is, except it's not an exercise. It's an operation. Come here." Selim tried to pull Ahdaf's head onto his shoulder.

"Wait, it's my turn," Ahdaf said, and made his own trip to the bathroom. When he returned, he gently eased himself back into the bed so as not to send it swinging, which he remembered happening the night before – not elaborately, but encouragingly. Rolling into Selim's outstretched arm, he buried his face in his thick patch of chest hair. "I think this is how I fell asleep last night. I have no idea what time it was."

"Me neither. It was a night without time."

Ahdaf rolled onto his pillow so he could look at the hundreds of photographs that crept up the walls. "Why only black-and-white?" he asked.

"With color, it's the physical objects I see first, especially if they're brightly colored. With black-and-white, it's the mood of the image I see first, the emotion it wants to convey. Its soul. Then I begin to focus on individual objects."

Ahdaf's phone, in his daypack in the living room, pinged. Instinctively he tensed; messages were almost always business.

It pinged again.

"I get the sense you want to check your messages," Selim said.

"I should, but I don't want to leave where I am. For sure it's business – my friends rarely text me – so there's probably a problem that I need to fix. But I don't have any clients, either!"

"Except for your two guests in your apartment."

"They aren't mine."

"I'll make coffee while you deal with your business." Selim left the bed and opened a dresser drawer. He pulled on boxers and tossed a second pair to Ahdaf. "Let's sit on the terrace," he said, before disappearing down the hall.

Ahdaf pulled on the borrowed boxers and took his phone to the terrace. Sprawling Istanbul was less enchanting than it had been the night before. The bright daylight exposed its gritty air, and its steady city hum had notched decibels higher. He watched the confusion of boats plying the Bosporus and wondered how they avoided collisions. He supposed there were water traffic controllers like there were air traffic controllers, but growing up in Raqqa – a desert town on the sluggish Euphrates – he had never thought about how things worked on the seas, let alone the crowded waterway dividing Europe and Asia.

The bright sun had had him angling his telephone screen this way and that until he could finally see the message, and he laughed when he read: DON'T FORGET YOUR TOOTHBRUSH! OR MINE! He felt flattered by Kalam's persistence, and was still chuckling at his message when Selim appeared with two mugs of coffee.

"It must not have been too serious," he said.

"No, it was a joke from a friend."

"I thought you didn't have friends who texted you."

"Actually, he was a client before we became friends. You saw him. He was the second guy in the van when I picked up Derya."

Selim set down the tray. "I hope American coffee is okay. For me, Turkish coffee is too gritty for the first cup of the day, and I hate those home espresso machines because they litter the world with plastic capsules. There's cream and sugar if you want."

"Black's good for me."

"Me, too." Selim lifted his mug. "Good morning, after a very good night."

"Not a 'very good night.' An *exceptional* night!" Ahdaf declared.

"Truly exceptional," Selim agreed.

"Have you had sex with a lot of men?"

"Not many."

"You seemed to know what to do last night."

Selim shrugged. "I've watched videos on the Internet, though I've never gone that far before. Plus, like you, I need to be careful."

"Why, if you're an American?"

"I can be kidnapped and executed in God's name like anybody else. It just takes the wrong person finding out. Also, secrecy is part of my job. The irony is, in the past, if somebody found out that you were gay, it would've ended your career. Now it doesn't matter. It's even an asset because it opens doors that used to be closed – especially hotel room doors."

"You've done that?"

"Four times. We never did anything too intimate. Just touching. They wanted more, but I wanted to keep it safe. I didn't find any of them attractive enough to want more."

"Was it weird?"

"It was what it was: a job. If it got the men talking and me into their rooms to look around, why not? In one case I stopped an attack. In the second, the existence of Malik's cell was revealed."

"Who did they think you were?"

"I won't say because I might have to use those covers again. I *can* say that they were all glad to find someone they could have even mediocre sex with who wasn't going to blackmail them or become a problem in their lives."

"Why'd they trust you?"

"Probably out of desperation. Eventually gays have to gamble and trust somebody, or go crazy from horniness."

"Are you trusting me out of desperation?" Ahdaf asked.

Selim laughed. "Yeah, last night was all about desperation. Now let's talk about today."

Ahdaf paused on the sidewalk before entering the mosque courtyard. Increasingly with every step, he felt the enormity of what he'd committed to do. Crossing the threshold through the gate was his binding signature. He felt he had no other choice except to disappear, to flee Istanbul as he'd fled Raqqa. Suddenly, the notion of joining Kalam in Greece had more appeal, but then he'd still be a fugitive of sorts. Always fearful. Always glancing over his shoulder for some official whose job was to try to keep him out of whatever country. No, he had to follow through on the commitments he'd made. It was too late to undo any of the twisted threads he'd already tangled. They'd unravel on their own.

A few old men sat on the benches in the verdant garden of the mosque. They'd stay for hours, enjoying the companionship and the bright day. Ahdaf, nervous, headed for the WC. Suleiman, in his standard beige kaftan, sat on a bench along the footpath. Ahdaf greeted him and the older man stood up. He said, quietly, "I told Malik that I followed you to Galata Tower where you met the CIA man. Then I followed you back to the Tropicana. When

211

I saw the light in your room come on, I went home."

"Why are you helping me?"

"Malik is an evil man."

"Why do you help him?"

"Like you, I have no choice."

Ahdaf nodded, understanding, and wondering what sin, in Malik's judgment, the older man had committed. Homosexuality seemed unlikely; he was just an average middle-aged guy with a drooping belly and a wife at home. Maybe he'd had an affair with someone else's bored wife. In Islam's hierarchy of forbidden sins, adultery was a notch less abhorrent than homosexuality; and both, from the fundamentalists' point of view, were punishable by death. "Tell him I'll come to his office in five minutes. First I need the WC."

The men split up. Ahdaf took a couple of minutes to relieve his nervous bladder before going to find Malik. He'd never had a reason to be in the mosque's administrative building which housed the *medrese*, and was surprised, given the building's ornate exterior, how the interior had been chopped into boxy offices with only one room large enough for religious classes. Malik's office was directly across from it. Doors to both rooms were open to each other.

Ahdaf paused where he couldn't be seen by Malik but could see into the classroom where teenage students – boys only – huddled over their desks, scribbling while the teacher recited Koranic verses. He paused at the end of each one to thank Allah for his wisdom, which the students repeated, before transcribing the next recited verse. Ahdaf recalled how ISIS emphasized religious education when it overran Raqqa. To attend a *medrese* was to pledge allegiance and obedience. He wondered how those memorized verses could possibly prepare the young men in the classroom for a future in the much more secular world of Istanbul. As soon as he thought it, he realized they were preparing themselves for the world they expected to create on the ashes of Istanbul. They were educating themselves for *their* world.

He knocked on Malik's open door and stepped into his office.

Malik, fidgeting with a pen at his desk, said, "Please come in and shut the door behind you. The noise from the classroom can be annoying."

As Ahdaf closed the door, he imagined it was more intimidating than annoying to have the headmaster able to constantly watch them.

"Please sit," he said, and waved Ahdaf into a chair.

"Thank you, but there's no need to disturb you," Ahdaf replied. "I'm only here to get the money for the Greek captain."

"You can update me on the latest plans. I insist."

"There's nothing to update. You already know the exchange has been delayed until dawn."

"Which means you have time for a tea," Malik pointedly said.

Obliged, Ahdaf sat as the headmaster dropped sugar cubes into two short glasses and filled them from a steaming kettle. Holding one glass by the rim, he gingerly set it on his desk close to Ahdaf, who picked it up to blow across it. He took an exploratory sip. Still too hot. He blew across it again, wanting to drink it quickly, take the money, and go.

Malik, though, seemed to have something on his mind. He set down his glass and said, "Your reputation is that you're resourceful, and it appears to be true."

"I have to be," Ahdaf replied. "In my job, so many things can change."

"Tomorrow, what might change?" Malik asked.

"The sea is always unpredictable. Weather can change in a shorter time than it takes to make the crossing. It's a narrow channel, so everything gets accentuated. That makes any weather more dangerous for rafts. When I think it's going to be too

213

dangerous, I rebook my clients unless they insist on still crossing. I can probably rebook with the Greek but shouldn't need to; a fishing boat can handle a much rougher sea. What I can't predict is if there'll be Coast Guard and police around, which might force the Greek to turn back. Then there are things I can't even know about. Who had a clue about the police ambush last week?"

"I sense that you're always making contingency plans," Malik remarked.

"I know what to do about missed connections, getting spaces on a raft, and finding crutches or powdered baby formula. I don't know what to do about a shootout except to run."

"Which was the right thing to do. You brought two brave fighters to safety. We could use your skills. Your resourcefulness. You're a strategist, too, and can figure out what to do in any situation. We want to rely on you. We want you to join us."

Ahdaf's heart sank. He'd just had a job interview with ISIS without knowing it. "Join who, exactly?" he asked.

"Soldiers of Allah who help other soldiers of Allah."

"You mean a cell of ISIS?"

Malik nodded. "Yes, and other groups aligned with them."

"Did you plan the Athens attack? Is that why Serhan and Özan are here?"

"Turkey was always a possible escape route. That's why I approached you. To be ready."

"Then why do you need me? You're just as resourceful. It's obvious that you're a strategist, too."

"We're in a war," Malik reminded him.

"I don't even know how to shoot a gun."

"You wouldn't have to. You'd help plan operations and arrange transportation."

"What do I get out of it?"

"My protection."

"Until I'm killed in a shootout, that is."

"It's an honor to be a *shahid*."

"I don't want to be a martyr for Allah, or anybody or anything. I'll take my chances with Allah's final judgment on how I live this life, if I'm allowed to live this life and do the many things I hope to do. I've helped you once and easily could've been killed, along with my friend. Tonight, I'm helping a second time, in a very big way. I can't help again. It's an impossible situation for me. I can't even go to my own home!"

Malik's expression hardened. "Timur confessed."

"Timur? From the hammam?"

"He told us the men who like to be touched."

"The men who like to be touched? It's the attendants' job to touch us. They scrub us."

"Some men ask for more."

"I'm not one of them."

"Why would Timur lie?"

"To try to save himself. People lie to save themselves."

"Then he lied for nothing." Malik set aside his tea and took, from a drawer, four thick money pouches. He slid them into Ahdaf's reach. "Five thousand euros in each. If the crossing is aborted, you bring back the money."

Ahdaf picked up a pouch to test its heft in one hand. Five thousand euros felt like a heavy slab of meat draped over his palm. "How do you find so much money?" he asked. "I always thought mosques survive on donations made in *kurus*."

"We have benefactors for special operations," the headmaster replied.

"Apparently so." Ahdaf zipped the four pouches into his daypack. "I need the key for the van."

"You're taking it now? There's still several hours."

"Why risk having a problem later with heavy traffic? Or maybe someone will block the alley. I'll park it at Leyla's, where I'll wait until I pick up your two guys and we go to Assos. In fact, let your man Suleiman go home tonight and watch some television with his wife."

"How will I know what you really do?

"I assume Serhan has a way to contact you."

"Of course."

"If he doesn't contact you, then you know I showed up. I'll send a message when we cross the Osmangazi Bridge and a second message when the exchange has been made. If all goes as planned, I'll be back for noon prayers tomorrow, *inshallah*."

"*Inshallah*." Malik reached deep into his kaftan pocket for the key to the van and handed it to him. Then he mumbled a prayer for Ahdaf's success on his sacred mission. They touched their hearts and Ahdaf turned to leave.

"You could be a real asset for us," Malik said to his departing back.

He paused and, without turning around, replied, "I already said no. It's too dangerous. I'm a refugee from danger."

"Then I can't protect you, especially now that there are two accusations against you."

"They're lies." He turned around to look Malik in the eyes. "Did your soldiers of Allah torture my cousin to give them names, too, before they killed him? Or no, of course they didn't, they didn't have time to torture him. What did they do, perch him on the edge of the roof and promise to let him live if he gave the names of other men?"

Malik didn't answer, but his cold expression made clear that is what had happened.

"Whose names do you expect people to give if you're torturing them or threatening to kill them? All of us, we only know so many people. We only know so many names that you'll believe. I could say I've had sex with the president of the country. Would you believe me? No, you wouldn't, but you'd believe a man standing on the edge of roof, waiting for his own execution, who tells you any names that pop into his head in the hope of a pardon."

Ahdaf left the building, following the flagstone path that brought him to the door in the hedge where the van was parked. He climbed into the driver's seat and rolled down the window. The van was parked as he'd requested: facing the busy street, so he didn't have to back into it. He sat for a moment to calm his own nerves before starting the engine and rolling forward to the main road. As he waited for a chance to pull out, his imagination fast-forwarded through the next few hours. Fetching Serhan and Özan. Driving toward Assos. Launching the ÖKK's trap. Despite his talent for contingency planning, that day he was hard-pressed to have a plan for himself. The best he could conjure was simply to try to survive whatever was thrown at him.

He pulled into traffic. Up ahead, he saw Suleiman turn into a side street going in the opposite direction from where he was headed. He was glad he'd won the older man a night off, though he'd been somewhat deceptive in doing so. He claimed he'd be going straight to Leyla's, but instead detoured to Munir's. He had something to give Yasmin other than encouraging words.

He parked close to her apartment – and he thought of it as Yasmin's apartment, no longer Munir's – and walked the two short blocks to her door. The yards were weedy and the buildings drab, but from window to window and across sidewalks, people chatted brightly; from inside he heard laughter, televisions, kids playing, and babies crying. It was a neighborhood where people, sharing the same disappointments, also shared the same pleasures, and likely came together to help someone worse off than them. Or so that was Ahdaf's wishful hope as he rang Yasmin's doorbell.

She buzzed him in.

Plodding up the two flights of stairs in the stagnant air robbed him of some of his optimism. When Yasmin opened the door, she looked, if possible, even more sallow than the day before, her eyes more bloodshot and the circles under them darker. He asked perfunctorily how things were, though he could see nothing had changed. Three-year-old Samir was watching his cartoons. The infant Fatima, too weak to manage a full outraged cry, whimpered and fidgeted in her cardboard crib. Yasmin herself seemed almost too exhausted to return to her chair at the small table.

"Is it Baba?" Samir asked, squinting in Ahdaf's direction.

"It's Baba's friend, Ahdaf," she told the boy.

"Baba?" he asked plaintively.

"Maybe tomorrow, sweetheart," Yasmin replied.

Ahdaf sat opposite her and asked, "Have the children eaten?"

"The boy has. We shared the chicken and he finished all the cookies."

"Samir!" he called. "Did you save a cookie for me?"

The youngster shook his head no. "Mama told me to eat all I want!"

"Has the baby eaten?" he asked Yasmin.

"I have milk, but she won't … she won't …" Her voice trailed off.

"Not even the formula?"

Yasmin shook her head. "I tried."

"Okay, I have an idea. But first we have some business."

"Business?"

"You'll see." He plopped his daypack on the table and reached inside for one of the leather money pouches. He handed it to her.

"What is this?" she asked.

"Open it." She did and looked confused to see the thick stacks of euro bills. "It's 5,000 euros," he told her.

She blinked. "I don't understand."

"It's for you."

"Was Munir supposed to be paid something?"

"No. Munir was a volunteer. A hero, not a mercenary. This is something I've arranged separately."

"Did you steal it?"

"I promise that I didn't steal it." He pushed it to her side of the small table. "Hide it somewhere safe. Someplace one hundred percent safe, because I can't rescue you again. This time, there are special circumstances. I can't tell you more than that. Tie it to your body; that's probably the safest thing. The pouch has loops to make it easy."

Yasmin put her hand on the pouch to be sure it was real. "I don't know what to say. It's a special circumstance for me, too." She couldn't believe her good fortune; and not because it was a fortune, but because it would rescue her family.

In her cardboard crib, Fatima woke up with a squeaky cry. "She's hungry," Yasmin said. "Will you hand her to me?"

He gingerly reached into the box tucked behind him and picked up the newborn, who felt no heavier than her soul. But her kick at the unfamiliar touch, accompanied by a hiccupped wail, convinced him that she still had her soul to keep for some time to come. He passed her to Yasmin, who turned away from him, enveloping the child in her robe while somehow offering her breast. She clucked and cajoled, trying to get the child to nurse; instead, the baby only cried. Yasmin's body slackened with disappointment, but still she cooed and rocked Fatima until the girl quieted down.

While she was doing that, Ahdaf took the baby formula from the cupboard, read the instructions, and in a small bowl made a milky paste with it. "Let me try something," he said, and reached for the baby. Cradling her, he asked, "What did Munir call her when he walked her?"

"*Habibat albi,*" Yasmin said.

Ahdaf smiled. "'Love of my heart.' That's sweet." He nuzzled Fatima's neck and said, "*Habibat albi … Habibat albi …* Are you my *habibat albi*?" He walked her and called her by her father's pet name, and she soon grew calmer. The next time he nuzzled her

219

neck, she cooed. He took that as his cue to dab her lips with the milky formula, repeating *habibat albi habibat albi habibat albi* .... She started to push him away but didn't persist; then, after reluctantly tasting his fingers, she hungrily sucked on them. "That's my *habibat albi* ... *habibat albi* ..." He handed Yasmin the bowl of milky formula. "I think she'll nurse now. Put some of this on you to help her start."

"Please look away," Yasmin asked, and he did while she dabbed formula on a nipple. "Okay, I'll take her now. Yes, sweetheart ..." she murmured, as she took Fatima in her arms. "Yes, sweetheart ... yes, yes ... yes, my sweetheart ..." Turning away from Ahdaf, she pressed the child to her breast. A long silence ensued, or so it seemed to Ahdaf, anxious as he was for the baby to nurse. When Yasmin started to sob, he felt the grief of failure. His experiment hadn't worked, or so he thought, until Yasmin murmured, "Yes, sweetheart, you're going to be all right. Yes, sweetheart, yes ..."

Teary-eyed, Ahdaf shouldered his daypack and let himself out.

A small truck pulled out of a space across from Leyla's Café and Ahdaf took it, parking the *medrese's* bulky van in it. As he got out, he could see Leyla watching him from behind her cowboy bar. It was a popular hour, and the café was crowded inside. He wound through the tables, dodging legs and daypacks before settling on a barstool under the gaze of Hollywood cowboys. As usual, no one else sat at the stubby bar, though a dozen cell phones adorned its surface with their tangled cables. Leyla stubbed out her cigarette.

"You don't have to put that out for me," he said.

"I know you don't like it."

"You've got a sexy voice. There's *that* to like about it."

"I've had this voice since I was 16."

"What happened that year?"

"I met the Marlboro Man."

Ahdaf was impressed. "You did? The guy on the horse?"

Leyla laughed. "Ahdaf, sometimes you're so naïve. So gullible. If I said there's 19 dead cats in the men's toilet, you'd believe me, wouldn't you?"

"I'd use the women's toilet."

"You're so practical. That too. Back to the Marlboro Man. I wanted a man like that, and if I needed to smoke to meet him, I'd smoke."

"Did you meet him?"

Leyla laughed and pointed to the hats nailed to the arch overhead. "They were all my Marlboro Men."

"You mean –"

"Yes, that's what I mean. But don't worry, you're too skinny to be a real Marlboro Man – though if you ever wear a cowboy hat, I'd be glad to keep it as a souvenir. Now you're *really* blushing!"

Ahdaf knew he was; his face felt hot. Even so, he protested, "It's stuffy in here."

"Why do you have the mosque's van?" Leyla asked.

"They needed a driver for an event tonight and I volunteered."

"Is that why you're dressed all spiffy in your new white polo shirt?"

"I needed a clean shirt. In my closet, they're hard to find."

"Do you want a beer?"

"I shouldn't, if I'm driving."

"What time's your event?"

"In a couple of hours."

"You've got time to have two beers and still sober up."

She pulled one from the fridge, poured him a glass, and put it back to stay cold. "I didn't know you could drive," she remarked.

He took a short sip and set it aside, planning to nurse it. "Everybody knows how to drive," he said.

"I don't."

"I'm surprised. You're so independent."

"Once people have cars, they get dependent on them. What kind of independence is that?"

Ahdaf shook his head. "You'd never survive in Raqqa. Not as a woman. How'd you get to be so independent?"

"My mother was a whipped dog," Leyla answered. "If she had had a tail, it would've always been tucked between her legs. I promised myself I wouldn't live like that."

"Most women can't imagine making that choice."

"Don't ever believe we can't imagine it. Every woman imagines it. It's men who can't see how things could be different. They've brainwashed themselves into believing inequality is natural."

"My mother was different, too," Ahdaf said. "She had a job."

"You've told me. An English teacher."

"She's why I was one, too, until the war. Schools were finished and eventually I had to leave. I could teach here, but it's not permitted for refugees to have real jobs."

"You could teach privately."

Ahdaf shook his head. "It's too risky."

"Hey, Leyla!" a customer called from the tables.

She glanced his way. He held up a tea glass and four fingers. Another caught her eye with a beer bottle and two fingers. "I have a job, too," she said, "only not as respectable as an English teacher."

"But a lot more interesting."

"That's one word for it." Leyla squeezed past the end of the bar to make her rounds.

Ahdaf sipped his beer and turned to face the room, but stopped halfway, his eyes roaming over Leyla's montage of cowboy pictures with a new appreciation. He'd had real sex twice in three days. Previously, he could only fantasize about Leyla's cowboys; he now had tactile memories to project on them. He couldn't take his eyes off one looking straight at him, in a cocky pose, leaning against a wall with his thumb tucked into his belt buckle and his hat back off his forehead to reveal his fair hair. *He could be Kalam,* he was thinking, when Leyla returned and said, "That's Paul Newman. He's handsome, isn't he?"

"He reminds me of someone."

"Perhaps your new client?" Leyla asked.

"How did you know?"

"I've got eyes, too."

"He's no longer my client," Ahdaf told her. "He's already made it to Greece."

"That was fast."

"He had a chance and wanted to go. He wants to stay in touch in case I eventually cross. We might try to hook up and help each other."

"That's a quick friendship," Leyla said.

"We have a lot in common."

"I'd already guessed that."

Ahdaf, sensing something in her tone, gave her a curious look; but she was already distracted by the overhead television. "There's breaking news," she said, and reached for the remote to turn up the sound.

The monitor displayed photos of two men side by side, full faced; but they weren't mug shots. They looked like most men in Istanbul: dark and bearded. Regular guys, who'd turned into killing machines – and who were currently holed up in Ahdaf's apartment. Offscreen, a newsman said, "Authorities have tentatively identified the suspected terrorists in last week's Spartacus Club attack in Athens."

"Fuck! That's Serhan Yildiz!" someone shouted.

"And Özan!"

To Ahdaf, it seemed extraordinary that people in Leyla's Café would know them. Özan said he came from Aksaray, but it was a large district, and he never contemplated that they might have crossed paths or have mutual acquaintances.

"… Serhan Yildiz, on the left," the reporter continued, "and Özan Kuçuk on the right. Both from Istanbul and known to be ISIS sympathizers."

"They've never had souls," Leyla muttered. "Look at their eyes."

Ahdaf did, and saw the same cold expressions that she did.

"After what they did in Athens, and on that beach, now I'm sure of it," she added.

"Do you know them?"

"They're from this district, and came in here and caused me trouble a couple of times."

They focused again on the reporter. "A third terrorist found dead on Big Rocks Beach, apparently from burns sustained in the attack in Athens, has tentatively been identified as Taner Yildiz, the twin brother of Serhan Yildiz. All three are Turkish nationals. The two surviving terrorists are believed to be in Turkey based on forensic evidence linking the attacks in Athens and Assos."

"They're no terrorists!" someone shouted. "They're heroes for killing fucking faggots! Local heroes! They're from right here!"

Immediately the room exploded into arguments. Serhan, Özan, Taner: their names were tossed about and derided or revered for what they'd done. Leyla muted the television, which caused the ruckus to gradually die out. "Nobody deserves to be killed when all they're doing is having a good time with friends, 'faggots' included," she said to everyone in the room. "If you feel they do, you can say so on the sidewalk, but not inside Leyla's Café."

"You're always preaching free speech!" someone shouted. "That sounds like censorship to me!"

"Enough with the speeches!" someone else shouted. "And enough with the news! Put on the music!"

Leyla did, while leaving the television muted, and the whole mood brightened. "I'm not surprised it's them," she said to Ahdaf. "They barged in here once, knocking over beer bottles, threatening Allah's wrath for drinking alcohol, all that fundamentalist stuff."

"How'd you stop them?"

"My customers stopped them. Twice. After the second time, I went to the police. I don't know what they did, but they haven't been back. Then I heard they'd gone to Raqqa, but everything's a rumor."

"They went to Raqqa," Ahdaf confirmed, realizing too late that he had just confessed to knowing them.

Leyla's eyes narrowed. She asked, "Does your 'event' tonight have something to do with them?"

"Huh?" Ahdaf looked at her as if she were crazy. "Why would you ask that?"

"Because it's too coincidental," she said. "You're driving the van from the same mosque they attended until they left."

"It's my mosque, too. I don't remember seeing them."

"You're also working for Selim Wilson."

"Why would you think that?"

"You've met with him where you're sitting. I don't know exactly what Selim does, or what he's having you do, but if the Athens attackers are back in Turkey, my guess is that he's involved in the case, too."

Suddenly it dawned on Ahdaf. "You work for him, don't you?"

"I tell him which boys he can trust."

"Why?"

"Because he asks me, and he leaves big tips."

"You told him about me? Why?"

"You seem trustworthy. I'm on his side, and I think you are, too. I don't want an attack, like what happened in Athens, in my place. I don't want the fundamentalists to win, because if they do, I'll be asking you to organize my place on a raft."

225

"Who else in here works for him?"

"I wouldn't necessarily know."

"Or tell me?" he asked.

"That's true, too. In this town, it's almost a game. People have spies watching their own spies. He hasn't asked me for anyone for a long time. Obviously, he has other resources for what he needs done." She glanced over his shoulder and said, "I'd better serve some tables."

She filled a dozen glasses on a tray with steaming tea and added a couple of beers from the refrigerator. She also placed Ahdaf's half-empty bottle in front of him. "You look like you might want more of that before I'm back." She squeezed past the bar, hoisted her tray, and zigzagged between tables, delivering drinks.

She'd unsettled him with her confession that she'd brought him to Selim's attention. Suddenly it made him doubt Selim's sincerity. Was he the victim of an elaborate honey trap? Why had Selim approached him so publicly, even handing him his card at the cowboy bar? What had all that accomplished? As soon as he asked himself the question, he knew: it had provoked Malik to try to recruit Ahdaf, in the process setting him up to become a double agent for Selim.

"Ten minutes," Ahdaf, seated in the van, said into his phone. "Be outside on the sidewalk. Bring whatever food you have left, too."

"What food?" Serhan complained. "Özan ate it all."

"We'll stop at the first service station. There's a nice one just before we cross the bridge. Ten minutes, on the sidewalk, and don't let anyone see your rifle." Ahdaf clicked off his phone and chucked it into his daypack. He clutched and reversed a few centimeters before pulling the van onto the road. As he did, he glanced back into the café. Sure enough, Leyla was watching

226

him. She knew nothing of his plans, though her unyielding stare made it clear she was frightened for him.

When he turned the corner onto his street, Ahdaf could see the light go out in his window at the end of the block. Selim claimed that the ÖKK had staked out his place, but he saw no evidence of it. No trailing cars. No sidewalk surveillance. No anything, from what he could tell. *But wait.* Was that guy really chatting up that girl while staring at Ahdaf's window? Was some guy parked in a dark blue car and smoking a cigarette just coincidentally facing his building? Was that dog walker talking to her dogs, or into a Bluetooth microphone?

As soon as Ahdaf pulled up to his building, the front door opened and his two guys came out. Serhan had wrapped his rifle in Ahdaf's towel. They slid open the side door of the van, bringing with them their individual fetid clouds: Özan smelling moldy in Ahdaf's clothes, which hadn't dried thoroughly, and Serhan sharing his sour sweat. "Perfect timing," Ahdaf remarked.

"Özan was watching for you. He's all nervous."

"Why? Did something happen?"

"You haven't seen our pictures on TV? We're famous!"

"Yeah, famous until someone recognizes us," Özan griped. "Then we're dead."

"I saw the news, too, and I wouldn't worry," Ahdaf said. "I don't think people will recognize you from the photos they're using. Besides, they'll assume you're hiding in Istanbul or Raqqa. They won't be looking for you in Greece. But just in case, why don't you sit all the way in the back, where people can't see you."

"Do you need my GPS?" Özan asked before switching seats.

"I already have it set up on my phone."

He drove off. In the rearview mirror, he watched a car make the same turns and follow him back to the main road. Ahdaf couldn't be sure, but he thought it was the blue car he'd seen in front of his building. It reassured him to think he was being followed.

It was well past the last remnants of rush hour. Traffic was light even on surface streets. He followed the directional signs to the national road. Merging onto it, he watched the blue car fall in behind him. He couldn't go fast in the *medrese's* clunky van, and most cars would have passed him, which convinced Ahdaf he *was* being followed – as part of the ÖKK's operation, he assumed, but realized he couldn't be sure. And he was even more puzzled when the blue car finally did speed past him and disappear.

He'd watched his passengers doze off and jerk back awake at every stop and turn. "There won't be so many turns now," he told them. "You should stretch out and get some sleep so you're rested for tomorrow. You already look tired."

"Who wouldn't be, after two nights with this snore machine in the room?" Serhan said, indicating Özan. "You wouldn't think someone so scrawny could make so much noise. No wonder you're not married, you snoring prick!"

"Women snore, too," Özan defended himself.

"Not when they're sleeping with me! Which reminds me, what happened to the two women we ordered?"

"I didn't see anybody I could ask. It'll be easier in Greece," Ahdaf assured him.

"I should've fucked your French neighbor. She wanted it. Why else was she cooking for us?"

"Because she likes me and thought you were my cousins. You left her alone, didn't you?"

"Yeah, but I shot her dog. That yappy bitch was another reason I couldn't sleep."

Ahdaf looked at him in the mirror hoping he'd make some sign that he was kidding, but he just stared right back. Finally, Özan burst into laughter, which prompted Serhan to smile and say, "I told you he'd believe me. Where the fuck did *you* sleep last night?"

"Probably with our two women," Özan snickered.

"Nothing so exciting," Ahdaf lied, recalling his night with Selim. How he wished his face were pressed against the CIA man's burly chest again, wrapped in his safe arms instead of chauffeuring two lowlifes into a dangerous ambush.

"Are we on the road to Ankara?" Serhan asked.

"Yeah. It's a couple of hours before we split off."

"Is it also the road to Syria?"

"Why are you asking?"

"Because we may have a last-minute change in plans."

"How's that?"

"I don't trust Malik. He's mouse shit. We'd plan operations, and at the last minute he'd call them off. That's why we went to Raqqa. We were tired of talking. We wanted to be fighting. Isn't that right, Özan?"

"Especially Taner."

"Don't start about my brother," Serhan warned.

"He hated faggots. He wanted to kill them. Athens was his idea."

"I said don't start!"

"To be honest, it doesn't matter to me if he hated faggots," Ahdaf said, wanting to diffuse the friction between them. "That doesn't make him special. A lot of people hate faggots. It also doesn't matter to me if you go to Greece or Syria, except I can't enter Syria. You'd be on your own at that point."

"We'll find a way to Raqqa," Serhan said. "We did once before."

"You weren't fugitives before," Ahdaf reminded him. "You weren't wanted for killing six cops. Other cops might not treat you very well."

"I think he's right," Özan said.

"Who asked you to think?"

"I'll tell you what, guys. You don't have to decide for a couple of hours. Get some sleep because if you decide to go to Syria, you're going to have to help drive."

"You get in the back seat," Serhan told Özan, "and try not to snore!"

Özan moved, and immediately complained, "It's cold back here, with the windows open!"

"It wasn't me who shot them out," Ahdaf reminded him. "I'll turn on the heater; maybe that'll help."

Once again, the two men lay flat on the short seats, heads resting on their daypacks and knees braced against seats across the narrow aisle. They shifted a bit and adjusted their packs to make themselves more comfortable. Serhan set his rifle on the opposite seat and concealed it with the towel, which, five minutes later, he used to cover himself for some warmth. Soon both men were snoring, Özan gagging on his tongue and Serhan expelling air like bellows fanning a fire. Ahdaf took a deep breath, calming his own nerves, enjoying a respite from the fear of being killed at any moment.

Only minutes later, Ahdaf approached the first toll station. Almost everyone in Turkey used a transponder to pay tolls, but for the rare few who didn't, there was always one lane to pay with cash or a credit card. Selim, when handing Ahdaf a debit card, had told him that the ÖKK had arranged for the far-right booth at all three toll stations to be the only ones accepting cash and cards. "Don't make it look easy," he advised. "You need an excuse for dropping it later."

As he braked for the toll station, Serhan bolted upright and grabbed his rifle. "Why are we stopping?"

"Toll station," Ahdaf replied. "It takes cash, so there's probably someone in it. Hide your rifle and sit out of sight."

There was someone. Ahdaf, trying to use the debit card, ex-aggerated the difficult reach from the van's high seat to insert it into a slot. The tollkeeper, noticing his difficulty, said, "Let me do that for you, sir."

He took the card and ran it through a toll machine inside his booth. As he handed it back, he said, "You have a good evening, sir." Then he winked. It was quick, but intentional: a clear message that Ahdaf hadn't been abandoned. Or so he wanted to interpret it.

By the time the booth had disappeared from his side mirror, Serhan had already fallen back into a wheezing sleep. Özan hadn't woken up at all, and fortunately, his gagging had lessened. Half an hour later, they approached the second toll station. As Ahdaf braked, Serhan dropped a hand on his rifle without sitting up. Again, Ahdaf exaggerated the long stretch to pay the toll. As the barrier lifted, Serhan snorted, already asleep again.

Ahdaf knew he had about another half hour to the third toll station. Thirty minutes to showtime. There was nothing he could do to change what would come next. His challenge was to survive it.

A road sign informed him: TOLL STATION 500 M.

Again he wanted to throw up. He wanted to run the van off a cliff into oblivion. Instead, he aimed for the rightmost lane, to the only booth open for cash or cards. As he braked to a stop, again it roused Serhan, who instinctively reached for his rifle. "It's our last toll station," Ahdaf told him. "Put your rifle on the floor and go back to sleep. It's another 30 minutes to our turn-off."

Serhan dropped his head back onto his daypack.

Ahdaf braked, ready to come to a stop when he said, "Shit!" A road cone had been positioned against the curb at the toll machine with STOP AND PAY! written on it in bold black letters.

"What?" asked Serhan, suddenly alert.

"It looks like the barrier is broken. It's still up in the air, and they've put a road cone to remind people to pay."

"Why pay?" Serhan asked. "Just go through."

"I'm sure there's a policeman on the other side waiting for people to do that. I don't think we want to get stopped. Go back to sleep."

Ahdaf stopped abreast of the toll machine, now a real reach for the debit-card slot; and, it dawned on him, this was by intent. It wasn't an inconvenience. It was a prop for his performance. He had an extra excuse to squirm while trying to reach the card reader, and was almost waist-deep out the window when he cried, "Shit! I dropped my card!"

The dark blue car pulled up behind him, the driver flashing his lights, wanting him to move.

"Let's go!" Serhan cried.

"We can't, without the card!" Ahdaf pointed ahead. "There, I see it in our headlights. The wind must've blown it."

The driver behind started honking as well as flashing his lights. As Serhan shook his fist at him through the back window, Ahdaf grabbed his daypack off the passenger seat and jumped out of the van. He dashed past the tollbooth, running harder than he'd ever run before, expecting any moment for the windshield to be blown into his back. He was an open target on flat asphalt. Then he heard shouts. A sustained barrage of weapons and shattered glass. A sudden silence. No pleas for mercy. No screams of pain. Serhan and Özan were dead.

Ahdaf kept running as fast as he could. Ahead of him, on the shoulder, a sedan had pulled over, taillights flashing. As he got closer, an arm shot out beckoning him. A glance confirmed that Selim was the driver, and he scrambled into the passenger seat.

As they sped off, he planted his elbows on his knees and held his head in his hands, catching his breath and shaking uncontrollably. Selim dropped a comforting hand on his back. "Are you hurt?"

"You can't believe how scared I was!"

"I believe it. But relax. It's over, and you're safe now."

When he'd caught his breath and stopped shaking, Ahdaf sat up and asked, "Where are we going?"

DAY 9

His father was teaching him to fly a kite in a dream when Selim pulled off the road, causing Ahdaf to bump his head on the window and wake up. "What's wrong?" Ahdaf asked, instantly alarmed.

"We're almost at Assos. This might be our last chance for a pit stop."

Selim parked on the crest of a high hill. The sun hadn't risen yet. Only an essence of its reflection colored the watery sky. A hill, covered with olive trees, dropped steeply to the attractive village wrapped around the harbor. They got out of the car and, with their backs to each other, relieved themselves. A telephone pinged.

"That was yours," Selim said.

They got back into the car, and Ahdaf checked his messages. "They're on their way to Big Rocks Beach," he said and read aloud: WE JUST CAST OFF. CAPTAIN G SAYS TO HEAD FOR BIG ROCKS BEACH. DID YOU REMEMBER YOUR TOOTHBRUSH???

Ahdaf chuckled at the last line.

Selim pulled back onto the road. "'Did you remember your

toothbrush?' What's he mean by that?"

"It's his joke. He wants me to join him. He wants somebody to travel with him to northern Europe."

"Are you thinking about it?"

Ahdaf shrugged. "I have, but not too seriously."

"Did you remember your toothbrush?"

"Yes."

"So you *are* thinking about it."

"It's my father's influence. He's a dentist, and made sure we took toothbrushes on any trip. When the war started, he insisted we take them everywhere, in case we couldn't get home."

Selim started the car. As they wound their way down the hill, Ahdaf tried to piece together what little he recalled from the night before. Abandoning Serhan and Özan in the *medrese's* van, he'd raced to Selim's car, where he'd collapsed on the seat, feeling his heart ready to explode from the combination of fear and exertion. Selim had driven off, and some minutes later received a call. After listening for a moment, he'd replied, "He's still catching his breath, but no injuries." He'd clicked off and reported to Ahdaf, "Serhan and Özan are dead. Malik has been arrested. You did a good job. You're safe now." Ahdaf had sobbed in relief as Selim squeezed his knee. "The scary part's over," he'd said. The adrenaline that had kept Ahdaf pumping all night drained from his body, and he'd passed out, remembering nothing more until he bumped his head on the car window only minutes earlier.

"I guess you need to decide," Selim said, breaking into his thoughts.

"Decide?"

"If you're going with your friend to Greece."

"I admit, I'm tempted to go. What do I have in Istanbul? I'm down to a toothbrush."

"Also a new shirt."

Ahdaf smiled. "Yeah, also a new shirt, and I'm glad to have it

– because it's become my only shirt!"

"You also have a new friend."

Selim's remark caught him off-guard. "You?"

"How many other new friends have you made since we met?"

"Actually, I don't have many friends," Ahdaf admitted. "I'm in the wrong business. Everybody I meet wants to leave."

"You're also gay," Selim reminded him. "That complicates friendships in Turkey, though it shouldn't complicate ours."

"Are you trying to tempt me to stay?"

"I'd like to be friends if you stay and let it evolve from there."

"You weren't thinking we'd be friends when you first met me."

"Because I hadn't *met* you. As soon as I did, that changed."

"It doesn't change why we met," Ahdaf replied.

"What do you mean?"

"You used me as bait for Malik. You knew what he knew about me. If he thought he had access to you through me, and I refused to help him, he'd threaten me, which he did and which gave you access to him."

Impressed, Selim said, "You should have my job."

"So I'm right?"

"Half-right. Yes, I wanted to know what Malik was up to. You don't send three cell members to Raqqa without people wondering what you're planning. We found out the hard way in Athens. We'd have preferred to find out another way."

"He didn't send them to Raqqa," Ahdaf said. "They left because Malik would plan operations and call them off at the last minute. They wanted more action. More attacks."

Selim grunted. "They succeeded. They did what they went to do and they probably never really expected to come back alive."

"I don't know what they thought," Ahdaf replied. "Malik implied they had an option to return to Istanbul, but no matter how many contingency plans he might have had, he couldn't have foreseen the massacre on the beach. That changed everything."

Closer to the village, Selim braked and turned right, heading north. Roughly parallel to the coastal road, they followed a narrow strip of asphalt that soon became a dirt track zigzagging between farmhouses in the olive groves.

"Where are we going?" Ahdaf asked.

"To a safe house."

"Like a spy safe house? Out here?"

"That's right. Out here and out of sight."

They continued another short distance, catching glimpses of the craggy shore until Selim pulled into a clearing in front of a simple stone house, bordered on both sides by vegetable gardens. A farmer on a short ladder was picking fruit off a tree. "That's Otar on the ladder," Selim said. "He and his wife used to be journalists. Even before the attempted coup, they didn't like the government's efforts to control the media, so they quit and bought this farm. It has an extra bedroom for journalists on the run."

"If you have them, why do you need me?" Ahdaf asked.

"They don't organize transport. They provide a hideout and meals, that's all."

"We're all just links in a long chain except you," Ahdaf remarked. "You're the guy pulling the strings."

"Trust me, someone pulls mine, too. Let me go check on the women."

"The women?"

Selim, without answering, got out of the car and walked over to shake Otar's hand. They exchanged a few words before Selim went to the house and knocked on the front door. Ahdaf didn't see who let him in. Otar, trim with a few days' growth of gray whiskers, came to the car to show him the bright orange fruit in his cloth sack. "Persimmons," he said. "Take some. The rain washed them clean last night. They'll never be better."

Ahdaf pinched one, sniffed it, and knew it was perfect. He ate it in a minute and devoured a second one as quickly. Otar urged him to take all of them. When he resisted, the older man said, "You'll be doing my health a favor. How many persimmon pies do you think a man my age should eat? Or persimmon cakes? Or persimmon omelets? Or persimmon –"

"Stop ... I get the point!" Ahdaf cried. "Don't worry, your persimmons will be eaten. I'll take a few more if you like." He moved his daypack to make room for the sack of bright orange fruit between the front seats.

The door to the house opened and Selim emerged, followed by Derya and Meryem. Ahdaf touched his heart and whispered a prayer of thanks. How many times had he prayed for their safety? How many times had he silently begged Meryem's forgiveness for his role in her family's tragedy? Or Derya's forgiveness for abandoning her on Big Rocks Beach? He had had no idea about Selim's arrangements for their safety. Suddenly, it became clear: Selim had hijacked *his* arrangements to return Serhan and the terrorists to Greece. Instead, he'd eliminated them and had two alternative passengers for Captain G.

"You planned this the whole time, didn't you?" Ahdaf asked.

"Not the whole time. Only from the moment you gave me the idea."

"How is it my idea?"

"By originally coordinating two operations: Malik's and mine. Now I'm coordinating yours and mine."

"What's my operation?"

"Going to Greece or not. It seems to be part of your plan today."

"And your operation?"

"It's both of ours: getting these two women to safety, and you're the one making it possible. Now they might have real lives. They might actually *live*." Selim touched Ahdaf's knee. "You're a man with a real heart."

Otar and Selim opened the back doors of the sedan. The women tucked their robes around them to slide onto the seat. They waved goodbye to a woman who'd appeared at the house's door: Otar's wife, Ahdaf assumed.

Across the top of the car, Selim said, "Thank you, Otar, for another rescue."

Otar took a shallow bow. "Always and anytime."

The men got back in the car. Selim turned the car around to pull back onto a dusty track through the olive groves. He looked across at Ahdaf. "Any more word from your friend?"

"Not yet."

"Do you know the pick-up spot yet?" Derya asked.

"Big Rocks Beach again," Ahdaf replied. "I hope you're not superstitious."

"I'm not, and we're only five minutes from it."

In another 200 meters, Selim cut down an even rougher dirt track to the coastal road, and then turned north.

Derya, looking out the window and remembering her fright and flight a couple of nights earlier, said to no one in particular: "The other night I came up this way, and your friends' safe house saved me."

Selim, with a sympathetic smile, said, "I'm glad for that. Let's hope we don't need a safe house today." He parked the sedan in the exact spot where Ahdaf had parked the *medrese's* van.

Ahdaf wasn't especially superstitious either, but being in that exact spot made him uneasy. "Do you have binoculars?" he asked.

"There's a pair in the glove compartment."

He took them out. Though they remained in a long shadow cast by hills, dawn had broken out at sea, and he scanned the water for Captain G's boat. He thought he saw it, but couldn't be sure. DO YOU SEE OUR FLASHING HEADLIGHTS? he texted Kalam, and told Selim to flash them.

Seconds later, Kalam replied, I SEE YOU. CAPTAIN G SAYS FIF-TEEN MINUTES.

"That's our boat," Ahdaf confirmed to everyone. "Let's get to the water."

As everybody got out of the car, Ahdaf made sure to help Meryem. Selim, with an unhappy expression, watched him sling his daypack over his shoulder. The women each had packs, too. "You two go ahead," he told them. "I need to talk to Selim. You may need to help each other over the stones. They're rough, and it's a steep slope at first."

"I remember," Derya said.

"Don't trip this time," he replied.

"You saw my report where I was running in the video?"

"It made me feel guilty that I'd left you."

"You had no choice."

"I know, but that doesn't make me feel any better. I'll be glad to see your first report from Greece."

"I'm waiting to see my next broadcast from Turkey," Derya replied.

Puzzled, Ahdaf asked, "When will that be?"

"When the current government falls."

The women, clasping hands, started down the tricky embankment.

"It's creepy to be here," Ahdaf told Selim. "I keep expecting somebody to run out from behind the rocks, shooting at us."

"You're brave to come back."

"I didn't know I was coming back. We need to talk about paying Captain G. He has what Derya paid the first time, and Malik gave me more."

"Let's wait and see what the Greek demands. I have enough with me to sweeten the deal."

"When they get to Greece, Meryem will probably end up in a camp for a while, but what's Derya going to do?"

"Don't worry about Derya. She's all set. Uncle Sam and CNN will take care of her. Why?"

"Malik gave me money for the captain. I think I should give it to the women."

Selim thought about it and shook his head. "Split it between yourself and Meryem. She needs it, and you earned it. You'll need it whenever you make the crossing, and it looks you're intending to do that today."

Ahdaf shook his head in denial. He hadn't made his decision, and asked, "Why do you think that?"

"You're carrying your pack, and I doubt if it's because you want to brush your teeth with salt water."

"The money's in my pack. Besides, this way I'm prepared if something decides for me at the last minute."

"It *is* the last minute. Or at least the last five." Selim exhaled, saddened by the notion. "Let's join the women."

They'd reached the pebbly beach when Ahdaf stopped to examine the ground. "This is where Munir died. That's his blood on the stones."

Selim put a hand on his shoulder. "I'm sorry about your friend."

"I feel sorrier for his family. Now they have to survive without him."

"Give his wife some of the money Malik gave you."

"I have already."

Selim draped an arm over his shoulders and whispered into his ear, "That's why I'm falling in love with you."

"What is?"

"You have a good heart. You're a kind man. I don't want you to leave. I understand why you're going – if you go. But if you don't like it where you end up, or change your mind, don't be too proud to come back. I think we're meant to be together." He gave Ahdaf's shoulders a squeeze before dropping his arm.

Ahdaf's thoughts were in a turmoil after Selim's declaration. He realized he'd been wanting an excuse to join Kalam in Greece, and Selim had provided it: take for himself some of the money Malik had given him. That way, he wouldn't arrive in Europe a beggar. He'd already convinced himself that Kalam would be a

241

fun companion for however long they stayed together. He didn't have Kalam's need for the glamor or excitement of Hollywood, though the money in his pack could take him there and back. Wouldn't any life almost anywhere else be better than a refugee's life in Istanbul, with its constant insecurity and dangers? That thought, more than any other, influenced his decision. When he saw Captain G's fishing boat chug into sight, the hope he felt reaffirmed it.

When they joined the women, Ahdaf said, "There's no dock, so we'll have to wade out and use a rope ladder to get onboard. Probably up to our knees, or maybe a little higher. Shoes off, and put them in your packs. You're going to need both hands, so pack straps over both shoulders. Someone will pull you onboard."

"I'm not sure I can climb a rope ladder," Meryem worried.

"I'll help from behind," Ahdaf said and added, "Meryem, can I speak to you privately? Just over there."

They stepped away as Selim and Derya, hobbling from one foot to the other, took off their shoes. "This is far enough," Ahdaf said. "I only need to give you something."

"I'm already so scared," Meryem admitted. "What is this new mystery?"

He opened his daypack and pulled out one of the three remaining money pouches. He handed it to her saying, "Hide it in your pack."

"What's in it?"

"Five thousand euros."

She looked at him in disbelief. "Five thousand euros? How –?"

"Don't ask. Put it in your pack now." As she did, he continued, "Wear your pack over both shoulders on the boat so you don't accidentally drop it in the water. When we get to Greece, I'll ask Kalam for a piece of rope to tie the money to your body. That's the safest thing, and the pouch has loops for that. Try never to carry it in a pack or a purse. No matter how careful you are, you'll get pickpocketed. They're more clever than any of us. Okay?"

Meryem nodded, bewildered.

"You don't need to be scared. You'll be fine," he said confidently. "I know Derya will help you. The boat's here. Let's join the others."

"Wait! My baby is kicking! I want you to feel it." She pressed his hand to her belly, and he grinned when he felt the baby move. "Yusuf wanted a new life for all of us," she said. "My baby will have a new life because of you. I'll name him 'Ahdaf.'"

"What if it's a girl?"

"It's also a girl's name."

Ahdaf smiled. "So it is; and I'm touched, here in my heart. Ready?"

Selim had also taken off his shoes, and rolled his pants up to his knees. "Why are you going in the water?" Ahdaf asked him. For a moment, he thought Selim had decided last-minute to make the crossing, which he instantly realized was ludicrous. Selim required no smuggler's boat. He could fly to Athens legally, and meet him on the other side.

"I thought you could use an extra couple of hands to get people onboard. It's never easy without a proper dock, and that's a high bow."

The sun peeked over the hills, warming their backs as they watched Captain G's boat enter the long cove. At its bow, feet spread apart for balance, stood Kalam, phone camera pressed to his eye, videotaping the approaching shore. In the morning's bright rays, he looked every bit the Hollywood golden boy he dreamed of being.

"Is that your friend?" Selim asked.

"Yes. My client and friend."

"Is he why you want to make the crossing now?"

"He's a temptation."

"I can see why."

They heard the engine reverse to stop the boat where it was, about 10 meters from shore. Kalam, dropping a rope ladder over the side, shouted, "COME ON! COME ON!"

They all dashed into the water, splashing furiously. Meryem stumbled, but Ahdaf caught her. "I'm afraid I'll hurt my baby climbing up the side of the boat," she moaned.

"I'll make sure you don't," he reassured her.

Selim reached the boat first and held the rope ladder steady for Derya. It was a clumsy apparatus, providing no firm grip or foothold, and even small movements in the water caused it to sway. From the deck, Kalam reached for her hand, but she was too afraid to let go. "I need a push!" she shouted, and Selim pushed his shoulder into her buttocks, hands gripping the unstable ladder's ropes, and nudged her high enough that Kalam managed to pull her aboard.

Next, Ahdaf held the ladder steady for Meryem, who planted both feet on the lower rung but decided to go up sideways to minimize the risk of banging her belly against the side of the boat. Ahdaf, climbing right behind her, gave her a shoulder to half-sit on while she pulled her way up, until she was high enough that Kalam could reach under her arms and pull her over the boat's rail.

Selim started to walk back to shore through the water.

Kalam asked, "What about him?"

Ahdaf answered, "He's not coming."

"That's everyone!" Kalam shouted to Captain G, who immediately started the engine to reverse out of the cove. "Shit, I'm missing my shot!" Kalam disappeared from sight.

"I could use some help too!" Ahdaf shouted, to no avail. On his own, he struggled up the unsecured ladder and over the rail.

Kalam had claimed his spot at the point of the bow to film their retreat from the cove. The two women were huddled together on a middle bench, comforting each other with simple touches and whispered encouragements.

"This is so cool!" Kalam exclaimed, camera to his eye. "It's like watching our arrival in reverse! I'm thinking I'll show this on a split screen. The coming and the going at the same time. Do you think that's a cool idea?"

"Yeah, it's great. It's clever," Ahdaf said.

"Somehow, the landscape is even more beautiful going backward! I can't explain it!"

He looked past Kalam to see what he was seeing, and what Ahdaf saw was different. He saw Selim, already back on shore, watching the boat slowly reverse, his face a study in heartbreak. Kalam, distracted by his camerawork, missed the real emotion of the moment. He probably always would. He'd be making movies or dreaming of other Hollywoods instead of seeing what was right in front of him.

Ahdaf, on the other hand, did see what was right in front of him, and realized he wanted to be with Selim. He wanted to be with a man who didn't ignore two distraught women but instead risked his life to save them. He wanted to be with a man who had pictures of all humanity plastered to his walls. He wanted to be with a man who already loved him enough that he looked at his departure so forlornly instead of forgetting to look at him at all.

Had he missed his chance? He decided not. They weren't halfway out of the cove. It would be an easy swim back to the beach; but first, he had to square things with the captain. He scrambled to where the Greek sat with his hand on the tiller, guiding them backward. "How much do I owe you?" he asked.

"One woman already paid the other night," Captain G replied.

"There's a second woman."

"Are those men dead yet?"

"Who? Serhan and Özan? Yes, they're dead."

His faced hardened when he said, "That's payment enough. They killed my son in Athens. He was at that nightclub for queers …. He never told me about himself. I had guessed it. I wasn't proud he was queer, but I wish I had one more chance to tell him I loved him."

"He knew you loved him. It doesn't always have to be said."

"When they – those scum – started bragging about how many 'faggots' they'd killed in Athens, that's why I radioed the police in Assos."

"You made the tipoff?"

The captain sighed. "Those poor policemen. I didn't expect what happened. All I wanted was justice for my son."

"You got it. How much do I owe you?"

"You were part of catching them?"

"Yeah. I can say I was."

"Then I've been paid back. Keep your money."

That was enough for Ahdaf.

He hurried back to the bow and dropped one of his last two money pouches at Kalam's feet. "Here's something to help you succeed," he said.

"What is it?"

"Your ticket to Hollywood."

Holding his daypack over his head, Ahdaf jumped overboard, kicking hard to avoid sinking below the surface and keeping his phone and last money pouch out of the water. His head went under, but not his pack. He surfaced, rolled onto his back and held it aloft while kicking himself toward shallower water. The women, seeing him jump over, cried out in alarm and rushed to the rail. He must have floated into Kalam's view when the fair-haired youth shouted, "What are you doing? Did you fall overboard? This is great!"

Those weren't the shouts he was tuned into, but he was to Selim's cries. "I'm coming! I'm coming to help you!" He could

246

hear his splashing feet getting closer, and then Selim was there to relieve him of his pack. "It's shallow here. You can stand up."

Ahdaf stood, and they embraced.

"I'm so glad you came back," Selim said.

"I could see you were sad. Me, too."

They started to slosh their way to the shore.

"You know, I'm not going to be a spy."

"You won't miss the excitement?" Selim asked.

"Never."

"You're a great strategist. You might get bored teaching English. You might want a challenge."

"Teaching the subjunctive will be challenging enough!"

Selim slung an arm around Ahdaf's shoulders. "Were that I knew it!" he exclaimed as they helped each other climb onto the slippery pebble beach.

ABOUT THE AUTHOR

Raised crisscrossing America pulling a small green trailer behind the family car, Timothy Jay Smith developed a ceaseless wanderlust that has taken him around the world many times. En route, he's found the characters that people his work. Polish cops and Greek fishermen, mercenaries and arms dealers, child prostitutes and wannabe terrorists, Indian Chiefs and Indian tailors: he hung with them all in an unparalleled international career that saw him smuggle banned plays from behind the Iron Curtain, maneuver through Occupied Territories, represent the US at the highest levels of foreign governments, and stowaway aboard a "devil's barge" for a three-day crossing from Cape Verde that landed him in an African jail.

Tim brings the same energy to his writing that he brought to a distinguished career, and as a result, he has won top honors for his novels, screenplays and stage plays in numerous prestigious competitions. *Istanbul Crossing* won the Leapfrog Global Fiction

Prize in 2023. *Fire on the Island* (Arcade Publishing, July 2020) won the Gold Medal in the 2017 Faulkner-Wisdom Competition for the Novel, and his screenplay adaptation of it was named Best Indie Script by WriteMovies.

Another novel, *The Fourth Courier*, set in Poland, published in 2019 also by Arcade Publishing, received tremendous reviews and was a finalist for Best Gay Mystery in the 2020 Lambda Literary Awards. Previously, he won the Paris Prize for Fiction (now the Paris Literary Prize) for his novel, *A Vision of Angels*. **Kirkus Reviews** called *Cooper's Promise* "literary dynamite" and selected it as one of the Best Books of 2012.

Tim was nominated for the 2018 Pushcart Prize. He's an avid theater-goer and playwright himself. His stage play, *How High the Moon*, a gay love story set in Nazi-occupied Warsaw, won the prestigious Stanley Drama Award.